Other novels by the same author

The Embracer

Shaya

Alternating Worlds

Workshop of the Second Self

The Kicker of St. John's Wood

Voyage of the Mind Carriers

GARY WOLF

iUniverse, Inc.
Bloomington

Voyage of the Mind Carriers

iUniverse books may be ordered through booksellers or by contacting:

iUniverse
1663 Liberty Drive
Bloomington, IN 47403
www.iuniverse.com
1-800-Authors (1-800-288-4677)

ISBN: 978-1-4620-0433-1 (sc)
ISBN: 978-1-4620-0434-8 (ebook)

Printed in the United States of America

iUniverse rev. date: 03/23/2011

Whatever has been, is what will be, and whatever has been done is what will be done. There is nothing new under the sun. Sometimes there is a phenomenon of which one says: "Look, this is new!" But it has already existed in the eras that preceded us. Just as there is no recollection of former things, so too, of future things that are yet to be, there will be no recollection among those of a still later time.

—Ecclesiastes 1: 9–11

The mind must transmute into a possession the remembrance of its passage through the ages of the world.

—Jacob Burckhardt, *Reflections on History*

AUTHOR'S PREFACE

I often marvel at the unintended consequences that arise when one becomes immersed in a new avocation. One is liable to be a magnet for questions, pronouncements, and outbursts of verbal bravado that sprout in conversation like mushrooms after the rain.

Such has been the case with my foray into the philosophy and literature of the ancient world. Without any purposeful action on my part, I have been the locus of spontaneously erupting discussions with scholarly overtones. Though some of these encounters have imparted a large portion of erudition, many have been characterized by superficiality and misinformation.

The phenomenon of unintended consequences was on display at a social event that took place about eighteen months ago. An ex-diplomat of my acquaintance had invited me to a dinner party at his elegant dwelling in Manhattan. I was privileged to benefit from such hospitality because I had once supplied the gentleman with some ghost writing. His heartfelt appreciation of my craft earned me a berth in his stockpile of "interesting people," called up for social occasions the way the Yankees call up baseball players from the minor leagues.

The soirée—taking place on that proving ground of urbanity and sophistication, Central Park West—included on its list of invitees the self-appointed shepherdess of moneyed Gotham intelligentsia, a woman I shall call Mrs. Forsythe. (The need for pseudonyms will be explained later.) As fate would have it, she established temporary residence in the modernist leather and steel armchair at my left flank. Mrs. Forsythe drew upon her sixty-odd years of experience in the art of social chatter to crack me open, as she undoubtedly did to many a lobster claw on Martha's Vineyard.

"How long have you been in New York?" she inquired.

"A few hours," I replied, as my fingers extracted an olive from a dish on the coffee table. "I'm just visiting."

"Have you been to the Metropolitan Museum?"

"On this trip, no."

"No?" she declared, at high volume, causing a couple of nearby heads to turn. "Then you *must* go. I insist."

I began nibbling on the olive, wondering where all this was heading.

"They have a wonderful show of Greek and Roman sculpture, from the new excavation in Sicily. Oh, it's just splendid. Have you heard about it?"

"No, I can't say that I have."

Mrs. Forsythe turned her face away slightly, displaying just enough astonishment to indicate her disapproval. "What do you *do?*" she asked, with eyebrow raised.

"I'm a writer."

"Oh, how interesting," she said. Her features seemed to transform into a sentient strain of marble, reminiscent of a mutation in Ovid's *Metamorphoses*. "You could write an article about the Sicilian excavation for your local newspaper. There's an exotic angle here, you know."

"What would that be?"

"Some of the objects are said to be from the lost city of Atlantis. You know, the legend handed down to us by Cicero."

"I believe it was King Solomon," opined a middle-aged man sitting on the sofa across from us.

I released a muted groan and rolled my eyes. I was just about to get up and leave the room, when a conflicting impulse—the need to set the record straight—came to the fore. "Well if you really want to know," I said, "the legend of Atlantis was handed down to us by Plato. The story may have been brought to Greece by Solon, who heard it from the Egyptians. In any case, Plato's account is the earliest we have a record of."

"Are you certain?" asked Mrs. Forsythe.

A man who had been chatting with a group off to our right, his back to us, turned around and approached. "I heard this gentleman's statement," he said, motioning toward me with his cocktail. "And it is correct."

Mrs. Forsythe, not missing a beat, introduced me to the man I shall call Dr. Cartwright. His demeanor fit my preconceived image of a distinguished yet unpretentious professor of archeology: his straightforward speech, his simple dress, the average height and weight, and the short brown hair that lacked a hairstyle. I immediately took a liking to him.

Mrs. Forsythe and the promoter of King Solomon could not long endure the conversation's new flavor. They excused themselves to search for greener and more familiar argumentative pastures. This enabled Dr. Cartwright and me to engage in a tête-à-tête.

Whatever the aesthetic virtue of the ancient statues at the Metropolitan, Cartwright considered the trove to be fascinating. He explained that the vast majority of the objects, found in a Sicilian villa from the first century BC, were more or less standard, precisely what one would expect in such a setting. There were several statues, however, of an older vintage, and hewn from a type of stone not indigenous to the region. Moreover, the stone showed signs of prolonged exposure to salt water. These oddities had fueled some wild speculation about the lost city of Atlantis.

"Atlantis is just a myth, isn't it?" I asked.

"Probably," replied Cartwright. "If it were true, what is the likelihood that absolutely nothing be found during all the centuries since Plato? And with all of our technology?"

"I see your point. But how do you explain the older statues, the ones that were underwater?"

"I don't, necessarily," he said, pausing for a moment to reflect on his contrarian statement. "An explanation will present itself. We might learn, for example, that the statues were brought over from Carthage, but the ship sank in the harbor during a battle. Then, many years later, an enterprising nobleman recovered the freight. Such occurrences were fairly common. Don't pay attention to Mrs. Forsythe; she's getting her information from the popular press."

"So it's an interesting project, but nothing extraordinary."

"Correct."

"You seemed more enthusiastic a moment ago," I ventured.

Cartwright shut his eyes and lowered his face. Then, after slowly emerging, he addressed me in an adamant tone. "Tell me something, sir. Do you enjoy controversy?"

"It depends on what kind," I replied.

He smiled. "A good answer. Allow me to rephrase the question. Do you relish taking a stand that runs counter to the trend of thinking in society?"

"Yes, now that you mention it, I rather do."

There was a flash of excitement in his visage before it returned to its usual attitude of pensiveness. "I may have a proposition for you. But let me sleep on it. Could you phone me tomorrow, say, in the late afternoon?"

"Certainly," I said, taking the business card from his outstretched hand. "I will call you."

He soon departed. A short while thereafter, I also quit the premises, content to be alone with my thoughts amid the bustling streets of New York City.

The next day, brimming with curiosity, I visited the Metropolitan Museum of Art, heading straight for the Sicilian exhibition. It was a fairly impressive collection of classical statuary, but nothing much out of the ordinary, as per Dr. Cartwright's summary. Several pieces were pockmarked, these being the "underwater" specimens.

I telephoned the professor at two-thirty, admittedly a tad on the early side of the late-afternoon call that he had requested. My fingers seemed to dial the number of their own accord, so palpable was my desire to get to the bottom of this affair. He asked me to meet him, at five o'clock, at a Starbucks café in Grand Central Station. He was to board a train for Boston, and we could chat for a while prior to his departure.

"My dear sir," he began, after we were seated with our cups of Sumatran Roast coffee. "I have decided to share with you an aspect of the Sicilian project that has not been publicized. But before I do, I must, in good conscience, warn you that this conversation may alter your life, and rather irretrievably at that."

I laughed, in spite of myself. "Alter my life? Just from hearing what you have to say?"

Cartwright hurled a penetrating glance in my direction. "Yes. That's exactly right."

"Fine," I said. "I'll take my chances."

"Okay, then. What, in your opinion, is the date of the first document ever written?"

"First document ... hmm ... Do you mean on paper, or do stone and clay qualify?"

"Anything."

"Well, let's see ..."

"Give me the absolute earliest date. Go back as far as you need to."

"Well, to be certain, I'd say there was nothing prior to four thousand BC."

"Close enough," said Cartwright. He lifted a finger as if he were going to emphasize some forthcoming words, but none ensued. His brow had become compacted to the point of redness. Finally, the bombshell arrived: "What would you say if I told you that I have a document that is forty thousand years old?"

"What!" I exclaimed. "Did you say *forty thousand years old?*"

Cartwright eyed me with satisfaction, as if he had won a grueling game of tennis. "Yes, my dear sir. That is precisely what I said. The age of the document, or rather the scroll, has been determined by the usual methods. And we're not talking about a tally of births and deaths. It is rather a story, a veritable novel."

I was at a loss for words.

"It is written in a dead language. A friend and colleague of mine, an expert in ancient dialects, worked with me for months to decipher the text. Luckily, we have computers available these days to assist in this labor."

"Is it something like hieroglyphics?"

"No, not at all. There's an alphabet, with distinct words and punctuation. The words are placed in columns, going from top to bottom, and then left to right. We translated it, as best we could."

"That's amazing," I said. "Where is the scroll from?"

"I found it at the Sicilian site, a couple of years ago. But we have yet to determine its place of origin."

"What's the story about?"

"That's a bit complicated. The subject of another conversation."

I took a sip of coffee, and became aware that we were sitting in a cavernous railway terminal. People were darting every which way, some of them coming within a yard of our little bistro table.

"Where do I fit in to all this?" I asked.

"Ah," said Cartwright, "that is the question. I need someone to perform an act of literary restoration. In other words, to complete the story, to fill in the missing pieces. A few segments have decayed over the years, and are no longer legible."

"How much is missing?"

"Approximately one quarter. In addition, our dry, academic translation must be retrofitted to its original mold. Re-novelized, if you will."

"And this is what you would have me do?"

"Yes."

"Well, thank you," I said. "I'm flattered that you would consider me worthy of the task."

"Don't be so quick to thank me," said Cartwright, as his previous look of satisfaction evaporated. "An impartial observer might conclude that you've been selected to be a sacrifice at the altar of some flaky obsession. Not long ago, I circulated a synopsis and some excerpts of the scroll to an elite group of academics, all of them sworn to secrecy. Would you care to speculate as to the result?"

"I really couldn't say."

"The responses ranged from polite rejection to strident rebuke. The word crackpot appeared more than once."

"They're crazy."

He chuckled. "You have to be a crackpot to say that."

"I guess I'm a crackpot, then."

"A perfect demonstration of why I selected you."

"But seriously," I insisted. "How could they say such things? Are these people real scholars?"

"As real as it gets."

"How can they dispute the dating of the document?"

"By concocting various conspiracy theories. Like one distinguished gentleman who admitted that the materials were of the age I claimed, but alleged that I had reworked and reassembled them using some sophisticated method. Then there was that woman at Oxford who, while likewise asserting foul play in the construction of the scroll, added the accusation that I am a closet Theosophist attempting to revive their discredited theories. It was futile explaining to her that my conclusions are based on an artifact, and not on some mystical tradition."

"You would think they'd be interested in the facts, in looking at evidence."

"Normally, that would be true," said Cartwright. "But we are not dealing with normal circumstances." He grabbed both sides of the table and leaned toward me. "The scroll is clearly the product of a highly developed culture. The place was in full swing forty thousand years ago. What is our usual impression of that era? The word Neanderthal sums it up. At best, a simple form of social organization with the most rudimentary technology. As for art and other intellectual pursuits, one conjures up nothing more than primitive cave paintings.

"The shock arrives when an advanced civilization, lost in the mists of time, suddenly resurfaces. Our habitual perception of history, of a linear progression, is thrown into disarray. The reality is too vast for the minds of most individuals, and maybe somewhat indigestible for the rest of us, whether we admit it or not."

"I'm not so sure about that linear progression," I countered. "Technologically, yes. But intellectually and culturally, a case could be made that far more advanced civilizations than ours existed long ago."

"Yes, yes, of course," he said, with a little wave of the hand to dismiss my remark. "But all of that is within the recent past, relatively speaking.

Your own estimate of four thousand BC for the earliest document is only six thousand years ago—a mere infant compared with our geriatric scroll."

"True."

"Now, in the spirit of full disclosure, I must inform you of yet another reason for hostility toward the project. It has to do with the content of the story itself. Much of that content is, how shall I say it, not quite politically fashionable. This will become apparent as you read the text."

"That cannot deter me," I declared.

"Very well. So, as I was saying, don't be so quick to thank me. Any connection to this affair has the potential to sound the death knell of your career. I can't imagine any but the most marginal support during the foreseeable future, unless corroborating evidence be uncovered."

Some silence passed before I returned the discussion to practical matters. "You're looking for a ghost writer, essentially."

"Not a ghost," said Cartwright, emphatically. "I prefer that you publish the final text under your own name. That will make it easier for me to work in the background, pursuing further research on the subject."

"So the book would be published as a sort of novel, with myself as author."

"Correct."

"With an explanation of how it all came to be."

"Yes, but don't mention my name. If you want to talk about me, or anyone else connected with this affair, use a pseudonym."

"Do we know the name of the original author?" I inquired.

"No, unfortunately we don't. It was written in one of the segments that has decayed."

I leaned back in my chair, took a deep breath, and pondered this extraordinary offer. Everything had happened so fast, leaving me dizzy with excitement. I probably should have asked for some time to consider my options, but an internal voice told me that it was the chance of a lifetime.

"I'll do it," I said.

"Excellent," said Cartwright, his voice vibrating with enthusiasm but his expression tempered by a germ of melancholy. "We'll be in touch very soon." He shook my hand, grabbed his rolling suitcase, and disappeared into the throng of travelers.

We met again a few days later at the professor's home on Long Island. He gave me a manuscript of the translated text as well as copious documentation detailing the procedures used to date the scroll. After we hammered out the minutiae of our agreement, my host filled two glasses with cognac, and we toasted the launch of the project.

Now, dear reader, you understand the genesis of this exceptional undertaking.

Some technical notes are in order. In adapting the rough translation, and filling in the missing pieces, I have endeavored to fashion the text using our contemporary idiom. When it comes to names, I have used forms drawn from our own society, so that they have meaning for us. The etymology has stumped the translators, and the names in their original form are discordant to our ears. For example, one of the main characters is called *hqlstnoponthx*. In one case only was it appropriate to preserve the original name, and that was for the leading lady, of whom you will make the acquaintance in due course.

In the world described in the scroll, the week is composed of ten days. They are named by their ordinal designation; that is, Firstday, Seconday, Thirday, Fourthday, etc., up to Ninthday. The tenth and final day of the week, which corresponds roughly to our notion of the Sabbath, is called Brainday. The story opens on a Thirday.

The calculation of months and years, as well as the relation of these to the weeks, is complex in the extreme. Since the subject has little, if any, bearing on the story, I have decided to spare myself the task of elucidating it.

Weights and measures have been converted to the United States Customary System; that is, inches, feet, miles, ounces, pounds, etc.

Without further ado, I present to you the ancient tale. I leave its interpretation to your good judgment.

Gary Wolf
April 2011

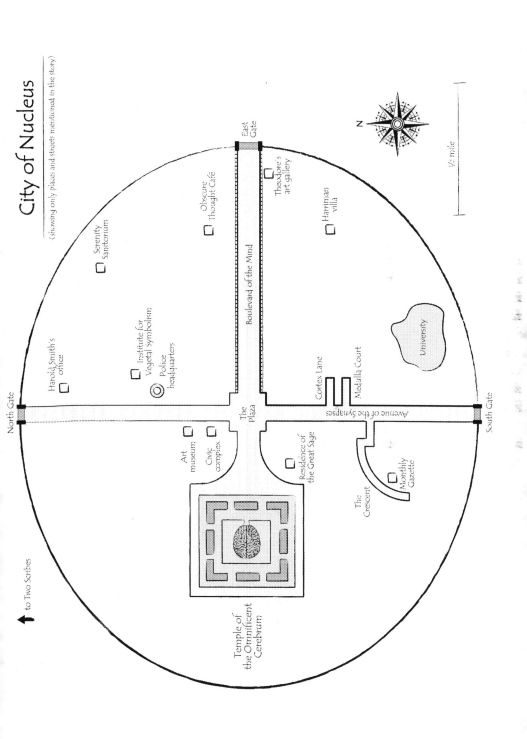

City of Nucleus

(showing only places and streets mentioned in the story)

to Two Scribes

North Gate

Harold Smith's office

Institute for Vegetal Symbolism

Police headquarters

Serenity Sanitorium

Obscure Thought Café

Boulevard of the Mind

East Gate

Theodore's art gallery

Harriman villa

The Plaza

Art museum

Civic complex

Residence of the Great Sage

Avenue of the Synapses

Cortex Lane

Medulla Court

University

The Crescent

Monthly Gazette

South Gate

Temple of the Omnificent Cerebrum

N

½ mile

I. THE INSPECTOR

A sense of awe settled upon Simon Baxter as he viewed the dead body on the floor. This was one of the most methodical homicides he had beheld in all of his twenty-three years as police detective. It was death by poison, and apparently it had been quick. There was no sign of struggle, no blows to the head, no vomit, no blood, and no damage to the furnishings in the room. The victim was found on his back, clothes in perfect order. A dignified aura surrounded him, like a deceased monarch lying in state. His face was serene—to say angelic would not be a gross exaggeration. He seemed pleased to have been relieved of his mortal burdens.

The other officers at the scene stood by without uttering a word that might disturb the veteran investigator. They knew from experience that Baxter would squat alongside the corpse and stare at it for quite some time. Then he would scrutinize every inch of it, touching here, scratching there, even mobilizing his nose for an olfactory probe. No one thought of hindering the master; such a blunder would be akin to accosting an astronomer as he gauges the movement of the heavenly spheres.

At last, Baxter rose to his full height and stretched the tense ligaments in his legs and back. Having reached the age of forty-eight, he could no longer drive his body with impunity. His waistline was expanding, his joints were not quite as limber, and the news-scroll was no longer in focus at the usual distance. Yet he was healthy, with neither broken bone nor surgical incision on his medical record. Nature had blessed him with a strong frame and superior endurance. Baxter cut an impressive figure: six feet tall with almost all of his youthful muscle intact. He boasted a fertile crop of curly brown hair, imbued with a tinge of red. Hardly any gray had seeped into the mix. The forehead was prominent, but not overly so; the brow similarly well-defined yet not out of proportion. High cheekbones, protruding above a thick beard, combined with a broad chin and a ruddy complexion, announced tenacity and ruggedness. These attributes were reinforced by a strain of hoarseness in the voice. The only component of the portrait liable to cause dissonance was the mouth, which was diminutive and fine, as if transplanted from a more delicate human specimen. To the discerning observer, it augured a refined spirit; by most people, it was overlooked, subsumed under the coarser features by which it was surrounded.

After conversing with the servant who had discovered the body, and listening to a summary of events presented by the officer who first arrived on the scene, Baxter conducted an inspection of the room and its contents. Despite the meticulous technique, not a single piece of noteworthy information was obtained. In fact, no progress was made, aside from a determination that the victim had been dead for approximately half a day. Undaunted, Baxter surveyed the remainder of the house. The task was time-consuming, being that the dwelling was a colossal villa, ranking among the most splendid in the city. Combing the profusion of intricate decorative objects and ornate furniture required great patience and the dexterity of highly-trained eyes and hands.

Once again, the labor was for naught. No objects or traces of activity related to the crime were found. At the conclusion of the tour, Baxter dictated a preliminary report to a scribe, who recorded the words on a small scroll. Finally, the coroner arrived, and confirmed Baxter's appraisal of the time and cause of death. Two police officers wrapped the body in a sheet, loaded it onto a stretcher, and removed it from the premises.

Stepping through the front doorway of the residence and onto the spacious portico, Baxter inhaled the warm, dry air. The summer sky was cloudless, the temperature perfect, and a gentle breeze was blowing. The city of Nucleus was drenched in the glowing light of the mid-afternoon sun. Relishing the moment was impossible, however, as soon as Baxter confronted the crowd of journalists awaiting him in the yard below. He considered a mad dash to freedom, laterally along the colonnade, but the risk of negative publicity was too great. The encounter could not be avoided.

He stood face-to-face with the seekers of information, who were now bobbing up and down for attention. Baxter noted, and not for the first time, the discrepancy between their mode of dress and level of manners. Most of them donned the blue and white tunic normally worn by playwrights, teachers of high rank, and other members of the learned classes. Such people would never shame their colors by exhibiting the type of behavior currently on display: yelling, jostling, and thrusting of hands wildly in the air.

"Gentlemen," declared the detective, his thumb and forefinger tugging at his prominent chin. "John Harriman, spokesman for the Bioprimalist movement, was found dead a short while ago right here in his home. It is probably a homicide, and it looks like poison. We are launching an investigation. That's all I can tell you." He began descending the stairway connecting the portico to the front yard. The reporters converged on his person.

"Are there any suspects?" hollered one of them.

"Not at this time," replied Baxter.

"Mr. Inspector," gasped another, "is it possible that Harriman was assassinated by the government?"

A clamorous chatter surged from the throats of the news-scrollmen.

"And what if they *did* assassinate him?" declared a man wearing a plain tunic, someone Baxter had never seen. "One cannot repeatedly insult the Omnificent Cerebrum, in public no less, and expect to get away with it. The guy had it coming."

Another uproar, more vigorous than the first, rose from the assembly. Baxter took advantage of the verbal melee to wiggle his way past the crowd. He slipped through the front gate and emerged into the street. He could still hear the argument raging behind him as he widened the distance between himself and the murder scene.

The newfound solitude enabled him to begin the next stage of the investigative routine: the walk home. His mind would be free to engage in some light meditation on the freshly-committed crime, quietly processing the numerous stimuli absorbed by his senses. This was the prelude to a much deeper session of meditation, normally performed in the privacy of his own abode.

Walking to all destinations was common practice in the city of Nucleus. Old and young, rich and poor, sages and unskilled laborers all used their legs as the primary mode of urban transportation. This did not pose an undue hardship, being that Nucleus was a mere two miles across, and densely packed. The neighborhood in which the murder occurred, with its grand villas and extensive gardens, was exceptional. Generally, the residential areas were filled with contiguous multifamily dwellings.

Baxter approached the end of the street. He quickened his pace, simply out of habit, for he was about to turn onto Boulevard of the Mind, the magnificent thoroughfare that crossed the city from east to west. Strolling its length was an uplifting experience. The pavement was an intricate patchwork of colorful tiles that formed images of the cerebrum. These images, showing the organ in cross-section, seemed to repeat themselves. In reality, however, each one represented a slice located at a small interval from its neighbor, so that over the course of the Boulevard the span of the entire brain was covered.

The storefronts were separated from the street by a vaulted arcade that culminated in majestic columns, the capitals of which provided a base for the façade of the upper floors. In between the columns were potted shrubs and small trees. Each plant was trimmed into shapes suggestive of human creativity; a musical instrument, for example.

Animals were not permitted to set foot upon Boulevard of the Mind. One might surmise that this ordinance had been enacted to preserve the aforementioned handiwork, but the actual reason was symbolic: the realm of the mind belongs exclusively to humans. Other sentient beings have no role in the drama.

It was fitting that Boulevard of the Mind have these adornments, because it served as the pathway to a sanctuary that was sublime—the center not only of Nucleus, but of the entire world: the Temple of the Omnificent Cerebrum. When Baxter first turned onto the Boulevard, the Temple could be seen in the distance; its appearance as a relatively small object in the panorama did not interfere with his meditative efforts. As he approached, however, his consciousness was gripped by its spiritual radiation. He began to ponder the object that constitutes the centerpiece of the Temple's rite: the Omnificent Cerebrum, the vast Brain that fills every inch of the universe.

A perennial question presented itself. Were his own thoughts, and those of his fellow human beings, formulated by the cosmic Brain itself, leaving the individual mind carrier with only the illusion of autonomous fabrication of thought? Probably not, was Baxter's conclusion. After all, the entire world—the Temple, the city of Nucleus, the hinterland stretching to the edges of the island, the great ocean of the surface, the subterranean ocean, and the dome of the heavens—was but a single cell in the Omnificent Cerebrum. A multitude of additional cells, populated by other races of mind carriers, filled the remaining gray matter of the cosmic Brain. Thus it stands to reason that a thought on the immense scale of the cosmos would never be manifest, in its entirety, within a solitary human brain. As it says in the Tomes of Ancient Thought, a whale does not give birth to a minnow.

There seemed to be no doubt, however, as to the validity of the opposite tendency, that the intellectual output of a cell's inhabitants finds its way into the machinery of cosmic cognition. The process is inconceivably complex, but one can say with certainty that the Omnificent Cerebrum, when constructing a thought, harvests the labor of a multitude of cells. Thus it was vital that the Home Cell (that is, Baxter's world), like all the cells, function properly, with the keenest intellect being deployed at every moment. And if this were true for the individual going about his daily business, how much more so for the learned classes—not to mention the sages of the Temple in the discharge of their duties. It is said that in the interior of the Temple, in the section where no layman may tread, there is a model of the cosmic Brain in which the location of the Home Cell is indicated. Baxter shuddered to think of the impact one miniscule error could have in such a rarified environment; how detrimental it could be to the health and stability of the cosmos.

At the geographic center of the city lay the intersection between Boulevard of the Mind and Avenue of the Synapses, the latter being the north-south axis of Nucleus. The four sides of the intersection were recessed about a hundred feet to form a square, known as the Plaza. If the Temple was the city's spiritual heart, the Plaza was its intellectual hub. Here, at any moment of the day, one could find all sorts of erudite activity, such as duos engaged in study of the Tomes of Ancient Thought, or discourses delivered to eager crowds thirsting for knowledge.

Crossing the Plaza, Baxter veered left onto Avenue of the Synapses, which was narrower and less embellished than Boulevard of the Mind, yet still one of the city's more impressive arteries. Along its length one could find civic institutions, a sports arena, the art museum, and noteworthy commercial establishments.

Baxter's apartment house was located on Cortex Lane, a cul-de-sac jutting eastward from Avenue of the Synapses. His residence, like the surrounding structures, was a bit above average: spacious, well-equipped, and built with quality materials, yet lacking the luxurious appointments one would find in the grand villas. The façade of the six-story building was severe, with no ornamentation to speak of. The same tan-colored stone was used throughout. Windows were small but plentiful. The border between the stories was demarcated by the protrusion of a slab several inches from the plane of the surface. This provided some relief from the monotony, as did the main entrance, which contained a portal sculpted into the shape of a man's head, in profile.

Baxter passed through that portal and into the lobby, where he waved to George, the doorman and superintendent of the building. George had some familiarity with the iniquity of the underworld, and appreciated the work of the police. He was friendly, reliable, and proficient at his duties, one of which was to keep the lobby clean and well lit. This task was not onerous, being that the space was sparsely furnished and the walls were bare, except for a mosaic rendering of several passages from the Tomes of Ancient Thought. The oil lamps were plain, without the decorative flourish found in more upscale buildings.

After the three-story climb to his flat, Baxter removed a key from his pocket. He unlocked the ponderous wooden door, pushed it open, and stepped into the foyer.

"Hi, Daddy," came a young woman's voice from an interior room.

Hearing his daughter Elizabeth call out to him as he entered the sanctuary of his home was music to Baxter's ears. He always paused, froze his position, and waited to receive the greeting. If it failed to arrive, he experienced a letdown.

"Hi there," he replied. After closing the door, he reached through the breastflap of his tunic, unstrapped and removed the sheath that held his dagger, and placed it on the breakfront. Moving laterally a step, he could see clear through the living room and into the kitchen, where Elizabeth was seated, doing her homework.

He marveled at how she had turned out to be so proper, so poised, after eighteen years under his roof. It certainly wasn't easy, especially when his beloved wife Eleanor passed away after contracting a mysterious illness just prior to Elizabeth's tenth birthday. Baxter at that time lost his nervous equilibrium and sank into despondency, a condition that led to a stay of several months in a sanatorium. Though his recovery was robust, it had never been within his power to entirely escape the clutches of that distressed frame of mind.

As an only child, with the mother deceased and the father melancholic and withdrawn, it fell to Elizabeth to be the rock, the anchor of the family. It was almost miraculous how the girl could demonstrate such resolve at that tender age. Apparently, a strong feminine instinct for nurturing had been aroused by the death and its aftermath.

Baxter wondered how much damage had been caused by the brutal rupture of Elizabeth's formerly carefree childhood. In general, she was cheery, gentle, and not at all resentful. But occasionally he detected on her features the signs of a gloomy retreat into her deepest self. His grief upon witnessing this behavior was compounded by a feeling of guilt, that his own unwholesome gloominess had been transmitted to Elizabeth, like a contagious disease.

"You're home early," she remarked, after he had joined her at the kitchen table. "Were you investigating a crime?"

"Yes, in a villa on the East Side. Appears to be a murder."

"What kind of weapon?"

"Poison. Quite expeditious."

"Would you like something to eat?"

"No thanks, I'll wait until dinner."

"But I have some delicious calf's brain, fresh from the butcher. The kind you fancy, with the butter and garlic."

Baxter smiled. "You're a sweetie. I'll enjoy it this evening, don't you worry." He smiled again, but with more restraint. He was never sure how much free rein to allow his emotions. Elizabeth, at eighteen, had blossomed into a beautiful woman, and he was a very lonely man. She did not seem to restrain her affection for him, though it always remained within appropriate bounds. If she were married, having the outlet provided by those relations, the tension would be eased. How to get her out of the house was the question. She had no interest in meeting prospective marriage partners. Well, thought Baxter, neither did he. The level of dependence between father and daughter had been a concern for quite some time, but lately it was filling him with consternation.

"What are you reading?" he inquired.

"Human anatomy."

"Excellent. You're going to make a great nurse, I'm sure of it."

Elizabeth looked at him with a benevolent pout, as one wears when reacting to a child's innocent silliness. "Daddy, you *know* that I haven't even started the nursing part of the program yet."

Baxter's heart expanded as he viewed his little girl. His mind conjured up a vivid image of her as a toddler, dashing to and fro, giggling constantly. The image faded, despite his wish to prolong the effect, like a person awakening from a delectable dream. He was thrust back to reality, compelled to acknowledge that across the table was an adult with the ambition to become a member of the medical profession.

Elizabeth, seeming to sense the inner movement of his spirit, stared at him with soft eyes.

"I'll let you get back to work," said Baxter, rising abruptly from his chair. He discharged a nervous cough, and left the kitchen. After making his way to one of the windows in the living room, he opened it, stretched his back, leaned forward onto the sill, and peered outside. The ubiquitous scent of Nucleus, sandy and desiccated, like earthenware left to dry in the sun, wafted across his face. It was joined at intervals by wisps of smoke from the city's innumerable chimneys. The field of view consisted exclusively of the buildings across the street, except for a sliver of Avenue of the Synapses, peeking out, with its enticing urban charms, from behind the apartment house on the corner.

The Temple of the Omnificent Cerebrum was only a few hundred yards distant; being on the third floor, however, Baxter's vantage point was too low for even a glimpse. He wished that he could afford a dwelling with a view of the hallowed shrine. The fourth floor in some of the buildings on the west side of Avenue of the Synapses would be adequate for this purpose. On a detective's salary, though, comfortable as it was, he could hardly expect to see the fulfillment of his desire. Be that as it may, he was thankful to be living in close proximity to the Temple, benefiting in no small measure from its spiritual radiation.

Baxter left his perch at the window and entered the extra bedroom that served as his home office. The room's walls formed a square of only about seven feet on each side, yet somehow it managed to hold a wooden desk, a chair, an elegant scrollcase that had belonged to Baxter's grandparents, and a day bed. On the wall were hung a painting of the Temple, an old map of Nucleus, and a finely-woven tapestry with a black and gold geometric design. Everything was covered in a thin layer of dust, which the homeowner was reticent to dislodge, as if by doing so he would remove from the artifacts an aspect of their venerability.

Baxter stretched out, prone, on the narrow bed. He closed his eyes and let his head settle into the feathery pillow. His nostrils were greeted by the odor of his own accumulated saliva, which after repeated applications had seeped into the pillow, becoming inseparable from the fabric. The sensation was comforting; it provided a cozy familiarity, as ingrained smells often do.

All was quiet; the street was distant, and Elizabeth knew that during a meditation her father was not to be disturbed. In his mind's eye, Baxter saw the tranquil face of the victim, John Harriman. The servant who found the body said that he was not aware of Mr. Harriman granting an audience to anyone that morning. This story was corroborated by the man's colleagues. They all believed the victim to be reading quietly, alone in his study, as he was wont to do. They insisted that no one besides Harriman and the domestic staff was present in the villa. Were they lying? Not necessarily; the story was plausible, given the immensity of the house and the presence of multiple entrances. Someone could have slipped in and out undetected.

Baxter imagined the following scene: the poisoned Harriman, feeling ill, slumped over in his chair. The killer then "helped" the incapacitated man lie on the floor. Next, the criminal announced that he was leaving to summon medical assistance. He escaped via the roof, or some other secretive route, and left Harriman to expire.

Who wanted to end this man's life? The list of antagonists probably contained more than a few names, as Harriman was a controversial public figure who doubtless had acquired enemies. Baxter did not know a great deal about Bioprimalism, the movement for which Harriman was a spokesman, but he was aware that it constituted a challenge to the authority of the Omnificent Cerebrum and its worldly intermediaries.

Baxter emerged from the meditation and sat on the edge of the bed. It was time for his appearance at police headquarters, to satisfy the requirements of administrative procedure. But first, he headed to the nook on the far side of the living room, where the family's Cerebral Shrine was located.

The centerpiece of the shrine was a life-sized ceramic model of the human brain, colored in tones of gray. On the wall behind it hung an artistically embellished diagram of the Temple. Off to one side of the model was a potted miniature bush, carefully trimmed into the shape of a scroll. This was an example of *vegetal symbolism,* more modest but of the same genre as the trees and shrubs along the arcade on Boulevard of the Mind.

The purpose of vegetal symbolism was to proclaim the triumph of man over nature; the dominance of intellect over the rest of the tangible world, be it animal, vegetable, or mineral. Being that man is an agent of the Omnificent Cerebrum, it is his duty to bring as much of the natural environment as possible into the realm of the mind. Thus within the city of Nucleus, one would not easily find a piece of flora, or even of naked earth, that remained in its raw state. Almost everything, from a lone tree to the magnificent gardens in the Temple compound, was sculpted to represent the supremacy of the brain and its creative faculties. This grand statement of purpose was reinforced by an example of vegetal symbolism in every single home.

Baxter recited the Declaration of Cognitive Achievement, in which he renewed the mind carrier's lifelong pledge to employ his intellect as productively as possible, pushing his brain cells to their utmost capacity. After discharging this obligation, Baxter said goodbye to Elizabeth, promising to return before sundown, at which time he would partake of the calf's brain she had offered earlier.

The route to police headquarters was simple: follow Avenue of the Synapses to the north, cross the Plaza, and continue for another five blocks. This latter stretch of the Avenue was dominated by major institutions, and many of the structures were marvelous to behold. For this reason, the short time necessary to traverse the route was often prolonged. There was an additional interruption: Baxter's customary stop at the Plaza, to observe the activity and to admire the incomparable Temple of the Omnificent Cerebrum, rising in the west. Its translucent dome, depicting the surface of the human brain, was accurate in its scale to within a fraction of an inch.

Baxter generally disliked the tasks he needed to perform at headquarters, but enjoyed the company of most of the people who worked there. He also felt himself in harmony, aesthetically speaking, with the building in which it all took place. The structure hailed from the old days of three-story construction, a trait meant to symbolize the three periods of creativity in the life of man: training, active production, and mature reflection. The stone was imbued with numerous hues, all within the range of the browns and reds. A grand archway framed the entrance. The entire edifice traced a perfect circle, as a harbinger of the day when crime would be eliminated, resulting in a smooth, "cornerless" society. The central courtyard was circular as well, presenting a captivating visual effect but causing a perennial headache for the maintenance crew.

Baxter's office, located on the second floor, adjoined the exterior wall. The large windows faced northeast, away from the Temple. The view was nevertheless engaging; just beyond the perimeter fence were the grounds of the Institute for Vegetal Symbolism. A sizable tract of land was dotted with the latest experiments in the exalted art. Baxter often gazed at these floral specimens of intellectual triumph.

Snug against the wall on the far side of the office was a small bed, or rather a cot, designed for meditation. It was simpler and more institutional than the one in Baxter's home. Most of the rooms in the headquarters complex were thus equipped, in accord with the universal custom.

At the moment of his arrival, the cot was inhabited by a junior member of the police force, Officer Phil Jorgensen. Instead of adopting the usual meditative pose—lying prone, body perfectly flat, hands at either side of the head—Jorgensen looked out of place: head tilted slightly upward, one leg bent, foot on top of foot. Baxter recalled that the man never seemed comfortable anywhere. Whether it was his interaction with fellow officers, or witnesses, or even socially, Jorgensen displayed the signs of chronic unease. This attribute did not detract, however, from his competence as a practitioner of law enforcement. An excellent performance at the outset of his career had earned him accolades from his superiors, and his reputation preceded him at all levels of the hierarchy.

Baxter took a seat at his desk, a rather crude block of wood as beat-up as an old police chariot. He unfurled the scroll left for him by the scribe who had taken dictation at the crime scene. The current task was to review the report, and make corrections and amendments as necessary. Baxter tried to marginalize his advanced cerebral functions so as to accomplish the bothersome duty with a minimum of frustration, but his mind wandered. He found himself gazing across the room. The light, at that moment still provided exclusively by the late-afternoon sky, had begun to fade, though not enough to warrant the lamps being pressed into service. A pleasant visual aspect was present, particularly among the numerous scrolls packed into the scrollcases. The natural light coated the parchment, accentuating the patches of yellowish brown that blotted the surface of the more aged documents.

Jorgensen's attempt at meditation began to unravel. One hand gripped the edge of the cot as a muffled groan slipped from his throat. He turned onto his side, so that he faced the interior of the office.

"I assume you're here because they assigned you to the Harriman case," said Baxter, as he corrected a spelling mistake in the scroll.

"You got it," replied Jorgensen, with a moan. He sat up on the bed. Although his meditation was a failure, he had gained some rest for the body, leaving behind a residue of grogginess.

"I want to know everything about our victim, including the philosophy he was associated with, this so-called Bioprimalism."

"Sure, boss. I'll churn the archives. Then I'll head over to the crime scene."

"No need for that," said Baxter. "We'll go there in the morning, when there's plenty of daylight and we're fresh."

Jorgensen stood up and stretched his lanky frame, as long and thin as a string bean. The shaggy mop of black hair was always unkempt, matching the wiry beard and wrinkled tunic. It was hard to believe that this same man was more proficient in the use of the dagger than almost anyone else on the force. "We'll comb the entire neighborhood," he said, taking a seat across the desk from his supervisor.

"You seem quite eager," remarked Baxter.

"Well, why not? There hasn't been a murder in this town for weeks. I'm sick of traffic detail and all that phony paperwork they shove down our throats." His knee was bouncing up and down, and more than once it smacked the underside of the desk.

"Can you stop that? I'm trying to write."

"Sorry, boss," said Jorgensen, altering his position in the chair. "We constantly have to file some kind of report. Who reads that stuff, anyway?"

Ignoring the complaint, Baxter made his final correction in the text, returned the quill to the inkstand, and rolled up the scroll. "Take this down to the archive. I assume you've seen it?"

"Yes, I did," said Jorgensen, as he leaned onto the desk. "Who do you think killed Harriman?"

"I have no idea," said Baxter, his voice sounding more gravelly than usual. "I'll be going upstairs to see the Chief, then home. Tomorrow morning, just after sunrise, we'll meet here and head over to the crime scene. You can let me know what turned up in your research."

"You don't really like the Chief, do you?"

A scowl covered Baxter's ruddy features. "Sometimes, Phil, you talk too much."

The junior partner rose from his seat, picked up the scroll, and made his way to the door. No words were exchanged, but a distinct swagger conveyed a message of defiance. There was a streak of immaturity in the young man, thought Baxter; he seemed to thrive on goading his elders into confessing their personal prejudices. The demeanor, though annoying, was never so trenchant as to be infuriating. On the contrary, it tended to arouse Baxter's paternal instincts. He perceived it as a cry for help from a forlorn individual, tough in so many ways, yet exhibiting a certain emotional frailty.

There was an element of truth in Jorgensen's assertion that Baxter harbored a negative view of the Chief. The problem was politics and bureaucracy. Baxter loathed these aspects of the police department, and the Chief, inevitably, was their prime exponent. When the two men were off-duty, the interaction between them, if not gratifying, was at least tolerable.

As it turned out, the meeting was rushed because of an administrative crisis. People were coming and going, and the conversation, if one could call it that, was punctuated by the Chief shouting at underlings in the adjoining rooms. All of this met with no objection from Baxter; the session had been mercifully brief, and he had discharged the obligation to update his superior.

Baxter's relief was short-lived. Upon exiting headquarters, he was confronted by a cluster of reporters. Though fewer in number than the group assembled earlier in the day at John Harriman's villa, the ruckus was equally enervating. He patiently presented the same story as before: Harriman was poisoned; it was probably a homicide; an investigation was underway; everyone would be informed as soon as there was a development in the case.

The detective was soon back on the street, homeward bound. The sun was now out of sight; though still above the horizon, it was no longer visible to a pedestrian in the midst of Nucleus. The air had cooled, providing a pleasant environment for a brisk walk. And indeed, Baxter's step was rapid, as he contemplated the dinner that would emerge from his daughter's capable hands.

When he opened the door of his apartment and stepped into the foyer, his ears were perked like those of a pure-bred hound.

"Hi, Daddy," came the melodic voice, without delay.

Baxter returned the greeting, as a sensation of comfort expanded within his spirit. He changed his tunic and presented himself at the kitchen table. He recited an abbreviated version of the Declaration of Cognitive Achievement, and the meal commenced. It fully met his expectations. As they discussed Elizabeth's day at the university, he let his opinion of the food be known, much to the delight of the chef. The calf's brain was as delicious as ever. He could feel his own mind sharpen as his digestive system repackaged and dispersed within his body the molecules of another creature's organ of awareness. Baxter never thoroughly understood the reasons for this transfer of force, despite having studied the topic in the Tomes of Ancient Thought. It did not make sense to him that the cerebral tissue of a sentient but non-intellectual being could have a positive impact on the brain of a mind carrier.

"How did it go at headquarters?" asked Elizabeth, as she cleared the dishes from the table.

"Oh, nothing exceptional. The usual nonsense with the Chief. Jorgensen is combing the archives, and we're going back to Harriman's villa first thing in the morning."

"And how is Mr. Know-it-All doing?"

"Just fine, thank you. By the way, Phil thinks highly of *you*."

She laughed. "Really? Does that mean he wants to add me to his collection of trophies?"

Baxter regretted his remark, annoyed at himself for failing to foresee the consequences.

"So," she continued, "you'd like to have him as a son-in-law?"

"I could do worse," said Baxter, unwilling to divulge the extent of his aversion to the idea.

"Okay, then tell him I'd like to meet with him as soon as possible."

"Please stop torturing me."

Elizabeth burst into laughter. Then, after glancing at her father with affectionate eyes, she placed herself behind his chair, rested her chin on his head, and draped her arms over his shoulders and chest. "Don't worry, Daddy, I was just kidding. About him, about anyone. I won't leave you."

It is difficult to describe the heartache experienced by Baxter at that moment. How could he indicate his displeasure at her remark, when at its root was an expression of profound fondness for him? And how could he crack the kernel of irrationality that informed her thinking? He had told her numerous times that he desired her departure from the house, on condition of course that a man with sufficiently high intelligence be found. She stubbornly refused to absorb this information, acting as if it had never been communicated. On the contrary, she cast him in the role of lonely widower, dependent on her care and affection for his very survival. Nothing he could say seemed to dent this attitude in the slightest degree.

Baxter went to sleep that night with a dose of angst in his spirit. As it turned out, the scene with Elizabeth was the prelude to yet another portion of anxiety. Although his sleep was usually peaceful, on occasion a bizarre and perplexing dream would leave its mark. So it was that very night. He dreamt that he was the commander of a military force that was camping in the field. The troops were awaiting his word to set forth. The terrain, with its sparse vegetation and sandy soil, was unlike anything he had ever seen. Behind the troops was a ridge of about fifty feet in height, topped by a promontory of sheer rock. It was a stark and vivid image, but it receded quickly.

Baxter lay in bed afterward for some time, awake but enveloped in nocturnal fog. The dream had unsettled him. Never before had he constructed such a scene in his mind.

II. THE COURTESAN

Shortly before sunrise, Baxter's half-conscious state was jarred by a pounding on the front door. He jumped to his feet, slipped into his tunic, grabbed his dagger, and moved rapidly toward the foyer. He saw Elizabeth standing in the living room, in her nightgown. Wielding the weapon, he approached the door.

"Who is it?"

"It's Phil."

Baxter opened the door. "This better be good," he said.

"It is, boss," said Jorgensen, smiling and pointing at the dagger. "You can put that down now."

Baxter obliged, setting the weapon on the breakfront. He motioned for his assistant to step inside.

"Hi, Elizabeth," said Jorgensen, after moving far enough into the apartment to catch a glimpse of the living room. Elizabeth scurried into her bedroom without saying a word.

"Well?" said Baxter.

"I have a suspect. We can wrap up the case right now. She's waiting for us at the Obscure Thought, you know, that all-night café on the East Side."

"Don't tell me. You threatened to arrest her."

"Correct," said Jorgensen. "I ran across her on another case. I know what she does—she's a harlot. Just now I said that if she doesn't wait for me to come back, I'll have her arrested for public solicitation."

"All right," said Baxter, giving up hope of delaying the moment of departure any further. He washed his face, put on his sandals, and fastened his dagger-sheath. The two officers of the law set out into the still-darkened city.

"I was at the archives until well past midnight," said Jorgensen, as they turned from Cortex Lane onto Avenue of the Synapses. "After leaving, I decided to take a leisurely stroll."

"Just a little stroll?"

"Yes, around John Harriman's villa. Not the complete sweep we're supposed to do today, just some poking around. So anyway, I arrive at the scene, check here, check there, and then, as I was about to leave, I saw our prostitute—her name, by the way, is Jiliada—doing some of her own poking around. I watched her for a while. She scanned the pathway, and then rolled a rock over with her foot. She's the murderer, for sure. Must've lost something and wanted to find it before we did. Tried to cover her tracks. The whole thing is obvious."

"*Nothing* is obvious, Phil," retorted Baxter. "There could be a dozen explanations for her behavior, starting with the simplest: Harriman was her patron, this was the appointed moment, and she was trying to figure out why the side entrance she always uses was shut. What did she say when you confronted her?"

"That she came to see Harriman, but first needed to find an expensive pair of earrings that she had lost during her previous visit last Ninthday. Don't tell me you believe that, boss."

"I don't know yet what I believe."

The two policemen reached the Plaza and turned right onto Boulevard of the Mind, on course for the East Side. They broke into a jog, enabling them to arrive promptly at the Obscure Thought. The café was located on a side street off the Boulevard, a few blocks from the Harriman residence. The old and venerable establishment had been part of the cityscape for several generations. At that time of night it was populated by insomniacs, workers on the graveyard shift, the lonely, the desperate, and other nocturnal figures.

They found the suspect in the back room, seated on a crude wooden chair next to a small table of similar construction. These simple furnishings matched the overall decor. The walls were entirely bare, coated with a smooth white plaster. The floor was a slab of dark cement that had sprouted numerous cracks.

Jiliada looked quite different from what Baxter had imagined. She wore a tasteful blue dress, plain sandals, and an elegant yet understated gold bracelet. She was slim, with silky, shoulder-length hair. The face was endowed with the richest appointments: thick natural eyebrows; large green eyes; smooth, glistening skin; and a prominent angle of the jaw, a trait that was prevalent among the learned classes. All of the parts fit together exquisitely, as if an artist had fashioned a statue using the most carefully calculated proportions.

None of this escaped the probing eye of the senior detective. Another aspect of Jiliada's persona that did not pass unnoticed was her resemblance to Elizabeth. It was subtle yet unmistakable. She had the same proportions in the figure, the same hairstyle, and the same distinctive facial expression, a clever and slightly mischievous look, as she awaited the opportunity for an astute remark. The resemblance was not so sharp as to be irksome; its primary effect was to kindle Baxter's curiosity and predispose him to be sympathetic in his dealings with her.

"I believe," he began, in a gentle tone, "that we owe you an apology."

Jiliada did not respond, but looked on with anticipation. Jorgensen rolled his eyes.

"My young partner is sometimes overzealous. Please forgive him. Now that we are here, however, I will ask for your help. If you decline, well, that is your right. You will not be arrested for any offense whatsoever. In fact, you can leave at this very moment if you wish." Baxter, tugging at his chin, leaned back in the chair.

Jiliada, her mouth tense, looked at Baxter and then at Jorgensen. The latter averted his eyes.

"How can I help you?" she asked, coldly.

"As you probably know, John Harriman is dead, apparently murdered."

"Yes, I was just informed."

"And I understand that you had … shall we say … a certain relationship with the deceased."

"Yes, I did."

"The relationship itself doesn't interest me. What does interest me is the information he may have shared with you. Things he may have told you about his life, his work, his associates, and—most important—his enemies." Baxter leaned forward onto the table. "I want to know who had a reason to kill John Harriman."

The waiter arrived, only to be dismissed by Baxter. A long silence followed. Jiliada was staring at the wilted flowers in the dilapidated earthenware vase that presumed to adorn the center of the table. Baxter noticed the beautiful form of the young woman's mouth. As he settled deeper into appreciation of this rare delight, he became convinced that he had once met her. He was unsure, however, of the time and place.

"I really can't help you," said Jiliada. "John talked about the Bioprimalist movement, and told me that he might be in danger, but it was always in a general sense. He never mentioned any names."

"Never?" asked Jorgensen, in a sarcastic tone.

"I believe that's the word she used," said Baxter. "Do you have any other information that might be useful to us?"

"No, I don't think so."

Baxter removed a small piece of parchment from his pocket, and handed it to Jiliada. "That's my name and the address of my bureau. The moment you think of anything, send a courier to let me know where I can find you. I realize that this is all very sudden. Perhaps if you meditate, an important detail will emerge. I would be grateful if you could share it with me."

She nodded and rose from her chair. Baxter also stood up. "May your intellect expand," he said, bowing slightly. As she left the room, Baxter followed her with his eyes. There was no longer any doubt in his mind that they had met previously.

"That's it?" said Jorgensen, throwing up his hands. "You let the whore go, just like that?"

"My dear sir," replied Baxter, slowly extracting the words from his coarse vocal chords. "We are not in the business of judging anyone's actions, unless it pertains directly to the case. And even then, we do it without emotion. Incidentally, I would not use the epithet with which you so rashly describe her. I would say, rather, that she is a *courtesan,* and of a rather urbane and gracious disposition. You youngsters are unaware of the role such women played in our society as late as a generation or two ago. Alas, it is a vanishing institution, as so many others in our day."

"Well, whatever you want to call her, boss, she gave us absolutely nothing."

"Patience, my boy, patience. As a general rule, Phil, we want all the mind carriers we encounter, including witnesses and even suspects, to work for us. Therefore, unless someone holding a blood-soaked dagger confesses to the deed, we want to win him over. So try to make the whole experience enjoyable, or at least non-threatening. Almost invariably, someone will let down his guard and lead us right to the killer's doorstep—even if he himself is the killer."

Jorgensen was shaking his head, evidently frustrated.

"The sun is rising," remarked Baxter, glancing at the exit as he stood up. "Let us conduct our sweep of the crime area. On the way there, you can tell me what you found last night in the archives." He placed a coin on the table, and they left the Obscure Thought Café.

During the walk, Jorgensen related the information he had gleaned from his research. John Harriman, at a relatively young age, inherited his father's business, a slaughterhouse. He expanded the enterprise until it became the largest of its kind in the Nucleus area. An enormous sum of money was earned in the process. After his early retirement, Harriman made the acquaintance of some teachers and low-level sages who were developing a new school of thought called Bioprimalism. According to them, the rite of the Omnificent Cerebrum is misguided, and some say demonic. People should embrace nature, not abuse and pervert it. Bioprimalists take an oath to desist from altering the natural environment in any way, unless absolutely unavoidable. Houses, to cite but one example, are constructed only on sites that require no landscaping. Vegetal symbolism is an abomination in their eyes, and will sooner or later result in catastrophe. The earth, inevitably, will wreak her revenge.

Harriman's contribution to the movement was more practical than theoretical. Most significantly, he organized the first publicity campaign, which was restricted to a thin layer of the learned classes. These inroads were tolerated by the authorities with the tacit understanding that it remain nothing more than a chic diversion, kept distant from the general public.

Baxter and Jorgensen conducted a thorough survey of the neighborhood in which the crime occurred. Next, they began a painstaking examination, or rather re-examination, of the interior of the Harriman villa. No corner was left untouched. Each person they encountered was questioned. Despite the extensiveness of the investigation and the punctilious methods employed, nothing of significance was gained. Alibis were solid. No motives were uncovered. No traces of the murderer's presence were found. There were no witnesses, and no suspicious activity reported by anyone. It was determined that suicide would have to be considered as a possible cause of death.

The two police officers returned to headquarters. They stopped at the Cerebral Shrine, and then headed for the cafeteria to partake in a hearty lunch. Following the meal, they went to the morgue, located in the basement, for the final inspection of Harriman's corpse prior to its release to the family. They were joined in this task by the coroner, who confirmed his earlier judgment, at the crime scene, of death by poison. He also confirmed his initial determination that the time of death was early in the morning. This meant that the corpse had been languishing for almost half a day prior to its discovery by the household staff.

Normally, the next of kin would transfer the body to an undertaker for burial. But the Bioprimalists, explained Jorgensen, refuse to bury their dead, claiming that cadavers discharge a toxic substance that pollutes the earth, endangering flora and fauna. To overcome the problem, they cremate the body and scatter the ashes over an area containing as much human settlement as possible.

No new information was acquired from inspection of the corpse. After thanking the coroner, Baxter dispatched his junior partner to handle a minor but essential bureaucratic duty. He then retired to his office for a midday meditative session on the cot.

The quality of the session was below average. The effort to clear his mind was disrupted by images of Jiliada. The tender contours of her mouth, and the way she moved—so similar to Elizabeth—distracted him, as did his inability to recall where they previously had met.

He sat up on the cot before the normal term of a meditation had passed. With a deep groan, he lifted himself, stretched his stiff back, and leaned onto the window sill. It was another gorgeous, sun-drenched day in Nucleus. He inhaled the fresh air and gazed at the outside world. About forty yards away, on the grounds of the Institute for Vegetal Symbolism, a man was busily trimming a piece of shrubbery. His companion stood close by, holding a small scroll in one hand while pointing at various spots on the plant with the other. The emerging floral sculpture seemed to be taking the shape of an inkwell.

Baxter pondered the information that Jorgensen had uncovered regarding the Bioprimalist movement. How was it possible to have such contorted beliefs and practices—building houses with no landscaping? Perhaps the cult was one of the periodic manifestations of intellectual disarray mentioned in the Tomes of Ancient Thought. In which case, thought Baxter, the aberration would be purged by the spiritual elite, who would take steps forthwith to counteract the cerebral virus well before it could threaten the Home Cell, let alone another cell in the cosmic Brain. If this cleansing process were underway, the murder of John Harriman might very well be an assassination. In similar cases in the past, however, the police were instructed to halt the investigation, and the matter was handled in some other way.

Jorgensen entered the room and noisily tossed a scroll onto the desk. "Here's that useless inventory document," he announced, "all ready for your signature." He sauntered over to the window, leaned his lanky frame onto the vacant side of the sill, and joined Baxter in his observation of the neighbors. "So what are they clipping over there in shrub-land? You'd think that by now they would have exhausted their imagination."

"Is something bothering you?" asked Baxter, calmly, without shifting his glance.

"Yeah, I'll tell you what's bothering me. Those guys at the Institute have the same intelligence grade as some people at the university. But they're nothing more than glorified florists. They find a shape they like, and then give a tree a haircut. Wow, I'm really impressed."

"Are you jealous?"

Jorgensen laughed. "You're kidding me, right? I could've worked at the Institute, I was qualified. Not for me, thank you."

"So you always wanted to be a cop?" asked Baxter, now looking at his partner.

The question seemed to pierce Jorgensen's armor of sarcasm, as his facial muscles reflected the tension of emotional distress. "It wasn't my first choice. What I really wanted to do was work in the Temple. Not necessarily as a sage, but something. I just missed the cutoff."

"That's a shame."

"What about you, boss?"

"My father was a captain on the force, as you know."

"And a great one, too."

"Yes, he was," said Baxter. "His father was commander of special operations. My maternal grandfather was the Chief of Police. There was never any doubt that I would follow in their footsteps. I was groomed for it since childhood."

"But is that what you wanted?"

"I wanted to do what was expected of me. That I actually had a choice never entered my mind."

"Did you have a passion for police work?"

"I have a passion to be as successful as my forebears."

Jorgensen scratched his beard. "What's your intelligence grade, if you don't mind me asking?"

"Bountiful."

"You're a *Bountiful?*" exclaimed Jorgensen.

"Correct."

"That's amazing. You could have been a teacher … or a sage."

"Yet I am not."

There was a knock at the door.

"Come in," said Baxter.

A short, overweight man, panting from his ascent of the stairs, entered the room. He was holding a rolled parchment sealed with wax.

"Hi, Ernest. What do you have for us?"

"A message, sir. Just arrived at the front desk."

"Thanks," said Baxter, taking possession of the document. Ernest returned to his post. With Jorgensen looking on, Baxter broke the seal and unrolled the parchment. It was a note from Jiliada. She was waiting for him at a certain address in Two Scribes, a village located about five miles from Nucleus.

"You were right about her stepping up, boss," said Jorgensen. "I guess I have a lot to learn."

"We all have a lot to learn."

"Do you want me to come with you? I could wait nearby in case there's a problem."

"There won't be any problem."

"Are you going to run it?"

Baxter chuckled. "I can't run that kind of distance anymore. No, I'll take a chariot for this one."

"They say that you used to run ten miles like it was around the block."

"A gross exaggeration. In any case, Phil, the operative term is *used to.*"

"And that you once finished third in the marathon."

"It was fourth place, actually."

"What should I do while you're away?" asked Jorgensen.

"Find out more about Bioprimalism and Harriman's role in it. Go see the Chief. You know how good he is with anything political. He has his finger on the pulse."

"Me, talk to the Chief? What, just waltz into his office and say I'm there to speak to him?"

"Why not? Say that I sent you, if you wish. He'll like it, don't worry. He craves attention. Massage his ego a bit; make him feel like an expert— which he is, actually, in these matters."

"Okay, boss, I'll see what I can do."

They left the room together before going their separate ways. Jorgensen went up to the third floor while Baxter descended to the stables to requisition a chariot. Soon, he was cracking the whip, speeding along Avenue of the Synapses toward the northern gate of the city.

Because of a revulsion from livestock, driving was not his favorite task. The odor of the horses, blowing constantly into his face, was distasteful to him in the extreme. This reaction was not unusual. People in Nucleus generally kept their distance from animals of all kinds, regarding them as a chilling reminder of the degraded condition that occurs when intellect is cast aside in favor of bestial instinct and emotion. In the rare event that someone owned a pet, it generally served as a decorative object, as in the case of fish. Moreover, no mind carrier would ever think of riding upon the back of a horse, donkey, or other animal. This would be considered undignified.

The road to Two Scribes began just beyond the city gate. It was wide, level, and well-maintained. It was also one of the principal highways of the realm, connecting Nucleus with the coast. Numerous points of interest, such as the great stadium and the largest quarry in the Home Cell, were found along its length. In the segment traversed by Baxter, there were several upscale suburbs, Two Scribes among them. The remaining terrain consisted of farmland and some patches of forest.

After crossing the boundary of Two Scribes, Baxter slowed his pair of horses to a trot. He drove to the local police station, and deposited the chariot at the stables. An officer instructed him on how to reach his destination. He set off on foot.

The police station was part of a cluster of commercial and civic buildings packed together on the main street. Beyond this downtown district were wide thoroughfares lined with splendid villas. The gardens offered the eye a wide range of vegetal symbolism, and of the very highest quality. Baxter passed through this pleasant environment before arriving at the designated address, a compound surrounded by a high brick wall. He followed the length of the wall until he came upon the carriage gate. It was made of thick wood, painted dark blue. All of the hardware—knobs, hinges, knocker, bell, and number-plate—was fashioned from a lustrous copper, which evidently had been polished quite recently.

He yanked the cord that was dangling from the bell. Very soon, the gate opened. An old man, dressed in a simple and neat tunic, indicated with a wave of the hand that it was permissible to enter the compound. Baxter stepped across the threshold. With the servant leading the way, they crossed a segment of the grounds, bypassing the villa itself. The three-story home was an impressive architectural achievement, replete with statuary, balconies, and a stunning portico. Baxter enjoyed the sight of the structure before coming to a halt at a patio of mosaic, which, like the pavement tiles on Boulevard of the Mind, depicted a portion of the brain—in this case the cerebellum—in cross-section. Alongside the patio was a small pond containing a collection of golden-colored fish, visible here and there under the lily pads that dotted the surface. The area was covered by a canopy of yellow fabric, which protected its occupants, and the furniture, from the sun.

Seated on one piece of that furniture was Jiliada. She motioned for her guest to sit in the adjoining armchair, and dismissed the servant. The old man retreated to a spot next to the house.

"Thank you for coming so quickly," she said.

"Thank you for inviting me," replied Baxter.

Jiliada responded to his graciousness by a nod and the thinnest of smiles. She was curled up, her legs fully within the confines of the capacious armchair. Her bare feet, resting on the cushion, were exposed below the hem of a red dress made from a fine grade of linen. Sharing the cushion with her was a pudgy black cat. The creature was examining the newcomer with distrustful eyes.

"This is quite a home," remarked Baxter, trying to recall the last time he had seen a mammalian pet.

"Thank you," said Jiliada. "The villa's not mine, though I've been here for over a year. I have a very generous patron. He lets me take care of his properties."

"Sounds like a convenient arrangement."

"It is," she said, scratching the cat's head. "Can we get you something to drink? It's warm today, and you must be thirsty from your journey."

"Nothing for me, thank you." He was distracted by one of the fish, whose brief emergence from the water caused a noticeable splash. Baxter returned his glance to the woman, trying to remember where they might have met. He also noted, with relief, that the resemblance to Elizabeth at that moment was minimal. This may have been due to the nonchalance of Jiliada's posture in the chair, a type of deportment his daughter would never allow herself to adopt.

"I want to help you," said Jiliada, her face acquiring a grave expression. "John Harriman was a special man. He looked after me, spoiled me in fact. He even took me on a trip to the coast. I'm telling you all this because I care. I feel distressed by the crime, and would love to see the murderer hang from the highest tree."

"We'll do our best to see that it happens. Tell me something ... Miss ..."

"Jiliada will do."

"Okay, Jiliada. How do you know it's not suicide?"

"Suicide? I don't think so. He was a man with a mission, and always positive, always optimistic. The last person in the world who would take his own life."

"How would you describe Mr. Harriman's financial situation?"

"Loaded."

"All assets in the clear? No debts?"

"Not that I know of. Why do you ask?"

"Financial difficulties are a prolific source of conflict," said Baxter, tugging at his chin. "Who will be inheriting this fortune?"

"I really don't know," said Jiliada, pulling the bottom of her dress in an effort to cover her bare feet. "I guess it would be his children. He has two sons and a daughter."

"Does your house belong to him?"

"No, to a different patron."

"Did you get a chance to meet any of his associates? His ideological cohorts, that is."

"Oh, you mean the Bioprimalists?"

"Yes. What do you think of them?"

"I ... well ... I don't know. Does it matter what I think of them?"

"They're a bit ghoulish, aren't they?"

A short burst of laughter escaped from Jiliada's mouth before she was able to hide it with her hand.

"In all likelihood," continued Baxter, "they would claim that the plants in your garden are as intelligent as your goldfish, and the goldfish are as clever as your cat. No offense to your cat, of course, who looks to be rather shrewd."

This time Jiliada let loose a full giggle, allowing her guest to view a true smile. "Well," she said, "the cat isn't mine; he belongs to the gardener. But yes, shrewd is the word."

"So you agree with me about the Bioprimalists?" he insisted.

"Yes, I do. It's a dangerous path."

"Now, Jiliada, I will ask you the same question I did when we first met at the Obscure Thought Café, under those lamentable circumstances. Who would have a reason to kill John Harriman?"

There was a long silence before Jiliada sat up in the chair, repositioning the cat in her lap. "There is someone, actually."

"Yes ..."

"It's a man named Ross Kinkade."

"Ross Kinkade," murmured Baxter, attempting to stimulate his vague recollection. "Ah … the curator of the art museum?

"Correct."

"How does he fit into all this?"

"Simple," said Jiliada. "Kinkade is one of the captains of Bioprimalism, and John's fiercest rival. John loathed him, and I believe the feeling was mutual. I met Kinkade only once, at John's house, and then only for a moment. That look of contempt in his eyes is an image I'll never forget."

"Kinkade knows about your relationship to Harriman?"

"No, he doesn't. The encounter was unplanned. John passed me off as a relative." Jiliada displayed her thin smile while fluffing her hair, causing Baxter momentarily to lose his train of thought.

"Well," he said, "I'll have to pay this Mr. Kinkade a visit. Thank you for that information. Just one last question, if I may, and then I'll leave you in peace."

"It's no bother. As I told you, I have an interest in seeing that justice be done."

"Of course. Tell me, Jiliada, did John ever say that he had enemies from the other side of the fence? In other words, individuals opposed to Bioprimalism?"

"Strange, but I don't recall anything. You would think that he'd have enemies galore from the other side of the fence, as you put it. Perhaps he did, but he never talked about it. John was fixated on his own organization, on rivals, on maneuvering."

Baxter digested the stream of information as he gazed at the little pond. A stout frog had established himself on a lily pad, and was now engaged in a vocal campaign to publicize the fact. Baxter had no further questions in mind, so he stood up. "Thank you very much," he said.

Jiliada gently placed the cat on the mosaic floor, rose from her armchair, and shook the detective's hand. "It was my pleasure to assist you," she said, glancing at the servant, who was still standing by the house, at his vigil. "I'll tell …"

"No need for that," interrupted Baxter. "I can find my way out. May your intellect expand." He bowed slightly, and took leave without further delay.

The preceding scene replayed itself in his mind as he retraced his steps to the police station of Two Scribes. The trip-wire of his investigative sixth sense had been jiggled; the alarm bells were ringing. Something didn't fit, though he couldn't put his finger on it. Was it that Jiliada had cast aspersions upon John Harriman's own people, instead of his ideological adversaries? Or that her body language and facial expressions didn't match her protestations of concern about the murder and the outcome of the case? Then again, it might have been her suspicious tone when responding to some of the questions, such as the one about Harriman's financial situation.

Baxter reclaimed his chariot from the police stables and returned to Nucleus, but not before sharing a pot of tea with the men at the station, at their insistence. By the time he arrived at his office, it was after sundown. Jorgensen had written a note announcing that he was leaving for the day and would return after breakfast. Baxter sent a parchment by courier to Ross Kinkade, curator of the art museum, requesting an interview for the following morning. He then left headquarters and headed home.

After eating dinner with Elizabeth, he immersed himself in a scroll that he had been reading for several weeks. It was a long essay on metaphysics, authored by one of the leading philosophers of ancient times. The subject matter fascinated Baxter, and the thoughts it stimulated usually set the stage for a peaceful sleep.

That night, however, he was visited by an anxiety-ridden dream. It was a continuation of the previous one. Again, he pictured himself as the commander of a military detachment. Alongside the camp was the same ridge, topped by the promontory of sheer rock. This time, he viewed the underside of the promontory. There was some kind of movement on its surface. He approached, until he was standing directly underneath. He discerned a number of creatures who were clinging, upside down, to the rock. It was a peculiar species, apparently a type of lizard with webbed feet. It gave the appearance of being a cross between animal and mineral; when stationary, it was nearly indistinguishable from the rock, having the same mottled grayish coloring. Baxter noticed that one of the creatures was having difficulty gripping the surface; one leg slipped, then another, and then a third, so that it was hanging by its right forefoot, now grasping the edge of a crevice with tenacity. The other lizards set upon it, biting it with their formidable teeth. It resisted, shrieking in a bestial wail. One of the larger rock-lizards clamped its jaw upon the victim's ankle, severing the foot. The body plummeted to the ground, landing with a great thump a few feet from Baxter. He turned his head to view the troops. They were going about their business as if nothing had happened. He returned his glance to the fallen creature, but it had disappeared. He looked up at the promontory. The swarm of lizards was still present, but there was no movement.

He felt a coldness in his bones, and then woke up.

III. THE MONKEY

Baxter rose quickly from the bed in an attempt to distance himself from the eerie nocturnal vision. He slipped into his tunic and stood at the window. The bedroom faced away from the street; the view consisted of the rear of the apartment houses on the next block. At that moment, just before sunrise, there was no one about.

The disturbing forms of the dream, still lifelike, hovered in his consciousness: the promontory; the bizarre rock-creatures with their webbed feet; the hideous shrieking of the one that fell to its death. Baxter was mired in the jumble of images, unable to snap himself into a fully awakened state in which a clear analysis of the dream might be possible.

He performed a short meditation and recited the Declaration of Cognitive Achievement. By the time he sat down to breakfast with Elizabeth, the usual calmness had re-established itself within his spirit. Watching his daughter's graceful step provided him with a sense of comfort, and it hastened the return to normal existence.

"Daddy, is everything all right?" she asked, pouring the tea. "You seem so pensive this morning."

Baxter smiled, watching her settle into her spot across the table. Her body was still young enough to have the last remnant of the jerky and insouciant motion of childhood, yet old enough to have a fully-developed womanly form. It made him think of his deceased wife Eleanor, who exhibited the same physique and the same characteristics when he first met her, also when she was eighteen.

"Everything's okay," he said. "There's nothing to worry about. Just a strange dream, that's all. It's the second time I had it."

"What happened? If you want to tell me, of course."

Baxter described the dream.

"That's so odd," said Elizabeth. "What do you think it means?"

"I have no idea," he replied, tugging at his chin. "Who can fathom the wisdom of the Omnificent Cerebrum, and the relationship between its thoughts and our little personal glob of gray matter?"

"Some little globs contain more interesting thoughts than others."

"Yes, my dear, like yours. Have you been storing any new medical procedures in that gray matter?"

Elizabeth laughed. "Daddy, we're not learning medical procedures yet. Just the science that medicine is based on."

"Oh yes, of course, I forgot." He buttered a piece of bread and took a bite of it.

"How's the new case going?" she inquired.

"Slowly. No witnesses, no suspects. So far the star of the drama is a courtesan who counted among her patrons the victim, the late Mr. Harriman. She thinks that the murderer might be a certain rival within his own camp. We'll be paying that rival a visit today."

"His own camp—you mean the Bioprimalists?"

"Yes."

"When I was at the library yesterday, I did some research on them. I read that they recently clashed with people in high places, including the Great Sage. There was no controversy as long as the group kept quiet, but the situation changed when they held a public meeting a couple of months ago. It was in the auditorium of the art museum."

"Very interesting," said Baxter. "Go on."

"A representative of the government attended the meeting. He warned that this new mode of activity would not go unanswered by the authorities."

"Interesting, indeed. I don't recall hearing about that."

"It was in a news-scroll from last month, buried in an article about vegetal symbolism."

"I see," said Baxter, wondering why Jorgensen was unable to uncover that same information. "Anything else?"

"No, that's all I found."

"You know, I might hire you as my research assistant."

"Well ... I don't think you would want me around all day."

"True. Maybe it's better that we have completely separate careers."

Elizabeth's eyes opened wide, a sign that her sharp intellect was at work. "Of course, I might decide to study forensic medicine. Then I could work at police headquarters."

"Why, do you like rotting corpses?"

"At least they're polite, and not very demanding."

"Like certain *living* people?" he asked, with a smile.

Elizabeth leapt from her chair, banging the table in the process, and threw herself into her father's lap. She hugged him tightly.

"Now, now, what's all this about?"

"Nothing," she said, withdrawing her head from his chest. "It's just that you were so cute before."

Baxter felt a coldness in his bones, not unlike the sensation at the end of his dream. "Okay, my dear," he said, gently detaching her hands from the back of his neck. "I'm afraid this cute policeman has to go to work."

She gave him one more hug before standing up. From the pout on her face, he knew that she was displeased by his abrupt termination of the embrace. He gave her a conciliatory kiss on the cheek, and left the kitchen.

On his way to headquarters, Baxter paused for longer than usual at the Plaza. He gazed at the Temple, pondering the wisdom of the Omnificent Cerebrum, and his own role in the cosmic drama that flowed therefrom. Why was he being compelled to struggle with his daughter in such a disconcerting fashion? He could see no easy exit from the maze. Ideally, she would marry a young man and turn her attention to raising a family. But she demonstrated no interest in the prospect. Too bad about Jorgensen, that his intelligence grade was a bit low. The nervous personality did not help matters either, though he had good intentions and was honest. In any case, Elizabeth vented her disdain for him at every opportunity.

What about the dream of the rock-creatures? A recurring dream is a serious matter, Baxter reminded himself. Three occurrences within a week—he already had two—and he would need to seek professional guidance. Such dreams carry vital messages from the Omnificent Cerebrum, and one would be ill-advised to ignore them.

Returning his attention to the Plaza, he noticed that a sizable group of people had congregated around a speechmaker. The man was standing on a stone pedestal, of which there were several scattered across the square.

"Reject all non-cerebral activity!" he wailed, shaking his fist in the air. "It is a trap. Creature comforts soften and destroy the mind."

"So no more steak, just bread and water?" said a man in the crowd, provoking a round of laughter among his fellow auditors.

"You may eat steak, but don't let it rule you. One cannot connect with the Omnificent Cerebrum unless one's brain is functioning at peak condition, like a sturdy, well-oiled chariot."

How many mind carriers, thought Baxter, were capable of such a regimen of drastically curtailed bodily pleasure? What about the need for recreation and exercise, which provide a release from intellectual tension? Rejecting all non-cerebral activity, as advocated by the speechmaker, might actually be counterproductive to the honing of one's cognitive powers.

Baxter was still pondering these questions when he arrived at the office. Waiting for him there was Jorgensen, who described his meeting with the Chief. It yielded approximately the same information about John Harriman and the Bioprimalists as the article mentioned by Elizabeth. As predicted by Baxter, the Chief had demonstrated openness to the approach of the junior officer. In fact, related Jorgensen, the Chief seemed intent on abbreviating any treatment of the case, preferring instead to wax nostalgic about his own experience as a young policeman rising through the ranks.

It was still early in the day when a parchment arrived from Ross Kinkade. The curator indicated his acceptance of Baxter's proposed meeting. Any time that morning would be acceptable. The two officers were out the door within a few moments, on their way to see the man said by Jiliada to be the primary rival of John Harriman.

The art museum was located a few blocks from police headquarters, in the cluster of civic institutions farther south along Avenue of the Synapses. It was set back a ways from the street; the grounds contained an expansive garden endowed with fine examples of vegetal symbolism, a smattering of sculpture, and some hybrids of both. Among the works of sculpture was one of Baxter's favorites: a life-sized statue of a man, in grayish stone, with hand extended. The hand was holding a glass hemisphere upon which were embossed the constellations of the heavens. The face was characterized by an inquisitive expression.

The building itself embodied the most tasteful traditional style, befitting the works that were domiciled within its walls. Steps of gleaming white marble provided the visitor's feet with a gracious ascent from ground level up to the wide colonnade that covered most of the façade. The doorways just beyond were shaped in the profile of some of the most illustrious heads in the history of the Home Cell. In this regard, they resembled the entrance to Baxter's apartment building; only here, needless to say, the craftsmanship was much more refined.

The lobby of the museum was airy and spacious, rising to the full height of the three-story structure. Its vaulted ceiling was punctuated by patches of stained glass, which diffused a soft, multicolored light across the space below. Speaking louder than a whisper produced an echo. When numerous mind carriers were gathered in the lobby, the result was a background din that served as a portent of the weighty works of art that waited patiently in the galleries for the arrival of appreciative intellects.

In the rear of the lobby was another staircase of marble, hewn from the same quarry as the steps outside. Engraved on the thick tube of copper that served as the banister were quotes from the classics of literature produced in the Home Cell down through the centuries. Moving upward, each stair was slightly narrower than its predecessor, so that when viewed from below, a vanishing effect greeted the eye. The narrow landing on the second floor channeled the visitors into the exhibit halls.

After presenting themselves at the information desk, Baxter and Jorgensen were accompanied by a museum employee to the office of Ross Kinkade. The room in which he labored was simple and bare, holding not much more than a desk, a few chairs, and a plain wooden scrollcase. Kinkade's heavy frame was covered by the blue and white tunic of the learned classes; the fabric was manufactured in the finest weave. A thick beard, bunched into knotty tufts, covered most of the face. The eyes, small and beady, exuded a look of savvy discernment. This was to be expected, thought Baxter; because of Kinkade's position at the pinnacle of the cultural world, one could presume a high intelligence grade.

"Can I offer you gentlemen something to drink?" asked the curator.

"No, thank you," replied Baxter, as he and his junior partner sat down in the two armchairs that were next to the desk.

"So you've been assigned to the Harriman case, then?"

"That is correct."

"Am I under arrest?" asked Kinkade, his mouth tense from a repressed smile.

"I don't know yet," said Baxter. "We haven't seen the museum's recent acquisitions."

The curator cackled with amusement.

"In all seriousness, sir," continued the detective, "we would like to thank you for granting us this interview, and we express our sympathy for the loss of John Harriman. I understand that the two of you worked together closely."

"Indeed we did," said Kinkade, his mien now somber. "John and I didn't always agree, but he was a great man. A *great* man."

"I heard that everyone liked him."

"Yes, it's true. He was hard to work with sometimes, but you would soon forget, because he had a way of endearing himself." The curator paused. "I can save you a lot of time by telling you right now who murdered Harriman."

"I'm all ears," said Baxter, calmly. He sensed that Jorgensen was fidgeting in the adjoining chair, and hoped that the temptation to speak would be resisted.

"It was the government," declared Kinkade.

"Why would they do a thing like that? Harriman was an important man, a wealthy merchant."

"It seems that wealth and safety aren't always convergent. John was a very bold man, Inspector. He helped us publicize some controversial ideas. You do know about Bioprimalism, I presume."

"In general terms, yes."

"Certain people, in very high places, consider us dangerous. I really don't see why. I mean, is there anything dangerous about having a garden where the plants grow wild, just as they do in nature? Is that hurting anyone?"

"No, I suppose not," said Baxter.

"Fair enough," interjected Jorgensen. "But don't you folks also have some things to say about the Temple, and the Great Sage?"

Kinkade tilted his head back so that he was looking down his nose at Jorgensen. "Yes, we've said a few things about them, it's true. But the reaction has been wildly exaggerated. Look, we're not against the Temple, or the rite of the Omnificent Cerebrum. We just don't think it should have a monopoly. Not every person wants to spend his life being a brain." Kinkade chuckled under his breath. "Why should I kneel down in my own house, twice a day, and stare at a model of the oatmeal we all have between our ears? They say that our world is a cell in the cosmic Brain. Fine, I have no problem with that. But does my entire existence have to revolve around the Tomes of Ancient Thought, vegetal symbolism, literature, mathematics, metaphysics, calf's brain for dinner, and evaluating everyone's level of intelligence? What if I prefer nature—wildlife, mountains, lakes, and soaking up rays of sun at the seashore? Or what if I simply wish to avoid the pathology that results from an unmitigated obsession with cerebral functions?"

"I see your point," said Baxter. "But what about art? Are you not, as curator of the museum, responsible for one of the Home Cell's most vital cerebral pursuits?"

"Ah," said Kinkade, his face brimming with excitement. "That is an excellent question. The answer is that art is not exclusively cerebral. Art is also about *feelings*. We cannot ignore our emotions; the softer, more sensitive part of our spirit. Enough, I say, of creativity that is hard, calculated, proportional, measured, thought-out, and precise. What Bioprimalism is introducing, among other things, is a new type of art, one that is connected with the earth, with nature, with life itself."

But would that be art, Baxter asked himself. He was tempted to pose the question, but was loathe to disturb his host's equilibrium, and risk turning a potential ally into an adversary. "Is anyone producing the type of art you describe?" he asked instead.

"Absolutely. As a matter of fact, we were set to exhibit several pieces here in the museum. Following the assassination of Harriman, however, I'm not so sure it would be prudent. I'd rather wait, Inspector, until you solve the case and bring the killer, or killers, to justice. But I don't envy you. With the government involved, it could get messy."

"We'll be okay," said Baxter, with an understated smile.

Kinkade shut his eyes and rubbed them. He then leaned back in his chair and viewed the police officers, alternating his piercing glance between the two, as if studying them. "Gentlemen," he said, finally. "Would you care to see a few pieces of Bioprimalist art?"

"We would be honored," replied Baxter.

Kinkade led the two investigators from his office to a corridor that took them deeper into the building. Near its end was a hefty red door, which Kinkade opened. He unhitched a portable lamp from a hook on the wall just inside, lit the wick, and proceeded to descend a narrow staircase. The others followed. In the basement, he lit a number of lamps, whose collective light was soon equal to the task of illuminating a handful of objects strewn about on the coarse cement floor. Kinkade stood alongside the collection. "Here they are," he declared, with a tentative smile.

Baxter and Jorgensen lowered their glance to see several planks of knotty wood, each having an area of about a square yard. On the surface of the planks were swirls of black paint, with no discernible pattern. The two men looked at each other, and then at Kinkade, with expressions of embarrassment.

"What do you think?" asked the curator.

"About what?" replied Baxter.

"About these works. Let me guess—you're not sure what to make of them."

"That is a true statement, I'm afraid."

"It's simply because you're not familiar with the *idea* behind them. Let me venture another guess: You assume that the artist must have completed the long cycle of apprenticeship with a master."

"Artist?" mumbled Jorgensen.

"Yes … artist," retorted Kinkade, in a peevish tone.

"I do admit to having assumed that the artist had to be fully qualified," said Baxter.

"Unfortunately, your assumption, reasonable though it is, is a faulty one. Because, gentlemen, these paintings were produced by a *monkey*."

Jorgensen began to chuckle, but restrained himself when he saw that his superior was viewing the scene with a serious face.

"A groundbreaking feat," continued Kinkade, "and never before seen. The animal actually held the brush between its toes."

"Interesting," said Baxter, folding his arms. "So what is the idea that you wish to convey?"

"Sometimes, Inspector, when a given sphere of life has drifted to one extreme, it is necessary to introduce a jolt, in order to bring things back to the center. Here, the extreme is our usual hyper-cerebral art, while the jolt is the monkey, who represents emotional, natural creativity, unfettered by cold calculation. This jolt returns us to the center, which is a balance between the two approaches." Kinkade squatted alongside one of the planks, and ran his hand along the wooden surface. He paused, and then stood up. "You know, our discussion has made me think. I'm no longer convinced that we should hang these in the museum. Perhaps somewhere else … ah, I know a gallery on the East Side that would be perfect. Start off slow, let the public get used to it. Introduce, in parallel, other aspects of Bioprimalism. Later, when the moment is ripe, have the big show here. What do you think?"

"Sounds reasonable," said Baxter.

"Well, gentlemen, I'm sure you have a busy schedule, so I won't detain you any further." After extinguishing the lamps, Kinkade led the others up the stairs, into the corridor, and finally to the lobby. They parted with an expression of thanks by the policemen, a pledge by the curator to provide any further assistance that might be necessary to resolve the case, and an exchange of blessings.

As soon as the officers descended the front steps of the museum, Jorgensen burst out laughing. "Did you see the look on that guy's face, boss? I mean, he was *serious*. They're hiring monkeys to make paintings!"

He began scratching under his armpit, and otherwise gesticulating and grunting in the manner of a monkey. "What's next—a lobster conducting an orchestra?"

Baxter could not restrain a chuckle. "It is rather odd, Phil, I grant you that."

"Odd? I'll say it's odd."

They crossed the yard of the museum and joined the pedestrian traffic on Avenue of the Synapses.

"How do you evaluate Kinkade's reading of the situation?" asked Baxter.

"What he's saying makes sense. After learning about Bioprimalism and seeing what's going on in that basement, I wouldn't be surprised if Harriman really was assassinated. Of course, we might still uncover another motive, like something connected to money."

"Assassination would seem logical. But why have we heard nothing from the government? In similar circumstances in the past, I was taken off the case, if I was ever given the case to begin with. It would be a simple matter for the authorities to bury the whole thing."

"I see what you mean, boss."

"What about suicide?"

"Nah," said Jorgensen, shaking his head. "Harriman was at the peak of his game. Rich as anything, a sense of importance, gorgeous women at his beck and call, just beginning a new project that he believed in religiously. He was going places."

"Going places, indeed," said Baxter, making a mental note of his junior colleague's perspicacious observations. "Why don't you spend the rest of the day tracking down and interviewing members of his family? Take a scribe with you."

"Sure, boss. But I hate prying into someone's life while he's in mourning."

"I know. A distasteful chore, but one to which we must accustom ourselves. It will be good practice for you."

They reached headquarters. After a brief interlude in the office, Jorgensen set out to fulfill his new task, while Baxter went to see the Chief. The purpose of the visit was to solicit the man's opinion as to whether an assassination might account for the death of Harriman. The Chief dismissed this conjecture, echoing Baxter's own conclusion that if the government were involved, the police department would be relieved of the case. He encouraged the detective to pursue other avenues of inquiry.

Feeling a slump in his investigative powers, Baxter decided to head home for an extended session of meditation. The walk was encouraging: the weather was fine, the translucent dome of the Temple gleamed in the sun, and his own little cul-de-sac, Cortex Lane, had been cleaned by the street-sweepers that morning. George the doorman greeted him courteously as he entered the lobby and ascended the stairs. Inside the apartment, all was calm. Elizabeth was absent. He removed his dagger and lay his body on the day bed in the little bedroom, anticipating a deep and productive meditation.

Instead of attaining the vaunted meditative state, however, Baxter fell asleep. Swirling through his mind were images drawn from recent days: Jiliada curled up in her chair; Jorgensen contorting with laughter on the steps of the art museum; Elizabeth throwing herself onto his lap as he ate breakfast. These scenes were pushed aside, as a single picture emerged, holding his mind in its grip like tongs. It was the dream, the dream about the promontory. He was standing underneath the jutting rock; the creatures, now numerous, swarmed across the rock and each other, producing a humming sound like bees emerging from their hive. One lizard plummeted to its death, and then another, and another. The scene went dark. Baxter felt pressure within his skull, and he woke up.

His heart was racing and there was an acute pain in his temples. He rose from the bed and began pacing around the apartment. The irritation was compounded by the realization that this was the third occurrence within the week, leaving no doubt that the dream was to be considered recurring. It was a foregone conclusion that the scenes he had constructed in his mind contained a message from the Omnificent Cerebrum. Baxter had no choice but to obtain the judgment of an expert, to help interpret the message and decide upon a course of action.

This was not welcome news. The last time a recurring dream had visited him was following the death of his wife Eleanor. On three successive nights, he dreamt that he was searching for her medicine, and each time forgot where he had placed it. A visit to an interpreter of dreams yielded an interpretation that was laced with anguish: The Omnificent Cerebrum was telling him that he had willed her death, so as not to be compelled to share the affections of Elizabeth. The impact on his spirit was devastating. Following the advice of friends and colleagues, he sought a second opinion. This move resulted in a benign interpretation. But the damage had been done; he was not able to forestall the breakdown that led to the stay in a sanatorium.

Eight years had passed since Eleanor's death, but at times it seemed to Baxter as if it were yesterday. This was one of those times. A feeling of loneliness engulfed him like a tidal wave. He sat at the kitchen table, doubled over from grief, torturing himself with images of their domestic life just before she had fallen ill with the mysterious disease. He recalled one scene that oppressed him because it was a reminder of the bliss and security he had felt in the presence of Eleanor. The two of them were seated in the living room one evening. Elizabeth, nine years old at the time, was doing cartwheels across the floor, something not normally allowed inside the apartment, but Baxter and his wife were swept along in the gaiety of the moment, letting themselves laugh and enjoy the occasion without compunction. When he made love to Eleanor that night, it was sublime. Baxter recalled how he gently slid his hand over the taut skin of her belly ...

It was too much to bear; he jumped out of his chair, ran to the door of the apartment, opened it, and raced down the stairs as if the building were on fire. He needed air, and urgently. George greeted him but he saw it as a blur, so intent was he to reach the outside. It took several blocks of rapid march to attain some sort of clarity. At that point, Baxter set a course for the Harriman villa, intending to plunge himself back into the case. He purposely took a roundabout route, weaving his way through the streets of Nucleus, so that he would be distracted by relatively unfamiliar scenery.

At the crime scene, he circled the block, not sure what he was seeking or what his strategy should be. He placed himself across the street from the villa and surveyed the property. He imagined the killer committing the deed, and then escaping through one of the windows or doors, of which there was no shortage. Despite the multiple escape routes from the house, the perpetrator still had to pass through the gate. Scaling the wall at the edge of the property would constitute a near-superhuman feat; the likelihood of such a maneuver, figured Baxter, was close to nil. If the master had not yet emerged from his chamber that morning, and no one had been admitted to see him, would not the sudden departure of a person through the gate have aroused some suspicion? Baxter nevertheless determined that it was possible—unlikely but possible—that someone could have slipped through. Given that the time of death was early in the morning, perhaps the murderer had spent the night in the villa, hiding in some obscure corner, unbeknownst to the household staff. After finishing his gruesome task, he stole out of the house and passed through the gate.

As Baxter pondered the scenario, he became aware of a man standing about thirty yards away who was busy examining a fractured slab of stone in the wall of the adjoining property. He was around Baxter's age and height, dressed in a plain tunic, and had a brown leather satchel slung over his shoulder. The detective's internal alarm had been triggered. There was no question in his mind that the man was there to observe him.

Baxter, with a nonchalant air, approached. "Nice day," he said, smiling and pointing at the sky.

"Uh … yes, yes it is," replied the man, evidently embarrassed.

"Are you from the neighborhood?"

"Yes … I mean no … I just …"

"You just," said Baxter, with a flat intonation.

"I just wanted to speak with you," he said, extending his hand. "I'm Peter Westlake."

The two men shook hands. Baxter noted that Westlake was sporting a sizable pot belly, and that his facial skin was dry and peeling.

"Sorry to be stalking you like that, Inspector. I'm a reporter with the *Monthly Gazette*."

"The monthly what?"

"Gazette," said Westlake, with a little laugh. "We're a new outfit, located in the offices of the defunct *Nucleus Chronicle*."

"Is that so? I used to work at the *Chronicle,* as a teenager, copying the news-scrolls."

"As many of us did. Anyway, I do special features, and right now I'm covering the Harriman affair."

"You know something, Mr. Westlake, you look familiar. I know I've seen you recently, but I can't remember where."

"It was right here, last Thirday, on the front steps of the villa. You were speaking with the press, right after the murder."

"Ah, yes, of course. Someone claimed that Harriman was assassinated by the government, and you said that if so, he had it coming, for insulting the Omnificent Cerebrum."

"Yes, that was me."

"Well," said Baxter, tugging at his chin. "How can we help each other?"

Westlake adopted a pose of absolute stillness, arms hanging motionless at his side, as if his entire physiology were diverted to his cerebral functions. "I don't know how to put this, exactly," he said.

"Just say it, straight out. We policemen are accustomed to being direct, and we're not easily perturbed."

The reporter's brow was knitted in an unusual manner, with one eyebrow raised and the other lowered. "I know that you've had contact with a courtesan named Jiliada. I saw your assistant interrogating her not far from this spot."

"Keep going."

"I wanted you to know that she's a key player in all of this."

"How's that?"

"She was close to Harriman, closer than you would expect. May I ask what she told you about the murder?"

"Is this off the record?"

"Yes."

"She thinks that the crime may have been committed by Ross Kinkade."

"Nonsense," declared Westlake, shaking his head.

"Why nonsense?"

"There's no motive. You know that, Inspector."

"She claims they were at each other's throats."

"So?" said Westlake, letting slip some emotion. "If that were a motive, we'd have a dozen murders per day in Nucleus. Anyway, Kinkade would never be so stupid. The Bioprimalists are on the rise, he wouldn't ruin that."

"What's your theory, then?" asked Baxter.

"Probably someone in a position of power. Government, intelligence agencies, the Temple—one of those. Or perhaps a concerned citizen. And you know what? They did us a favor. Bioprimalism must be stopped, Inspector. Stopped cold. It's a question of survival."

"Is the threat that severe? We've had challenges to authority from time to time. Yet we carry on, and the challengers fade into obscurity."

"This is different," said Westlake. "If we don't rid ourselves of the plague, the Omnificent Cerebrum will intervene. You recall what it says in the Tomes of Ancient Thought about the sedition of Lensic and his people."

"Yes, it brought about the Flood."

"Exactly. It wasn't enough that the Lensic clan be annihilated. The Omnificent Cerebrum took the steps necessary to cleanse the Home Cell of every trace of the disease. That is a treatment I wouldn't wish on my worst enemies."

"No, it would not be pleasant."

"But that is precisely where we stand today. We are dangerously close to the abyss, my friend. If you wish to hear further clarification, I would suggest an audience with the Great Sage."

Baxter chuckled. "You have an inflated view of my stature, Mr. Westlake. I can't just go knock on the door of the Great Sage. Even the Chief of Police would be reticent to take such a step, unless it were first coordinated with a higher echelon."

"In any case," said Westlake, "I urge you to carefully weigh my remarks. You are one of a handful of people who may determine the fate of the Home Cell. Handled correctly, we can rid ourselves of this insidious threat. But if we take a lackadaisical approach, thinking it's business as usual, disaster awaits us."

"And what would you have me do, exactly?"

"To answer that, I must ask you a few questions. Still off the record."

"Go ahead."

"Do you have any suspects?"

"No."

"Any leads?"

"Not really."

"Then it's possible that Harriman committed suicide."

"It's possible," replied Baxter.

"Let us say that it was his way of repenting for the terrible damage he did to our society."

Baxter displayed a stony face.

"I'll leave you now, Inspector. I think we understand each other. Feel free to get in touch with me at any time. May your intellect expand." Westlake bowed slightly, and took leave.

Baxter resumed his observation of the Harriman villa. He was finding it difficult to digest Westlake's discourse. Was the man overly agitated about the Bioprimalists? Or was his analysis correct, and a major threat was looming? Baxter did not believe that he himself was in a position to decide, at least not at that moment. One thing was certain: He would not entertain a premature determination of suicide, as Westlake had intimated. Baxter could not endorse such a course of action under any circumstances.

There was one opinion of Westlake's, however, with which Baxter found himself in agreement: Jiliada's implication of Ross Kinkade was far-fetched, and perhaps even fabricated. It was time, then, to pay her another visit, and persuade her to divulge the full extent of her knowledge.

IV. WHAT IS A DREAM?

Baxter returned to headquarters, where he requisitioned a chariot for the trip to Two Scribes. He did not provide advance notice, but wagered that Jiliada probably would not have left the house so early in the day. He considered the possibility of her absence to be a minor risk.

The trip was annoying. The road was caked in dust; when blended with the odor of the horses, it produced a particularly distasteful sensation. To make matters worse, images from the recurring dream invaded Baxter's thoughts, bringing in their wake associations to the earlier dream about his departed wife. He resolved to find a reputable interpreter of dreams as soon as possible, perhaps even later that day. The expert would reveal what needed to be revealed, and the matter could be laid to rest.

He arrived at the police station of Two Scribes and deposited the chariot and its horses at the stables. He then set out on foot, reaching his destination within a short while. Pausing in front of the gate to Jiliada's compound, Baxter tried to collect his wits and prepare a plan, however sketchy, for the upcoming interview. No strategy came to mind. He rang the bell. There was no response. The only perceptible movement was the fluttering of some birds who evidently had been alarmed by the sudden noise, causing them to abandon their perch on a nearby tree. Baxter again yanked the cord. Still no response.

Resigned to the failure of the excursion, he began his retreat to the police station. After walking a couple of blocks, he heard a woman, from afar, calling out his name. He looked back but saw no one. Then Jiliada appeared, turning the corner at a brisk pace. She was wearing the same blue dress that she had worn at the time of her encounter with Baxter and Jorgensen at the Obscure Thought Café.

"Thank you for coming to get me," said Baxter, feeling awkward. "I didn't mean to disturb you; I was just taking a chance that you might be available to talk."

"I'm available," she said, with a smile.

They returned to the compound. After passing through the gate, Jiliada announced that she was hungry, and suggested that they go to the kitchen to have an early lunch, or at the very least some tea and biscuits. Baxter at first declined, as it was his time-honored policy not to dine with suspects, witnesses, or anyone else associated with a case. But she insisted, and he did not wish to risk insulting her.

The interior of the house was as impressive as its exterior. As they walked through the vestibule and into the main hall, Baxter marveled at the elegant furnishings and decorative objects. They matched the standards of the most upscale boutiques in Nucleus.

Jiliada led him to the kitchen, where she invited him to take a seat at the table. The arrangement of furniture was not unlike that of his own apartment, though every item was of a quality far superior to anything he owned. Jiliada explained that because the servants were either out of the house or busy with other tasks, she herself would prepare the food. The scene was reminiscent of a meal with Elizabeth. Baxter's dark ruminations about his relationship with his daughter, along with the vexation of the recurring dream, returned to the forefront of his consciousness. It was only with some effort that he made the transition from small talk to the heart of the matter.

"I went to see Mr. Kinkade this morning at the art museum," he said, dunking a biscuit in his tea. "And I must tell you that I find your assertion about his involvement in the murder to be unconvincing."

"Why is that?" she asked.

"He doesn't exhibit any signs of having committed such a crime. And there's no motive. At this juncture, all signs point toward Harriman's real enemies—his ideological opponents."

Jiliada's eyes softened. "Are you all right?" she asked.

"What do you mean?"

"I don't wish to pry, but you seem upset about something."

All of the verbal parrying of their previous exchanges faded into the background of Baxter's consciousness. Now, all he saw before him was a beautiful woman who had succeeded in penetrating his defenses, his façade of stoic fortitude. Being the recipient of this feminine warmth and intuition left him disarmed, and it felt good. In the blink of an eye he had passed from the realm of the intellect to the realm of the emotions, and was not inclined to stop.

"Yes, it is true," he murmured. "I am upset."

"What happened?"

"I had a recurring dream."

"Go on," said Jiliada, leaning toward him.

"It was not particularly offensive, but it resuscitated all the unpleasant memories associated with my last recurring dream, which happened just after my wife's death eight years ago. I dreamt, back then, that I had misplaced some medicine that surely would have cured her. An interpreter told me …" Baxter paused, as a cloud of sadness descended upon him. "He told me that I had willed her death. Of course, I loved her more than anything in the world."

"I am certain of that. What caused her to pass away?"

"No one knows. It was a strange disease, and the physicians were not able to arrive at an unequivocal diagnosis. She died within a week of contracting it."

"I'm sorry," said Jiliada, in the most delicate of tones. "By the way, something very similar happened to me."

"How's that?"

"It was also eight years ago. I had been married just a few months when my husband was killed in an accident. He was a sage, still in his apprenticeship. It happened in the Temple."

"Oh yes, I remember hearing about that. It was …" Baxter stopped himself from uttering anything further about the event in the presence of the widow.

A tear rolled down Jiliada's cheek. "It was awful. And then afterwards, like you, I had a recurring dream. A hideous one. And the interpreter …"

"It's okay," said Baxter, repressing a desire to hug Jiliada. "You don't have to go on."

"But I want to. It was just like your story. The interpreter said that I had willed the death of my husband. I was distraught; it was more than I could bear. I was pregnant at the time, and I lost the baby. It was all because of my anger. You see, after my husband's accident, the Great Sage adopted me, took care of me. I spent two weeks in his house, with his wife and his servants. When I had the dream, he wanted me to go to the interpreter of the Temple. But I was angry at them, at everyone over there, blaming them for the accident. So I went to an interpreter they all despised."

"Who was that?"

"Conrad Burton."

Baxter's mouth was agape.

"What is it?" she asked.

"Conrad Burton was my interpreter, as well."

"Oh, no. Such a nasty man. So you know how he thinks, then."

"What do you mean?"

"His philosophy."

"No, I'm not familiar with it."

"He was an apprentice sage, just like my husband. A month or so before the accident, he was discharged from the Temple. The official reason was that he was interpreting dreams, which is something that apprentice sages are not supposed to do. But there's another, more important reason."

"What is that?" asked Baxter, feeling a surge of trepidation.

"He was a Bioprimalist."

"A Bioprimalist?"

"One of the first. The whole thing was in its infancy. My husband tried to stop it. I thought he was being narrow-minded; why be so judgmental, I told him." She wiped away some tears with the back of her hand. "I was so foolish. Look what happened in the end."

The two of them sat in silence for several moments, sipping their tea and absorbing the reverberations of their journey into the past.

"Tell me about the dream you're having now," said Jiliada, now composed and attentive.

Baxter tugged at his chin. "I'm the commander of a sizable military detachment, something approximating a regiment of infantry. We're in camp. On one side of us is a ridge, topped by a promontory of rock, jutting out quite far. Underneath the promontory are these peculiar creatures, clinging upside-down to the rock. It's a kind of lizard with webbed feet. They have the same grayish coloring as the stone. One of them, apparently in a weak condition, is attacked by the others. He falls to his death." Baxter leaned back in his chair. "That's it."

"I have heard about this dream," said Jiliada, looking grim.

"You have?"

"I overheard some sages talking about it. Funny, how one remembers certain things, how they stick in your mind. They say that the dream has an important meaning, something connected with the Temple."

She was looking at Baxter with warm, compassionate eyes. He allowed himself to become captivated by the magnetic gaze, but then, startled by its profundity, he abruptly severed the connection. He inhaled deeply and tightened the muscles throughout his body, as if constructing a fortress that could withstand the siege of his own emotions.

"Are you all right?" she asked.

Baxter presented a tentative smile. "I feel better, now that we talked."

"We've both been through a lot."

"Yes, we have."

"And our experiences are very similar."

"Yes, they are."

"Would you like to speak with the interpreter at the Temple?"

"I guess I should."

"I'll arrange it, then. I'll send you a parchment."

"Oh … well thank you, that's very kind," said Baxter, amazed by the result of the conversation.

Jiliada drank the remainder of her tea. "Is there anything else you wanted to know about John Harriman?"

"There is something, actually. After all that's happened to you, I would think you'd be less favorably disposed toward Harriman, being that he was a leader of the Bioprimalists."

"Perhaps you shouldn't judge so quickly," she replied, in a businesslike tone.

Baxter felt a yearning for the spiritual bond they had experienced only an instant earlier.

"I'm sorry," she said, reassuming her soft voice. "You deserve a better answer than that. But it's complicated. Maybe we could leave it for another day."

"Of course. Tell me something, Jiliada. Have we met before?"

"I don't know," she said, her face tense. "You do look familiar."

"Well, maybe it's nothing," said Baxter. He finished his tea, stood up, thanked her for her time, and announced his departure. Jiliada asked whether she could accompany him for part of the route. He consented. They left the house, crossed the yard, and exited the compound.

"Thank you for listening to my problems," said Baxter.

"I'm glad I could help. You listened to some of my problems, as well."

He felt an urge to hold her hand.

"Anytime you want to do it again, that would be fine," she continued. "Of course, you may find my stories to be a little tiresome after a while."

"I could hardly imagine a conversation with you becoming tiresome," said Baxter, who immediately regretted the remark as being too gallant.

They came to the street on which the police station was located, some two hundred yards distant. The sight of the building returned Baxter, quite rudely, to the mindset of detective. He stopped walking.

"One last thing, Jiliada. Do you know of a man named Peter Westlake?"

"Yes, the journalist. He's a muckraker and a pest, but honest. Used to hang around the Temple a lot. After the accident and my disastrous dream, he wanted to do an exposé on Conrad Burton, but it was too much for me. Why do you ask?"

"Just curious. I had a little talk with him. He expressed his opinion of the Bioprimalists."

"I assume that his opinion of them was less than glowing."

"Your assumption is correct," said Baxter. Unsure of how to take leave of the woman, he retreated a step and stretched his back. When he turned to face her, the police station again was looming in the background, next to her head in his field of view.

"Well, Inspector, I hope your visit was a success."

"Yes, it was. And in ways I never expected."

"As I said, anytime you want to continue, just let me know."

She extended her hand. Baxter grasped it and squeezed it gently. The gesture was more than a handshake, but not so intimate as to constitute an indiscreet overture. Nevertheless, the touch was sufficiently prolonged to give each of them a foretaste of the sensation to be derived from the contact of their flesh.

During the drive back to Nucleus, the dust from the street and the odor of the horses was of no concern to Baxter. He was too deeply engrossed in his thoughts. At the outset, they revolved around a sense of guilt. In his own estimation, he had failed to uphold the responsibilities and decorum of his position. This had never occurred in all his years with the police: Turning a meeting on official business into an occasion for personal gratification.

On the other hand, he reasoned, Jiliada's revelation that his recurring dream was connected with the Temple could prove to be an invaluable piece of information. The referral to the interpreter might very well lead to a clarification of his spiritual condition. If he were to consult a different interpreter, he might not acquire such knowledge.

He marveled that a courtesan would be the one to set up a meeting between himself and an official at the Temple of the Omnificent Cerebrum. It made more sense when he considered that her background—wife of an apprentice sage—made it almost certain that her family heritage was of the highest order, with an intelligence grade to match. Somehow, she had managed to remain in the good graces of at least one important personage at the Temple, despite her self-proclaimed rebellion. Was she still on familiar terms with the Great Sage, in whose home she had once stayed?

Baxter arrived at his office to find Jorgensen seated at the desk, cramming a sandwich into his mouth.

"Hi, boss," he said, the words mingled with the sound of chewing.

"Please don't spread crumbs all over the place," muttered Baxter, taking a seat across the desk.

Jorgensen took an exceptionally large bite out of the sandwich. He swallowed the food, and wiped his mouth with the back of his hand. "Did you have a good morning?" he asked, his facial muscles in the grip of a smirk.

"No, actually I didn't. I'm no wiser about the case than I was yesterday. What about you?"

"Well, to give you an indication of how wonderful my day has been, this stale calf's brain sandwich is the highlight thus far. It's leftovers from the dinner I had a couple of days ago with mom and dad. My brain is expanding as we speak."

"I am pleased to hear of your alimentary transformation."

Jorgensen burst into laughter. "You know what, boss?"

"What ,.."

"You're all right."

"Thank goodness for that. What did you find out about Harriman's family?"

"They're a weird bunch."

"In what way?"

"Let's see. I spoke with two of his three children, a son and a daughter. The son—he's the youngest—lives in a fancy apartment located a few blocks from the father's villa. He helps run the slaughterhouse. He has this awful tic in his face, and talks like a snob."

"What did he say about his father?" asked Baxter.

"That he had been completely wrapped up in the world of Bioprimalism. A real workaholic. Loved every moment of it, and talked about it constantly, especially about the future and how bright it looked. I think we can rule out suicide."

"You're probably right. What about the daughter?"

"She works at the art museum, down the hall from Ross Kinkade. Her name is Margaret. Another fruitcake. She gave me the whole Bioprimalism spiel, minus the monkey."

"Interesting. Did you come across anything that could point us to likely suspects?"

"Not really. Both of the children claim that the government is the culprit. But I couldn't get anything more specific. Oh, by the way, I have an appointment early this evening with the other son. That about covers the family. Harriman's wife is institutionalized; she went crazy a few years back. His parents are deceased. He had one sister, who died a long time ago." Jorgensen proceeded to eat the last remaining morsel of the sandwich, washing it down with a glass of water.

"Good overview, thanks."

"No problem, boss. You know what else was weird ..."

"Tell me."

"Neither the son nor the daughter seemed particularly upset about the murder. A bit suspicious, no?"

"Not necessarily, Phil. You'll see that people who are enduring great sadness often hide their feelings from us. It's when someone is effusive in his grief, in our presence, that I become wary."

"Okay, I'll keep that in mind."

"I spoke today with a man named Peter Westlake," continued Baxter. "He's a journalist. Ever hear of him?"

"No."

"He works for an outfit called the *Monthly Gazette*. Find out what you can about him, and see whether he wrote anything about Harriman or Bioprimalism."

Jorgensen looked as if he had bit into a lemon.

"What's the matter?" asked Baxter.

"When are we going to do some real police work already? No offense, boss, but I feel like a glorified scribe."

"What, pray tell, do you consider to be real police work?"

Jorgensen presented his ideal job description, replete with manhunts, stakeouts, interrogations, arrests, and visits to the hospital and morgue. Baxter settled back and enjoyed the display of youthful enthusiasm. It was a healthy sign, he thought, as long as it finds an outlet. Otherwise, it could lead to depression and bitterness.

The young man seemed to be suffering from a syndrome that afflicts officers who have advanced beyond their first year, but still lack significant experience. When one is a rookie, an aura of fascination surrounds every object, person, and action. Merely walking across the lobby of headquarters fills the spirit with satisfaction. At a certain point, however, usually in the second or third year, reality demands its rightful place at the table. This is where Jorgensen was situated, and quite in the thick of it.

"All right," said Baxter, when his junior partner reached a pause in his remarks. "Never mind the research. You want some real police work, eh?"

Jorgensen sat in rapt anticipation, like a child about to receive his favorite candy.

"Here's what you do. Tail this Westlake guy, for one entire day. Report back to me here, same time tomorrow. I want to know where he goes, who he sees, and what he does—every moment. Got it?"

"Consider it done, boss ... oh, wait. What about Harriman's other son? I'm supposed to see him later today."

"I'll do it. What's his name? Where does he work?"

"His name is Theodore. He has a shop—or maybe you'd call it a gallery—with antiques, art, and rare scrolls. It's on the Boulevard, just inside the East gate."

"Good. Well, what are you waiting for?"

Jorgensen, with a wide grin, left the room.

Baxter sat for a brief while, pondering the many events of the day. He then lay on the cot for a session of meditation. Contrary to expectation, the session was productive. Almost all of the noise was swept aside, vacating a mental space in which the mind could reach a state of pure concentration. This did wonders for Baxter's overtaxed nervous system. He rose from the cot feeling refreshed, with the brain sharp and primed to absorb new data.

He left the office, and walked to the gallery of Harriman's son. It was located within a row of upscale retail establishments on Boulevard of the Mind. Upon arrival, Baxter spotted an unusual lacuna in the urban environment: In front of the gallery, under one arch of the colonnade, a specimen of vegetal symbolism was missing. Normally, there was a plant under each and every arch.

He entered the shop. Wealth and sophistication oozed from every square inch. Statues, furniture, and objets d'art covered the floor. Scrollshelves, in ponderous dark wood, lined much of the wall space. Resting upon them were scrolls of varying age. On other parts of the wall were hung magnificent paintings and tapestries.

A young man greeted Baxter, and inquired whether he might be looking for something in particular. The detective showed his badge and stated the purpose of his visit. The young man disappeared into the back of the shop. He emerged a short time later accompanied by a man dressed in a tunic of archaic style, with frills of golden lace and a coat of arms embroidered on the chest. The man wearing the garment was Theodore Harriman, proprietor of the establishment and son of the murder victim. The shop assistant conducted the introductions, and withdrew.

"I believe you received a parchment from my associate," said Baxter.

"Yes," said Theodore. "He announced an impending visit." The art dealer looked as though he himself could be mistaken for an objet d'art, and not merely because of the uncommon tunic. He was tall and thin, almost meager, but standing upright, radiating vitality. His head was elongated and narrow, as was the nose. The beard, as well, fit the overall array, being closely cropped and shaped to follow the contours of the face.

"I'd like to ask you a few questions, if you don't mind," said Baxter. "It shouldn't take long."

"Certainly. Shall we adjourn to my office?"

They moved to a room at the back of the shop. The space was packed with objects; on the walls, on tables, piled on furniture, and scattered across the floor. The two men sat in high-backed wooden armchairs on which rested enormous leather cushions.

"First of all," said Baxter, "please accept my condolences."

"Thank you."

"This is quite an impressive place. How long have you had it?"

"About seven years."

"Were you ever involved in the management of your father's slaughterhouse?"

"Absolutely not," said Theodore, with a dismissive wave of the hand. "I abhor it. Someone else can inherit that foul and nauseating place."

"So you've always been interested in art and antiques?"

"Oh, yes. It gives me great pleasure to be surrounded all day by such beauty."

"That indeed would be something worth striving for. Now I must ask you a distasteful question. Who would desire the death of your father?"

"I have no idea, Inspector. I really don't. My father was widely respected. Even his servants adored him."

"What about his rivals? Ross Kinkade, for instance."

Theodore squirmed in his seat at mention of the name. "Ross Kinkade is a pompous fool."

"Was that your father's opinion, as well?"

"Yes."

"And Kinkade's of him?"

"Yes, or something equally negative, I'm sure. But to jump from that to murder? Not a chance. The man is a backstabber, but only in the figurative sense. Kinkade always got his way; if anybody should have been murdered, it was him. My father was a supporting actor in the play. Kinkade knew how to manipulate him, how to extract the utmost advantage from their partnership. Why kill someone whose life force you're sucking dry?"

"No reason to, I suppose. What about relatives? No distant cousins seeking vengeance for past wrongs?"

Theodore laughed. "No, nothing of the sort. Our family life is rather pedestrian. It would be more captivating, I admit, if we had some juicy scandals."

"Yes, perhaps it would," said Baxter, as a jewel-studded silver ewer caught his eye. "What do you think of this Bioprimalism business?"

"I think it's ridiculous and absurd. My father was a good man, Inspector, but naïve. He wanted everyone to be happy and at peace with those around them. He could never tolerate conflict or adamant opinions. The Bioprimalists provided him with the perfect outlet. Let's just exist, they say, without pretensions to all this brainy activity in which we indulge ourselves. Such an attitude was perfectly suited to his temperament. You see, Inspector, my father was never a real thinker. So he could support these people, these charlatans, and share in the supposed audacity of the great innovation. They promise the glory of intellect without actually needing to have any." Theodore halted his speech, and gestured with a sweep of the arm at the treasures on all sides. "Have you any idea, Inspector, what mountains of genius are represented by the objects in this room? Do you fathom the chain of transmission necessary to produce them? The sacrifice and discipline, the teaching and apprenticeship, built layer upon layer, for generation after generation? Those Bioprimalists would destroy it all, in the blink of an eye."

"Sounds like an ominous threat. But then why did you remove the specimen of vegetal symbolism that was in front of your shop?"

"It wasn't me, Inspector. I'd prefer not to discuss it; the whole episode is embarrassing. I arranged for it to be replaced." Theodore's facial muscles tensed, making his head seem even more narrow. "Let me show you something," he said, standing up.

Baxter followed him through the multitude of objects. Theodore stopped in front of a table, opened a drawer, and removed a large scroll. He pulled off the sleeve to expose the parchment, which exhibited a light green color. "Do you know what this is?" he asked.

"No, I can't say that I do. I've never seen parchment of that color."

"Can you keep this matter confidential?"

"Certainly."

"This scroll is the most important document of the Bioprimalists. There are only a handful in existence, and the leadership has forbidden the transcribing of additional copies. It is therefore priceless. The work is called *Humanity and the Harmonious Earth*. It was written by a man named Conrad Burton."

Baxter, hearing the name of his erstwhile interpreter of dreams, could not stop his face from momentarily expressing dismay.

"You've heard of him," said Theodore.

"Yes, in a different context."

"Burton is the philosopher, the prophet; the brains of the operation, if you'll excuse the term. In reality, of course, he's an intellectual midget and a *poseur*."

"I should speak with him."

"I'm afraid the conversation would be rather brief. Unless you enjoy conversing with ashes, that is."

Baxter cleared his throat. "When did he die?"

"About a year ago. They say it was a boating accident, but in reality he was attacked by a shark. He came too close to one of his beloved creatures of the harmonious earth."

"How did you come to be in possession of the scroll?"

"My father purchased it," replied Theodore, "after I had conducted a search on his behalf. It was delivered the day of his death. I'm not sure what to do. If I sell it, and my sister Margaret finds out, I'll never hear the end of it. Margaret, by the way, fancies herself as the new Conrad Burton."

"Why is it so controversial?" asked Baxter.

"I will show you." A few moments were required for Theodore to unfurl the scroll and roll it to the spot containing the passage he sought. "Read the columns that are now visible. I'd rather not defile my lips."

Baxter read silently to himself:

CHAPTER 6. Mother Earth, O wonderful, caretaking, affectionate Matron, who gives us life, who nurtures and sustains us. Let it not be denied that we have sinned against you. How can you forgive us? We are worthy of destruction, of ruin, of desolation. 6.5. Only by virtue of boundless love for your creatures are we spared. Because you sense, in the depth of your bosom, that we will return to the true path. Not all humans are the same; we do not act as one. Many are those who seek your warmth, but they are confused and despondent. For a cabal of evil and ruthless men have set themselves over us. 6.10. From their temples on high they sit in haughty judgment, even as they utter falsehoods and slander the very entity that gave them life. Their unctuous sages consider their own thoughts to be beyond your unfathomable wisdom, O Mother Earth. They deface your vegetative creatures in the name of their cult. They lead the innocent astray, beguiling widows and orphans without pause. It is a travesty and an affliction of the spirit. 6.15. Verily, I say, you will return your flock to the harmony of your womb. The blind will see, the deaf will hear, the disheartened will take heart. It shall come to pass that the idols are smashed, the sages slaughtered, the scrolls burned in the public square. As the Brain is torn asunder your rule will be restored to your creatures. You will reign forever, as humankind shares its love, one with the other, all with one, and the community with Mother Earth. 6.20. Never again shall a human being lift his hand against your soil, your air, or your water. Never again shall the selfish rob you of your treasures for their own benefit. Never again shall the arrogant few consider themselves to be superior to you or any of your creatures. In the Enlightened Days, all organisms—strong and weak, large and small, feathered and scaled, stationary and mobile—will share equally in your bounty.

Baxter looked up at Theodore; the glance they exchanged conveyed more effectively than words their sense of alarm. Theodore rolled up the scroll without delay. "Now you understand, Inspector, why no one must know that I am in possession of this screed. I don't have the strength to have my throat slit in the middle of the night. And it would be such a mess for the servants when they find me."

Baxter smiled. "I see your point."

"I am ashamed that people so close to me are involved in such scandalous activity. It has already been catastrophic for my family, and further damage is to be expected."

"Your concern seems justified," said Baxter. "In any event, I thank you for your cooperation. Please notify me immediately if you come across even the most trivial information that might assist us with the case. Likewise if you feel threatened for any reason."

"Thank you, Inspector. May your intellect expand."

They bowed to each other. Baxter exited the gallery and began a rapid, nervous march along the Boulevard, racing toward headquarters. But then it occurred to him: Why the rush? What good will come of it? Would it not be wiser to take a leisurely stroll? It was deserved, after the day's toil. He slowed his pace significantly, and turned his attention to the sights and sounds of the street. The vitrine of a butcher shop caught his eye; he approached, and viewed the calf's brain that was on display.

Why should he fret over the Harriman case, or become agitated by his dream? It will all work itself out, he mused; it always does. Even in death, the grand cycle of existence continues. Consider: a calf was slaughtered (probably under the supervision of Harriman's youngest son), and his brain ended up in this shop window. A mind carrier will consume it; the material is absorbed by the human's brain. When that person dies, his intellect is reassigned by the Omnificent Cerebrum to a body in another cell. So it has been since the beginning of time, and so it shall be for all eternity. Life will triumph. Why allow oneself to be vexed?

Eager to capitalize on his sanguine outlook, Baxter decided to go home and initiate a session of meditation. He would focus his cerebral force on the homicide whose solution was his solemn responsibility. The apparent intractability of the case must be an illusion, he surmised. Somewhere, there lurked a clue. In all likelihood, it was right under his nose. Only by clearing the debris from the surface of the pond would the shiny gem be visible at the bottom.

He reached the Plaza, which was burgeoning with mind carriers. A musician was playing his flute, much to the delight of the audience, many of whom were seated cross-legged on the ground. Not far away, an aspiring author was reading a segment of his epic poem. Baxter briefly lent an ear, and then continued his walk.

Just before he reached the far edge of the Plaza, a speechmaker, standing atop a pedestal, addressed him. "You, over there," he shouted, pointing at Baxter.

The crowd turned to see the target of the remark. Baxter froze in his place.

"You seem like an intelligent man."

Baxter said nothing. He observed the scene with a placid expression.

"What is a dream, my friend? What does it mean to you?"

The veteran detective tugged at his chin and surveyed the faces of the audience, all turned in his direction. "A dream is a message," he replied.

"Ah," said the speechmaker, smiling. "A reasoned response. One could hardly find fault with it. But I submit to you that it is not thus. Rather, a dream is the manifestation of an additional personality. Or perhaps more than one other. All are sharing the same consciousness. What say you to that, my good fellow?"

"A fascinating notion, but I do not accept it."

"And why, may I ask?"

"Because each individual brain represents a single consciousness, a single mind. So it is written in the Tomes of Ancient Thought."

"Of course," said the speechmaker, still in a friendly tone. "But do you not accept that we are all linked together within the cosmic Brain? Just as the cells operate in unison, and their output blends into a single thought at the highest level, seemingly distinct human intellects can mingle."

"By that token," said Baxter, "why limit yourself to dreams? Could you not also say that right now, at this very moment, you and I are sharing the same intellect?"

"Well said, my good fellow. But you shall see that dreams are different. They are a revelation of the innermost secrets of our existence."

Baxter bowed slightly, blessed the speechmaker and the audience, and continued on his way.

V. THE MISSION UNVEILED

He reached home in short order. After George greeted him in the lobby with customary good cheer, Baxter ascended the stairs, arrived at his door, unlocked it, and stepped inside.

"Hi, Daddy," came the sweet voice from within the apartment.

The feeling of surprise at Elizabeth's presence caused a momentary delay in his response. He acknowledged the greeting, and then made his way into the kitchen.

She was sipping some tea. There were several small scrolls on the table, two of them unfurled. Baxter took a seat. "I didn't expect to see you here," he said.

"My last class was cancelled; the professor was ill." She rose from her place and left the room, returning a moment later, parchment in hand. "This was delivered by a policeman, a little while ago. He said that a courier had dropped it off for you at headquarters. It was marked urgent, so the officer brought it here."

Baxter took possession of the parchment. He unrolled it, grumbling to himself that his plans for a peaceful meditation were in the process of being scuttled. The message was from Jiliada, informing him that an interpreter of dreams, a Mr. Henry Thompson, was waiting for him at the Temple compound.

"What happened?" asked Elizabeth, in a nervous tone. "Is it connected with the murder?"

"To some extent," said Baxter, rolling up the document and slipping it into his pocket. "I have to leave now."

"Wait, Daddy."

"What is it?"

"I need to tell you something. It's good, don't worry."

"Can we discuss it later?"

Elizabeth was wearing a childish pout. "It won't take long."

"Okay, then," said Baxter, suppressing his impatience.

The young woman's pout transformed into a smile as her eyes blazed with excitement. "I'm engaged!" she declared.

The communication wound its way through Baxter's ear canal, but could not penetrate the gateway to his brain. He sat, immobile, like a stone.

"Aren't you happy for me?"

"Uh … yes, of course, dear. I'm very happy. I just wasn't aware that there were any candidates."

"There weren't … well, it all happened so fast that I'm a bit in shock myself. He's an intern at the medical school, and my lab instructor. The nicest man, Daddy! We've known each other for a few months, but we met outside of class only twice, and both times within the last few days."

"It seems to me that this process is out of line. You can be engaged only when I approve the suitor, and I can't approve anything if I haven't met the man."

"But I *know* you'll approve it, Daddy. I know it."

"So how did it happen?" asked Baxter.

"I was in the library, looking for information about the Bioprimalists. Remember, when I found that article? Anyway, Gregory—that's his name—came into the hall. He said hello, looking really embarrassed. He's shy, you see, and then when he saw the article, we got into a big discussion about Bioprimalism. We talked for quite some time. About other things too, of course."

"And what does this Gregory fellow have to say on the subject?"

"He knows all about it. It's not what you think. Love is the most important part of Bioprimalism. Love for all people, for animals, for the earth. Respecting everyone else's inner spirit. Never taking more than you need."

Baxter's heart sank, but he maintained a neutral facial expression. "Okay, so that was the first meeting. And then?"

"And then this morning, after the lab, Gregory asked me to take a walk with him around the campus. He was so nervous, it was really cute. He said he's desperately in love with me, and has been since the first lab, but didn't know what to do about it. Then finally, in the library, he got up the courage. Isn't that wonderful, Daddy? So romantic!"

"Undoubtedly. When will I get to meet the lucky young man?"

"Anytime you want."

"How about this evening, after dinner? He could drop by for a little while."

Elizabeth's smile stretched from ear to ear. "Great! I know you'll like him, and you'll approve of our engagement."

Don't be so sure, thought Baxter. "Very well then. Please excuse me for now." He kissed his daughter goodbye, and left the apartment.

During his walk to the Temple compound, Baxter upbraided himself for not making more of an effort to find a husband for Elizabeth. This is the result, he concluded, of his neglect: She finds a wishy-washy type who doesn't have the guts to make his intentions known for months on end. And he's all in a sweat about Bioprimalism, about respecting everyone else's inner spirit. Baxter resolved to work him over that evening in the finest police tradition. At the sight of his breakdown, Elizabeth might think he's a little less cute.

So immersed was Baxter in thought that he approached the Temple area without being gripped by its spiritual radiation. It was only when he reached the security gate that a full awareness of his location took hold. At that point his mental alignment underwent a radical shift, causing his countenance to reflect the appropriate level of solemnity.

The interpreter's chamber was located in the office block, a simple structure adjacent to the gate. Neither this building nor the ground on which it stood had any elevated status in the rite of the Omnificent Cerebrum, yet still, the functions discharged within its walls were closely related to the rituals. A high level of decorum was obligatory at all times.

A sergeant of the Temple guards handled the admittance procedure. He escorted the visitor to the chamber of the interpreter of dreams, Henry Thompson. After introducing the two men, the sergeant returned to his post.

They shook hands. "Please, sir, have a seat," said Thompson. Baxter complied.

The man's appearance did not fit Baxter's preconceived notion. Instead of an old, frail, unkempt wizard, the real Thompson was relatively young, physically fit, and impeccably dressed and groomed. The voice was smooth, lacking any harsh notes. He looked ready-made to be a spokesman for the government or some large mercantile concern.

After a brief exchange of amicable chitchat, Baxter described his recurring dream about the promontory of the rock-creatures. He felt comfortable in Thompson's presence, to a great extent because the interpreter possessed excellent listening skills. He was subdued and attentive, like a wise physician.

At the conclusion of the recitation, the expert turned his concentration inward. He closed his eyes and breathed deeply, seeming to embark upon an impromptu meditation. Then he looked at Baxter with an almost frightening intensity. "What I am about to tell you ... well ... you may find it somewhat disturbing."

"Go ahead."

"We know about your dream."

"You do?"

"Yes," said Thompson. "Some variant of the dream visits a handful of people in each generation. It is a great privilege, but also a heavy responsibility. This group is selected by the Omnificent Cerebrum for a mission that is of supreme significance for the fate of an entire cell."

Baxter started to laugh, but restrained himself. "It's hard to see how a simple detective like myself could have any impact upon the fate of the Home Cell."

"I didn't say the Home Cell. I merely said *cell*. This is not quibbling over details. Your personal mission involves the fate of another cell, not ours. The reason you find yourself in the Home Cell is that the answer to your quest lies here. But that answer, once found, is meant to be applied elsewhere."

"What are you talking about? How is that possible?"

"It is possible because you have committed an error, one that anyone in your situation would commit. You assume that your normal, waking life is here, in the Home Cell, and that the world of the rock-creatures is the land of your dreams."

Baxter felt a coldness creeping into his bones.

"Your assumption is just that—an assumption. If we take a step back and expand our field of view, we find that there is another possibility, equally plausible: That your normal life is somewhere else, and your existence here is of a different quality."

"Are you trying to tell me," said Baxter, "that right at this moment, I'm living in some kind of dream?"

"No, and here's where it gets tricky. The word dream does not capture the essence of your existence in the Home Cell. I believe that *visitor* or *transient* are more apt. You, sir, are as real as anyone else; as real as me, as your colleagues, as the Great Sage himself. The difference is that your sojourn here has an expiration date. Beyond that point, you will once again experience the world of the rock-creatures as your sole, waking reality—which is actually your normal state, even though you cannot see that right now. In any event, when the expiration date arrives, all contact with the Home Cell will be lost to you forever."

"Are you saying that everyone I know here will be dead to me, and me to them?"

"Not exactly," replied Thompson, his bearing now more sympathetic. "There is some sort of parallel in your personal life between the two worlds. It is something we don't fully understand. There is a theory that your loved ones have a mirrored existence in the other reality. Only you, sir, can discover whether this is true in your case, and to what extent."

"And how can I do that?" asked Baxter.

"I will explain. During this final period among us, you will be apprised of the information you need to take back with you to the other world. Part of that process involves a deepening of your recurring dream. When you find yourself there, try to relax. See if it's possible to meditate within the dream. Are your meditations usually effective?"

"More or less."

"Good. You may not succeed on the first go. It will be difficult to reach such a level of concentration. But don't give up. Also, try to calm yourself as much as possible before going to sleep. Then, be aware of the surroundings. Gauge your situation in the world of the rock-creatures. Try to discover who is there and who is not. Do you follow me?"

"Only too well," said Baxter, repelling the shock to which his body was inclined to surrender. "So how exactly do I transport myself to the other cell, when my time here has expired?"

"Let us leave that subject for another day."

"Could you tell me about this critical information that I must take with me?"

"I am not able to do that yet. The dream is not sufficiently advanced. The scenes with the rock-creatures are common to all the people selected for the missions. It is only later, in subsequent dreams, that you are shown your actual life in the other cell. Therefore, you ought to come see me again in a few days. We'll have much more to discuss."

"What do I do now?" asked Baxter, with a note of resentment. "Am I just supposed to walk out of here, and carry on with my life? What of my daughter?"

"I am sorry to be the cause of your distress," said Thompson, softly. "It would be pretentious of me to assert that I know the answer to your questions. All I can say that may provide you with some consolation is that you are fulfilling a mission of the highest importance. The welfare of a multitude depends on you. You were selected because you have unique attributes and untold reservoirs of strength—strength which you are not even aware dwells within your spirit. I implore you to believe that you are indispensable to a plan of cosmic dimensions. If only you could see the result, I am sure that you would rush to accomplish whatever tasks stand before you. You would fly out of this place, frustrated at not being able to work fast enough."

Baxter rose from his seat. He thanked the interpreter for his time, and left the office. After passing through the security gate, he did indeed fly out of the place, but not for the reason suggested by Thompson. Beyond simple frustration and anger was an unwillingness to accept the decree. The entire scenario seemed like an unfortunate error, having no relation to his circumstances or to his spiritual constitution. He undoubtedly was a responsible man, performing his cerebral duties with a pure heart and a clear conscience. But he was a practical man, with practical ambitions. He wished to serve humanity, though in his own manner, one that suited his personality. These notions of a dual life, of dreams with cosmic significance, of fateful missions from the Omnificent Cerebrum—nothing could be more alien to the tenor of his existence.

He walked briskly down Boulevard of the Mind, not paying heed to the activity taking place around him. Perhaps it wasn't true, he thought. Could not the interpreter of dreams be mistaken? The people who serve in the Temple were known to be "in the clouds," divorced from the everyday world. Perhaps the whole split-reality story was a product of someone's hyperactive imagination. Furthermore, leaving aside the validity of the appraisal, was he compelled to obey? An interpreter of dreams is a type of consultant, like an attorney or an architect. No one is obligated to follow his advice.

In the course of his deliberations, Baxter had wandered to the far eastern edge of town, near Theodore Harriman's gallery. The spot was in view of the wall that enclosed the city of Nucleus. The sun was setting; it occurred to Baxter that he should be on his way home for dinner. Yet he needed more time. The turmoil in his mind was considerable. His daughter's suitor would be arriving, and Baxter needed all, or at least most, of his wits about him. The solution came into view across the street: a courier station. He hurried inside, and dispatched a parchment to Elizabeth, notifying her that he would not be arriving home until after dinner.

He began to stroll through the strip of grass and vegetal-symbolic shrubbery that bordered the interior of the city wall for its entire circumference. Continuing the analysis of his situation, he hit upon an interesting prospect. Thompson had remarked that the dream of the rock-creatures occurs several times in each generation. If the story were true, then there must be a number of "survivors" in Nucleus. Surely he could find them, using his investigative skill and, if necessary, some police authority. Could he assign such a task to Jorgensen? Of course not, was the immediate conclusion. No one close to him must know of this entire affair, at least not until some basic questions were answered.

Baxter continued his promenade. The subdued light of dusk had enveloped the city. A few mind carriers were about, stretching their legs after a long day of work. Some children were playing in a sandbox, engrossed in their feats of engineering. A squirrel darted under a bush, evidently fearful of Baxter's approach. The detective stopped at a bench and took a seat. He surveyed the scene. Was this not his life, his home? How could he belong to another cell, which Thompson claimed was his primary existence? What, without a trace in his brain, other than a cryptic dream that occurred for the first time at age forty-eight? Such was tenuous evidence. If he tried to present it as proof of guilt in a criminal case, he would be laughed out of court.

On the other hand, he reasoned, the revelation originated in the Temple. Nothing of the sort should be dismissed casually. To do so would be to manifest a despicable hubris. True, the Temple generated a bad egg every now and then, as evidenced by Conrad Burton, the Bioprimalist apprentice-sage who had to be removed from his post. But overall, the keepers of the hallowed site were among the most intelligent individuals in the Home Cell, and they carried out their functions under an ancient code that tolerated no deviation from its lofty standards.

It was fairly late in the evening when Baxter stood before the door of his apartment. Through the hefty planks of wood he could hear the excited voices and giggling of the two young people inside. He paused, pondering the distasteful task that awaited him: ruining plans for the ultimate happiness in life. This was a role he had to play countless times in his career with the police; spoiling fantasies was as natural to him as uprooting weeds is to a farmer. But when his own daughter was involved, things were far from routine.

He opened the door, stepped inside, and waited for the customary greeting. Instead, an expectant silence gripped the air.

"Daddy, is that you?"

"Who else would it be?" grumbled Baxter as he made his way into the living room. The young couple were standing in front of the sofa, looking awkward and embarrassed.

"Well, are you going to introduce us?"

"Yes ... yes, of course," stammered Elizabeth. "Daddy, this is Gregory. And Gregory, this is ... well ... my father."

Baxter approached, and they shook hands.

"Nice to meet you sir," said the young man.

"Likewise," said Baxter. He examined the suitor. Gregory was short and skinny. He had unusually light hair, as if his head had been bleached. His beard was nearly invisible, having the same pale tint and being quite sparse. The facial features were delicate and feminine. The eyes were in constant motion, as were the hands, as if Gregory could never find a resting place for them. Baxter surmised that he was dealing with a personality type that lacked fortitude, and could easily be rattled and confounded under interrogation.

"Sit down, please," said the master of the house. The couple retook their spot on the sofa as Baxter sat in the adjoining armchair. "I understand you're an intern."

"Yes, sir, that is correct," replied Gregory. His soft-spoken manner matched his frail appearance.

"When do you become a full-fledged physician?"

"In another year."

"Is your father a physician?"

"Yes, at the hospital. He specializes in skin diseases."

"And what will you specialize in?"

"Oh, nothing really. Just general medicine."

"Maybe we could have some tea?" suggested Elizabeth, regaining her usual poise.

"Sure, dear," responded Baxter. "That's a very good idea."

Elizabeth smiled and went into the kitchen. Gregory, with foreboding in his countenance, followed her with his nervous eyes.

"So," said Baxter, folding his muscular arms. "I hear you're a disciple of this Bioprimalism cult."

Gregory sputtered a jittery little laugh. "Well, I just like it, that's all. It really can't be classified as a cult, though."

"No? Then what is it?"

"A different approach to life."

"Life without the Omnificent Cerebrum?"

"I wouldn't say *without*. We prefer the two approaches together, side by side."

Baxter could feel his blood starting to boil. Normally, he would not care much about anyone else's beliefs. When it came to his daughter, however, the interest was magnified a hundred fold. "Aren't they contradictory, the two paths of which we speak?"

"Not necessarily," replied Gregory. "One can acknowledge the role of the intellect while realizing that we are part of nature. We can be truly happy only when we live in harmony with the earth."

"In harmony with the earth? Do the Tomes of Ancient Thought not say that the earth was put here for the sole purpose of assisting us in our cerebral tasks?"

"Yes, of course, but nature should not be abused. If we don't alter our behavior, then very soon Mother Earth will seek her revenge, and the consequences for humanity will be catastrophic."

"How can an inanimate object seek revenge?"

"Uhh ..."

"And if you people have your way, what will happen to art and music?" demanded Baxter. He caught a glimpse of his daughter standing at the entrance to the kitchen. There was a distinct look of anxiety on her face. It reminded him of a certain expression she had as a child, in the ominous days following the death of her mother. Strangely, it often appeared in close proximity to a display of tenacity and courage. Similarly, in the present scene, she was bravely introducing a young man whom she knew to be disagreeable to her father, yet lurking under the surface was a potent apprehension that was now finding an outlet.

"Art is still considered important," ventured Gregory, in his timid voice.

"But will your art be produced by humans?" retorted Baxter.

Gregory's eyes widened. "What do you mean?"

"I mean, do you plan on hiring any monkeys?"

"Daddy, what are you talking about?" asked Elizabeth, who had returned to the living room, and now was resting a tray on the little table in front of the sofa.

"I heard a rumor that there's going to be an exhibition of Bioprimalist work, somewhere in Nucleus, consisting of paintings produced by a monkey."

Elizabeth looked at her fiancé. "That's my father's idea of a joke."

"It isn't a joke," said Baxter, solemnly.

"Umm … I know about that," said Gregory, his bleached face growing even paler. "Look, it's just a one-time thing, to make a point. For centuries, art has been institutionalized, frigid, and morose. We're trying to shock people a bit by going to the other extreme. Later, it will settle down somewhere in the middle."

"Is that what you think of the masterpieces in the art museum, that they're frigid and morose?"

Gregory cast his eyes down. Elizabeth's look of apprehension returned, as she shifted her glance from one man to the other. "You know what, Daddy—Gregory graduated with honors from the medical school."

"Is that so?" said Baxter, not unhappy to be changing the subject. He gladly would have demolished the young man were it not for his daughter's expression of disquietude, so reminiscent of the darkest years of her life. He would need to reevaluate his approach in order to minimize the pain he was causing her. There was no question, however, concerning the young man on the sofa. He found Gregory to be effeminate, weak-spirited, and prone to flights of fancy. If Elizabeth were to marry him, he would turn her into a social leper, embarrass Baxter, and most likely endanger their safety, given the inevitable crackdown on the Bioprimalists. Why couldn't she bring home someone decent? One would think that young men would jump at the opportunity to court such a beautiful and intelligent maiden, and from a respectable family, no less. Baxter concluded, once again, that the dilemma was the result of his own neglect. He resolved to take steps immediately to ensure that the distasteful conversation he was having that evening would never be repeated.

They drank their tea. Elizabeth piloted the remainder of the discussion, which went from medical school to police work to Gregory's family history. Baxter remained calm. When a lull arrived, he stretched and yawned, remarking that the day had been extraordinarily long. Gregory took the hint, and announced his departure. Elizabeth accompanied him downstairs.

Baxter parked himself at one of the windows facing the street. He saw the young couple emerge from the lobby and walk slowly toward Avenue of the Synapses. Elizabeth, he mused, has a good heart. Was this not the same girl who, at age eleven, declared that she would become a nurse, in order to help save other little girls from the anguish of losing their mother? It was not merely a good heart, but a giant one, with ample room for all sorts of empathy. No wonder she could be captivated by a movement such as Bioprimalism. Their call to be respectful and loving had apparently worked its magic. She does have a rational side, but it was insufficiently robust to extricate her from her powerful emotions. Moreover, what the mushy appeal of Bioprimalism could not accomplish, her infatuation with Gregory did. Fortunately, Baxter reminded himself, she has a father with his head screwed on straight, ready to return her to reality. He would not approve the union; she would have no recourse. Case closed.

As he reached resolution on the issue of his daughter's engagement, another problem came to mind, that of the recurring dream. Baxter laughed to himself: Disposing of Gregory was a picnic compared to the real challenge that loomed before him. First, it was necessary to determine whether the scenario presented by Henry Thompson, the interpreter of dreams, was to be taken seriously. And then, if perchance the worst were to emerge, doing what was required to survive.

Returning his attention to the street, he saw his daughter, head bowed, returning alone from Avenue of the Synapses. He awaited her from his emplacement at the window. She entered the apartment, and was soon standing alongside him.

"You are a sensible girl, Elizabeth," he said, in a gentle tone. "You have always made wise choices in life, keeping yourself on an even keel. You emerged from the tragedy of your mother's death as a hero, saving yourself and those close to you from ruin. Schoolwork was never neglected. Shining brightly was your mind, as you positioned yourself for admittance to a vital profession. But alas, no human being is infallible. All of us make mistakes; left to our own devices, we would surely dig our own graves. That is why we have family and friends, trusted advisers, to save us from folly. Sometimes they can see things, dangers, to which we ourselves have become blinded. And thus we yield to their better judgment."

Baxter, with trepidation, awaited the reaction. At first she was quiet, seeming to be in shock. Then her lip quivered, her eyes widened, and the floodgates opened. She yelled and cried, hands flailing. She moved around the room, always directing her ire at the figure of authority, who, like a sentry at his post, did not budge from the window. Baxter absorbed the torrent, until at last her energy was spent. With one last wail, she stormed into her bedroom and slammed the door shut.

Her father sat for a while on the sofa, afflicting himself with images of Elizabeth's swelled and contorted face. The images faded, to the point where the specter of the dream returned to mind. He recalled Thompson's advice, to meditate before going to sleep, so that he would be able to concentrate during the dream. But first, there was another duty to fulfill. Baxter moved to the little nook at the edge of the living room to recite the Declaration of Cognitive Achievement at the family's Cerebral Shrine. He sat cross-legged on the floor, as was the custom, and beheld the little brain, pondering the unimaginable power of the entity whose model was before him. Who was he to second-guess the established, legitimate representatives of the Omnificent Cerebrum? Did he purport to have more knowledge of the cosmos than they? Maybe his predicament was even more severe than what he had been told, and Thompson was being merciful, not revealing the full picture all at once. Perhaps death was imminent. Who can say what the Omnificent Cerebrum has in store? Baxter regarded himself as a humble man, but was plotting to interview "survivors" of the dual reality the act of such a person? Or was it rather an expression of arrogance, thinking he could outsmart everyone, from the sharpest brains in the Home Cell to the ultimate Brain itself? He shuddered at the implications. Here he was, lecturing his daughter about making mistakes and being saved from one's own folly. He might be better advised to direct some of that wisdom to himself.

Baxter completed the Declaration and rose from the floor. He considered speaking with Elizabeth, but rejected the idea, preferring instead to let the worst of the storm pass. He went to his room and put himself to bed. The earlier resolution to meditate slipped his mind; fatigue, mostly of the mental variety, had taken its toll.

He soon found himself at the promontory of the rock-creatures. The scene was calm; the lizards were stationary, and the soldiers in the nearby camp were quietly going about their business. A trumpet sounded, in a series of shrill blasts. The soldiers hurried into formation. The trumpeter walked briskly over to Baxter, planted the base of his lance firmly in the ground, and thrust it forward.

"Yes ..." said Baxter.

"Troops aligned and ready for inspection, General."

Baxter was dazzled by the entire display, but had enough presence of mind to try and look the part. He was no stranger to the art of commanding, having on several occasions led detachments of police on special assignments. The trumpeter, meanwhile, stood immobile, awaiting the directives of his superior.

"Give me your lance," said Baxter.

The man's eyes widened with apprehension as he complied. Baxter took the weapon and turned it over and over, pretending to inspect it, though his sole purpose was to examine the spearhead. It was fashioned from a metal he had never seen, of a dark gray color. He ran his fingernail over the edges, noting the hardness, unlike anything existing in the Home Cell. After returning the weapon to its owner, he viewed the troops, who were about fifty yards distant. Several thousand of them were assembled; some were equipped with lances, and all with shield and sword. Each man stood as still as a statue of marble. At the front corners of the formation were the standard-bearers, holding massive black and gold flags that were fluttering in the wind.

"Are the men ready?" asked Baxter, in his gravest voice.

"May I speak freely, sir?" asked the trumpeter, in a hush.

"Of course."

"The General is very popular among the men. Our previous commander never gave such a large share of the spoils to the infantry. Not to mention the General's order granting leave for three days, to go into the city."

"I may have been too charitable, now that I think of it."

"There is no cause for concern," said the trumpeter. "They will take their leave in shifts, as the General instructed. That order will be implemented to the letter, on my personal responsibility. The main camp will never contain fewer than a thousand men under arms."

"That is good."

"The troops will not forget that their commander made available to them all the houses of pleasure in the city, for their exclusive use. Their loyalty is assured."

"That was my intent," said Baxter.

"Let us go without delay, for the men wish to show their appreciation before embarking upon their leave. And of course, the Emperor awaits us at the main camp."

Baxter nodded solemnly. They walked to the front of the formation. The movement of his limbs caused Baxter to take note of the equipment in which he was engirdled. A leather sheath, inlaid with gold and jewels, held a sword of the same gray metal as the tip of the trumpeter's lance. Thick boots covered most of the length of his calves. His head was compelled to support a helmet of great weight. Upon his finger was a ring with a seal of jade.

They took up position before the troops. "Men of the infantry," declared the trumpeter, "before you is the greatest general who has ever lived."

A whoop of celebration filled the air, until it seemed that the ground itself would crack open from its force.

After a few moments, Baxter raised his hand for silence. "Men, you have been valiant and loyal. For this you are being rewarded. Go forth and enjoy your leave. Spare yourselves no pleasure, because there will be much work to do when you return. The enemy has retreated to his cities, but he will surely renew his belligerence at the first opportunity. Many campaigns await us." Baxter nodded at the trumpeter. The latter sounded his instrument with gusto. Another cry of joy rose from the multitude, who broke ranks and ran in the opposite direction, toward the main camp.

The General and his trumpeter began to walk the same route. It was at that point that Baxter experienced his first recollection from within the other world. He remembered, albeit vaguely, a meeting that had taken place the day before, in the Emperor's tent. The Emperor was vexed by a crucial decision that loomed before him. His counselors were engaged in animated discussion.

As they descended the hill, a vast encampment came into view. Tents were pitched for what seemed like miles. There was much ado; soldiers running, deliveries of food arriving, men conversing with great vigor. Baxter looked around with unquenchable curiosity. His legs carried him forward as if they knew the route to the Emperor's tent.

The spot was thickly guarded. Impassioned salutes greeted the General as the phalanx parted to allow him and his aide to pass. He came upon the entrance, and paused. The trumpeter looked at him with a thin, wise smile, and entered the tent. Baxter turned his head and saw a woman about thirty yards away. It was Jiliada. She smiled and waved, and then continued on her way as if the situation were entirely routine.

He attempted to take a step in her direction, but found that his feet were stuck to the ground. He tried to holler, but his throat felt as if it had been stuffed with cotton. A flash of light turned everything a bright yellow.

Baxter opened his eyes and beheld the ceiling of his bedroom.

VI. IDENTITY CRISIS

Baxter lay in bed for some time. He resolved from the first moment to remain calm and concentrate in order to retain in memory as much of the dream as possible. Of all the images, the starkest in his mind was that of Jiliada. What struck him was the familiarity of the contact. There was no surprise in her expression; on the contrary, one would think that they had been together a short time before, with the expectation of being reunited very soon thereafter.

The interpreter Henry Thompson's assertion that the dream represents another existence in a different cell was corroborated by Baxter's nocturnal experience. Dividing up the spoils? Sending thousands of soldiers en masse to "houses of pleasure"? Such things have never come to pass in the Home Cell. Baxter reasoned that he would not be capable of extracting these outlandish notions from his own mind. Likewise, from where would he conjure up such vivid images of the metal he encountered on his sword and on the trumpeter's lance? No one in the Home Cell had ever seen material of that nature.

He glanced at the window. The intensity of the light indicated that he had overslept. He rose to his feet, stretched, and began the morning routine. Elizabeth was absent. Baxter ate a quick breakfast, and left the apartment.

He arrived at police headquarters a short while later. Jorgensen was waiting in the office, feet up on the desk, a wry smile on his face.

"I thought you'd never get here, boss," he said.

"Yet I am here," replied Baxter, placing himself in the unoccupied chair.

"You need to sign this document," said Jorgensen, removing his feet from the desk.

The detective glanced at the text in the little scroll, and affixed his signature. "So what do you have to report?"

"I tailed this Westlake guy, boss, just as you told me."

Baxter at that moment concluded definitively that his assistant would not be a suitable candidate for son-in-law. The habitual use of the word *boss* settled the issue. Though Baxter found the term endearing, it was indicative of a somewhat inferior intellect.

"Westlake has an interesting life," continued Jorgensen.

"Oh? Why is that?"

"He spent some time yesterday in the Temple compound. I didn't follow him in, but I spoke with the guards. They told me that he was going to see the interpreter of dreams."

"Interesting," said Baxter, tugging at his chin and wondering what else the guards may have divulged.

"But it gets better. From the Temple, Westlake was picked up by a carriage. Guess who was inside? Our little whore, Jiliada."

Baxter winced at hearing the slur. "Hmm ... What do you make of it?"

"Something's going on, that's for sure."

"It would seem so. Did you find anything else?"

"Why, wasn't that enough?"

"Just asking."

"No, nothing else."

Baxter stood up and stretched his back. "I think another visit to Jiliada is in order."

"Should we leave right now?" asked Jorgensen, moving his lanky frame toward the door.

"I think I'll go there alone, Phil."

Jorgensen let loose a grunt of frustration.

"It's better this way. I have a certain rapport with her, and it's fragile enough as it is. We can't risk ruining it."

"What else is part of that rapport?"

"I'll ignore that snide remark."

"Sorry, boss," said Jorgensen. He pulled the long, shaggy hair away from his forehead. "It's just that I want to be around for the good stuff."

"Why, tailing Westlake wasn't good stuff? You did your job well, and uncovered what might be a key link in the case."

"Thanks," said the junior partner. He still appeared crestfallen.

"Our goal is to solve the murder, not to find personal thrills. There will be times when I'm sitting here signing documents and you're out saving lives and making arrests."

Jorgensen lumbered back to his chair, and sagged into it like a sack of potatoes. "So what should I do while you're … umm … solving the murder?"

"Good question," replied Baxter. "What would you suggest?"

"I want to find out more about Westlake. Something tells me that he can lead us to some answers. For starters, I could go sniff around at his news-scroll, the *Monthly Gazette.*"

"Sounds like a wise course of action. You may have a future in this business."

"Thanks, boss."

"Let's rendezvous here later today, just before sundown," said Baxter. "Good luck."

They both left the office. Jorgensen exited the building, while Baxter headed for the stables to requisition a chariot. On the way, he was intercepted by the Chief, who asked for a quick update on the Harriman case. Standing in the hallway, Baxter did his best to explain the few threads that had emerged thus far. As was his custom, he downplayed the progress made, sounding more pessimistic than any of his colleagues, were they to find themselves in the same circumstances. The Chief showed no concern, assuming based on past results that an arrest was imminent.

This delay in Baxter's progress was followed by another. While speeding along the highway, one of the wheels on the chariot began to wobble. This had happened once before, about a year earlier; on that occasion, the wheel and the axle parted company. Fortunately, the present mishap occurred as Baxter was passing through a suburb, about a mile past the city gates. Knowing of a mechanic on the main road, he detoured to the man's workshop. Happily, he was present, and agreed to take care of this police business immediately.

As the mechanic was completing his labor, Baxter glanced at the highway and saw Westlake—with Jiliada at his side—pass by in a carriage. The heavy vehicle, hitched to a team of only two horses, was slow, traveling at not more than half the speed of a chariot. Baxter hurried into his vehicle, promising the mechanic that he would return very soon to settle the account. He sped away in pursuit of Westlake.

It did not take long to catch up. Baxter reduced speed and trailed the carriage at a distance great enough to maintain an inconspicuous presence. He endured the unpleasantness of the slow pace until at last Two Scribes could be seen ahead. After entering the village, the carriage turned in the direction of Jiliada's villa. Baxter followed it almost all the way to its destination. He brought the chariot to a halt on the adjoining block, tied the horses to a post, and glided silently to the street corner. From there he observed the unfolding scene.

The carriage was parked in front of the gate of the compound. Westlake and Jiliada were seated in the passenger compartment, engaged in conversation. The frequent hand gestures indicated a lively topic. Baxter speculated as to the nature of their relationship. Was Westlake a patron of hers? If not, what were they doing? Did it involve Baxter, the Harriman murder, Jiliada's relation to the Temple, or some combination of these? The more he thought about it, the more Baxter felt resentful toward Jiliada. It was clear to him that she had not been forthright. What was she hiding?

She stepped out of the carriage, walked to the gate, and pulled the rope that rang the bell. A member of the household staff opened the gate, and she stepped inside. The carriage, now holding only Westlake and the coachman, departed.

Baxter, his wrath kindled, scurried forward from his observation point. He yanked the rope with such force that nothing but a dull thud was heard from the bell. He repeated the action at normal strength. A few moments later, the gate opened to reveal a young servant with a sour face. "Yes?" he wheezed, tilting his head back and giving Baxter a condescending look.

"I'm here to see the lady of the house."

"I'm sorry, sir, but the lady of the house is not accepting visitors at the moment."

"That doesn't interest me," said Baxter, shoving the man aside as he surged into the yard.

"I'll summon the police!" shouted the servant, his fist in the air.

"I *am* the police," retorted Baxter, without turning his head. He entered the house by the front door. After passing through the vestibule, he poked his head in one room, and then another. All was quiet.

At last he came upon Jiliada. She was in a small parlor, standing quietly, with a melancholy look. Baxter was as tense as a wound-up spring prior to its release. The reddish tint of his facial skin matched that of his beard. "I want answers," he fumed. "And I want them now."

Jiliada inched forward until she stood just in front of her uninvited guest. Her expression of melancholy deepened as her eyes caressed his own. "I will tell you everything I know," she said, in a whisper.

Baxter inhaled deeply and sighed, as some of the burden was lifted from his spirit. Jiliada motioned for him to sit on the sofa. He complied.

She closed the door to the room, took off her shoes, and sat cross-legged next to him.

"I am sorry to see you so distraught," she began, in a voice louder than a whisper but still subdued. "If it's any consolation, I've been living with the same frustration for the last eight years. Ever since that incident in the Temple involving the death of my husband."

"That was tragic, indeed," said Baxter.

"What I didn't tell you last time is that it wasn't an accident. My husband died because of the dream. The same dream that you had, and that I will have very soon. Everyone who has the dream dies. Yet it's not exactly like that. Part of us dies. But part of us survives, only elsewhere. Did the interpreter of dreams tell you all this?"

"He told me that the dream is planted in my mind by the Omnificent Cerebrum. It's a sort of mission. I'm living in two worlds simultaneously."

"Exactly," said Jiliada. "Anyway, I wasn't supposed to find out the real reason for my husband's demise. That I did was a fluke; I overheard some sages who were gabbing carelessly, oblivious to their surroundings. It is said that when a mission has run its course, the person returns to live exclusively in his cell of origin. He dies in the cell where he was a visitor. But he's not really deceased. As the Great Sage put it, his life returns to his true world. For us, the Home Cell is the world we are visiting. We originate elsewhere."

"We?"

"Yes. You, my husband, and myself."

"But I thought you didn't have the dream."

"No, but I've had a waking vision that comes to me every so often. You see, when the forbidden knowledge was inadvertently passed to me, the normal process was disrupted. I shouldn't have connected with my other reality so early. It should have been buried in a place within my spirit that is so deep, only a dream could unlock it."

"Go on," said Baxter, repressing an urge to gather Jiliada in his arms.

"I discovered that I am from this other world, and that I'm just an interloper in the Home Cell. Our other world ..." Jiliada's head drooped slowly. When she again looked up, there was distress in her face. "The other cell, our real world, is called Luctor. I am the niece of the Emperor. And you ..." Tears began to well in her tender eyes. She raised a clenched fist to her mouth, bit her knuckles, and looked at Baxter with a mix of affection and dread.

"Tell me who I am," said Baxter. He spoke in a serene voice, bracing himself for the oncoming shock.

"You are General Hendrick, commander of the army, hero to all the people of Luctor—and *my husband*."

They both remained silent for some time.

"I saw you in my dream last night," he said.

"You were outside the Emperor's tent."

"Correct," said Baxter, no longer taken aback by the barrage of revelations.

"I was on my way to our own tent," said Jiliada, "to supervise the preparations for dinner. My father—your father-in-law and the Emperor's brother—was set to join us. We have a happy existence in Luctor. You are satisfied with your life's work. And I have a husband who cares for me and adores me."

"How long have you known about this? About me?"

"Since it all started, years ago. I always knew you were in the Home Cell; I could feel it, and powerfully, but I didn't know your identity here, and no one from the Temple would tell me. I pleaded with the Great Sage, but he refused to divulge anything, saying that too much had been disrupted already, it was too risky. Then I saw you in that dingy café, with your assistant, not long after the murder. There you were, my husband, interrogating me. You can imagine my distress."

Baxter smiled. "You seemed a little out of sorts."

"Now I am waiting for my dream to arrive. Then it will seem as though we are really there. Don't you feel that way in the dream, that Luctor is the only real existence, that there's nothing else?"

"Oh, absolutely. That is a fundamental characteristic of dreams. But don't you have the same feeling in your visions?"

Jiliada shook her head. "It's not the same. I'm awake when it happens. I see many things, and receive much information, but it's not the same." She suddenly stood up, as if by doing so she would cast away her frustration. "I want all of this to be behind us, so we can get on with our lives. I can't stand being here, in this place. I've made a mess of everything."

"How so?"

"You think I enjoy being a courtesan?" she cried, arms waving in the air.

"Evidently not. But why do you continue, then?"

"I don't know," said Jiliada, again biting her knuckles. She paced to and fro. "In the beginning I didn't think it would last so long. It started as part of a rebellion against the world, after my husband's death, the loss of the baby, and my discovery of Luctor. I lashed out at everyone and everything. If I would have had some real family, it might have been different. But I was an orphan, adopted and raised as an only child by an elderly sage and his wife."

"What happened to your natural parents?"

"They died just after I was born. The people who adopted me had no other children. And then they died before I was married. I have no one, really. I did stop my business a few times, but it wasn't easy. I changed my address, but my patrons found me, and pleaded with me to continue. For some of them, I was their only hold on life. One threatened to commit suicide. Another said that he had ceased to function as a normal human being. The whole thing was oppressive. Each time, I convinced myself that it would only go on a bit longer. And what does it matter, in the end? This entire existence is false; this world isn't mine. I hate it, I hate it ..." Jiliada hurled herself onto the sofa and began to sob.

As Baxter moved closer to comfort the distressed young woman, she sprang up and looked at him with dread. "Is it too horrible to bear? Do you despise me now?"

"Despise you?" he whispered, reaching out and placing his hand on her soft cheek, which was warm and moist from the tears and sweat. Jiliada closed her eyes and kissed his fingers, now working their way over her lips. Baxter pulled her gently toward him, bringing her mouth to his. She allowed a brief kiss, and then rested her head on his shoulder.

"Do I have to call you Inspector?" she asked.

"You can call me Simon."

"I like that name, Simon."

"I am glad. Is your husband there now, in Luctor?"

"No. He died completely, everywhere. Something went wrong in the Temple. When it is time to return to the cell of origin, the person must renounce his life in the other cell. My husband—I hate calling him that, his name was Michael—resisted; he refused to let go of his life here. This is forbidden, and he was cautioned. The whole procedure was wrecked. Michael wasn't from Luctor anyway, I'm almost certain. Once I confronted the Great Sage about it. He wouldn't deny that I spoke the truth."

"Tell me something, Jiliada. Would it not be possible to find people in the Home Cell who have passed through the entire ordeal, from start to finish? I'm talking about people for whom the Home Cell is the cell of origin."

"I have considered that too, many times, but it is strictly prohibited to make contact with them, as it could disrupt the process. The Great Sage warned me of it."

"He also warned you about looking for me, did he not?"

"Yes," she replied, releasing a sigh. "But you appeared out of nowhere. When something comes to me, I accept it. It is a sign of the Omnificent Cerebrum's assent."

Baxter held Jiliada's head snugly against his shoulder. He had forgotten the comfort that accompanies a situation of intimacy with a woman. A warm tingle spread through his limbs, and he savored it.

"Simon ..." she said, as her hand stroked his beard.

"Yes?"

"I began my life in the Home Cell as an orphan. My adopted parents are deceased. I have no one truly close to me here. But you have a family, don't you?"

"My parents are no longer living, and I am an only child, as you are. My other relatives are dead or far away; I hardly have contact with them. My wife died suddenly of a strange disease, as you know. In recent years I have had only one true friend, a fellow detective named Samuel. He was killed in a police operation just over a year ago.

"But I have a daughter, Elizabeth, who is more dear to me than all the gold in the world. What shall I do about her when the time comes for this dangerous ritual, in which my primary existence passes to Luctor, and I become dead for everyone in the Home Cell? Will I not die completely, like Michael? How could I possibly renounce my life here? What will I tell Elizabeth?" Baxter, choked with sorrow, ceased his discourse. Now it was his turn to spring from his seat and pace nervously about the room.

"I'm sorry, Simon. I don't have a good answer for you. We are both caught in the net."

"What happens if I simply refuse to go along with all this? Will the interpreter of dreams, Thompson, turn me in? Will the Great Sage have me arrested?"

Jiliada's eyes were brimming with sadness. She said nothing.

"Answer the question," moaned Baxter, in more of a plea than a demand. "What can they do if I refuse to go along?"

"They can do nothing, it is true. But you won't be talking this way after you discover the reason for your mission. Wait until you've had another dream or two, and then ask me again."

"Do you know the reason for my mission?"

"No."

Baxter rushed to the sofa and grasped Jiliada by the shoulders. "Please tell me, you must."

"I don't know, I really don't. But everything will be explained to you soon, first in your dreams, and then by the sages."

"Is Elizabeth there, in Luctor?"

"I don't know that either. You will have to find out when you're in the dream."

Baxter relaxed his grip and settled back into the sofa. He felt limp and despondent.

"Oh, Simon," said Jiliada, shaking her head. "I know how you feel."

They sat in silence for several moments.

"Is there anything else I can help you clarify?" she asked.

Baxter hardly had the strength to go on, but turned his head and caught sight of Jiliada's sympathetic gaze. "There is one more thing. I was wondering about Westlake."

Her expression became stern. "He annoys me greatly, that persistent little pest."

"He's a journalist. If he must be anything, it's persistent."

"Yes, but he's a bit too clever for his own good. All these years he hasn't forgotten the incident with Michael. You should have heard him just now in the carriage. He wants to revive everything, investigate, publicize. Oh, of course he makes it sound as though he's doing me a favor. Justice will be done, he says."

"Maybe he honestly wants to help," said Baxter.

"Maybe. By the way, Westlake recently got wind of the dual existence. I don't know how; I didn't tell him. The questions surrounding Michael's death, which everyone laid to rest, became rekindled in his spirit."

"Did you tell him about me?"

"No, of course not. He's been to see people in the Temple, though I couldn't imagine anyone there divulging information of this sort. It's simply not in their interest. They know he wants to smear them."

Baxter leaned forward, resting his forearms on his knees. "Jiliada," he said, with a sigh.

"Yes …"

"Let us speak no more of this today. My mind is saturated and I am weary." He turned his head in her direction. "Thank you for everything. I am in your debt."

"If I can help you avoid any of the pain that I went through, it is recompense enough."

She stood up. He did likewise, and embraced her. They remained immobile for some time. Baxter announced that he was compelled to return to the city. Jiliada accompanied him to the front door of the house, where they hugged each other one last time before parting.

After exiting through the carriage gate, Baxter walked to the next block. He unhitched the horses from the post to which they were tied, and led them to a nearby fountain. "Be happy that your life is simple," he said, as the beasts quenched their seemingly endless thirst. When they were satiated, their master mounted the footplate of the chariot, and the trip began.

Soon Baxter was hurtling down the main highway, headed for Nucleus. The air blowing in his face helped to clear the fog from his mind. Scrutinizing the affair in the light of day, it seemed to him out of control and intolerable. Jiliada and the interpreter of dreams, with all their good intentions, had backed him into a corner. Rarely in his life had he been subjected to such pressure. As far as he could discern, they were being honest and forthright, but could they not be in error? Might their explanation of the dream be nothing more than a fairy tale? Why should he swear allegiance to the Temple's interpreter of dreams? The man is surely fallible, like anyone else. As for Jiliada, she was an intelligent and attractive woman whose concern for him was palpable. But did that justify placing his fate in her hands?

On the other hand, how did she know about the scene in the dream where he was standing outside the Emperor's tent? This qualified as evidence in her favor. Yet prudence, thought Baxter, required that he investigate further; another explanation might be uncovered. In any event, how did this woman suddenly become his adviser on spiritual affairs? Even worse, she might be a witness in the Harriman case—and he *kissed* her. How about explaining that to the Chief? Things have gone too far, Baxter concluded. Much too far.

He detoured to the workshop of the mechanic who had repaired his vehicle earlier in the day. The detective gave the man a voucher which he could present at police headquarters for reimbursement. They parted with a firm handshake and an exchange of blessings.

Across the street was a well-known tavern, The Fisherman's Net. Baxter had enjoyed their hospitality on several occasions, though much time had passed since his last visit. He drove across the highway, and parked at the trough, so that the horses could also partake of refreshment and enjoy the company of their peers.

He entered the establishment and took a seat at the bar. The bartender recognized him, and initiated a convivial round of chitchat. Baxter gladly cooperated, as the diversion was most welcome. He ordered a glass of wine. After a few sips, the alcohol took effect; his rattled nerves began to settle. As the bartender gabbed away, Baxter surveyed the scene, deriving satisfaction from what his eyes absorbed. The Fisherman's Net was decorated in a maritime motif. Scattered about were nets, harpoons, oars, and other boat-related paraphernalia. The tables were made from fragments of old fishing vessels. On one wall was a mural depicting a ship being tossed about in a blustery storm. There were a fair number of patrons, all of them talking and drinking in relative quiet.

A man perched himself on the neighboring stool. Baxter glanced in his direction: it was Peter Westlake. The journalist laughed at the sight of Baxter's face. "No one is ever happy to see me," he said, "but this is extreme."

"Don't take it personally. I'm not feeling particularly sociable."

"I don't see how you can ever feel sociable in your line of work."

The bartender took the new arrival's order, a potent variety of wine.

"Do you come here often?" inquired Baxter, noting Westlake's eyebrows, which became misaligned whenever the man's speech took an emphatic turn.

"I've never before set foot in this place. But I was following you, and saw you come in here."

"You were *following* me?"

"Yes," replied Westlake, laughing again. The wine arrived, and he promptly downed half the glass in one go. "Ah ... that hits the spot. Anyway, yes, I was following you, all the way from Two Scribes. Do you think you're the only one who knows how to do it? Frankly, I'm surprised that a veteran detective like yourself didn't notice."

Baxter, with a pout, picked up his glass and swirled the liquid around.

"Does that wine hold the answer to the riddle of your recurring dream?"

Baxter's hand stopped its movement. "Okay, let's have it," he groaned, still looking downward.

"There are people, sir, who are taking you for a fool."

"Are they?"

"Yes. Don't tell me that the possibility never occurred to you. Let's start with Michael the sage. Surely you heard the story of his death from our little courtesan."

Baxter suddenly turned to face the journalist.

"Now, now, Inspector. You like Jiliada, and feel a strong kinship after she convinced you that you share the same fate. But let me remind you that she has a history of mental instability. She's a very kind—but very disturbed—young woman."

These words caused Baxter no small discomfort.

"Never mind that, let's get back to Michael, the deceased husband. The unsuspecting chump walked right off the cliff. Do you know what he died of? I'm speaking of the actual cause of death."

"No idea."

"I'll tell you. He had a heart attack. So what, you say. Well, he happened to be in his twenties, and in perfect health. Never hospitalized a day in his life. So I'd like to know the sequence of events that fateful day in the Temple." Westlake downed the rest of the wine in his glass and ordered another round, which was promptly served. "I have a theory."

"Oh?" said Baxter, in a friendlier tone. He was beginning to appreciate the counterweight of Westlake's challenge.

"I believe that Michael was literally scared to death. They destroyed his mind and broke his spirit. When the moment arrived for the supposed leap to the other world, he was already delirious. Bring someone in that condition to the inner chambers of the Temple, where no layman may tread, and all bets are off."

Baxter was tugging at his chin, rather intensely.

"There's more, Inspector. Several other young, healthy individuals met their deaths in the same manner as Michael. I have the coroner's report for each of them."

"Have you located any survivors, or someone now in the process? Aside from Jiliada and myself, that is."

"No, not yet. But I'm working on it."

"So why are they doing all this? Do you think it's some kind of conspiracy?"

Westlake smiled. "I don't believe in conspiracies. That's not the way the world functions. No, Inspector, the people in the Temple have latched on to this atrocious myth; they're as deluded as the poor mind carriers whose lives they've destroyed. We'd all be better off if they tended to their proper duties, at which they are quite proficient: managing the festivals, running the Temple, and ensuring that the rite of the Omnificent Cerebrum is passed down to the next generation. Enough of this hocus-pocus. I mean, is there anything more preposterous than claiming that you can regulate the movement of people between cells?"

"No, I suppose not."

"And now we have an urgent task, you and I."

"What is that?"

"We must ensure that the same fate does not befall *you*. And Jiliada, and anyone else who stumbles into the trap. To accomplish this goal, I need your help."

"What is it you seek?" asked Baxter.

"I'm going to write a major article about this affair, exposing the whole thing. What I need from you is testimony. I want the whole story, start to finish. If you gave it to me now, and I published the story as is, it would be powerful. But to be truly damning, we need to go all the way; all the way, that is, to the inner chambers of the Temple. So you play along with everyone—with Jiliada, with the interpreter of dreams, with the Great Sage himself. And then, at the last moment, as they get set to rob you of your life force, you bust out of the Temple and we expose the entire scheme."

Baxter soaked up the words like a sponge, allowing them to calm his fears. He felt jittery, however, about such a brazen challenge to the authority of the sages. "It all sounds logical, what you're saying. But let me think about it. We have discussed many matters, and now I must reflect."

"I understand, Inspector. Consider it all, and let me know what you decide. Either way, don't let them deflate your spirit."

"Thank you. May your intellect expand."

Westlake rose from the stool, polished off his wine, and threw a coin onto the bar. "We'll talk soon," he said, before turning to leave The Fisherman's Net.

Baxter lingered for a short while, thanked the bartender, and exited. He untied the horses, and continued the journey into Nucleus. Soon, he was passing through the gates of the city. As the urban vista unfolded before him, his heart expanded with new inspiration and courage. The discussion with Westlake had reinserted him into the life of the Home Cell. Yes, this was his true existence. *I live here,* thought Baxter, right here in this city, not in some fantastic dream or the still more fantastic interpretations assigned to it by people whose faculty of judgment was open to question.

He reached headquarters, and dropped the chariot off at the stables. The next destination was his office. It was devoid of activity; no Jorgensen, no messages, no documents to sign. He returned to the street and headed home.

Every stone along Avenue of the Synapses acquired new significance. The buildings looked majestic, particularly the art museum and the civic complex. At an upscale gourmet shop he purchased several expensive items for dinner. It was to be a celebration, a thanksgiving for his return to normal life. He hoped that he would be able to pacify Elizabeth to the extent necessary to secure her participation.

George greeted him in the lobby of the apartment building. Baxter opened one of the packages and gave the doorman a large piece of pickled herring, for which the reward was a profusion of thanks. Baxter, forgetting his age, bounded nimbly up the stairs. He entered the apartment and paused. There was no response from within. He went to the kitchen, where he stowed the comestibles. On the way to the little bedroom, he spotted Elizabeth. She was seated on the sofa.

"Oh, there you are," he said.

She lowered her gaze. Baxter sat in one of the armchairs, so as to be in close proximity, but without crowding her.

"How was your day?" she asked.

"Satisfactory. And yours?"

"Not bad. I'm sorry I yelled at you last night."

"I understand your distress. Are you still cross with me?"

"No," replied Elizabeth, looking at him with sad eyes. "I had a long talk with Gregory. He said that you are a good father, that you care deeply about me. He respects your position, and knows that the burden of proof is on him because he is the one breaking away from tradition. He also said that he would be honored to have children who come from such a line as yours."

Baxter said nothing. He observed that his daughter's demeanor, particularly her manner of speech, was remarkably mature.

"Gregory told me never to be angry at you, because that would be disrespectful. Anger is a terrible thing. Only love should exist in a family. That's what he said."

"Very nice," said Baxter, noting to himself that Gregory was no moron, having taken this soft-sell approach.

"And now, Daddy, I have something of my own to add. I'm not giving up so easily. Will you permit me to ask you again, at some point in the future, whether or not you have changed your mind about the engagement?"

Baxter smiled as his heart softened. "Yes, you may ask me again, though I don't see how my opinion could be different. And by the way, you don't have to stop being friends with Gregory. There's nothing wrong with that." He paused for a moment. "Perhaps what is needed is to let time pass. Everything was so sudden."

"It sure was," she said, now sounding more adolescent.

"I'm certain that we can work everything out."

"Daddy..."

"Yes?"

"You're not mad that I was thinking of leaving you?"

Baxter could find no words. His already conciliatory heart melted in a stream of sentiment. He castigated himself for even contemplating the possibility that he would "depart" from the Home Cell and abandon Elizabeth. It was simply not going to happen.

Seeing his emotional state, she gave him a strong hug. He reciprocated with equal force. Every aspect of her embrace reminded him of his departed wife: the way she held her hands at the back of his neck; the soft breasts pushing against his chest; even the scent of her hair.

He relaxed his grip, and she drew away. "I don't look forward to your absence," he said, "but I know that it would be better for you. Anyway, you could live nearby and visit often."

"Of course I will, Daddy." She glanced in the direction of the kitchen. "What was it you put over there?"

"Some delicacies for dinner. We're going to have a celebration this evening."

"A celebration?"

"Yes. We will rejoice in the simple fact of being alive, and being together."

Elizabeth was smiling, but her knitted brow betrayed her uncertainty as to the essence of the proposed event.

"It's a long story. Someday I will share it with you."

"Can't you share it with me now?"

"It would serve no purpose," said Baxter. He gave his daughter a kiss on the cheek before standing up and stretching his back. "I must return to headquarters. But I'll see you this evening. In the meantime, I have a decision for you to make."

"Yes ..."

"I'd like us to do something together, and the sooner the better. We could go to a concert, or to the theater, or a good restaurant. Whatever you wish, just let me know."

"That would be great," she said, looking and sounding thoroughly pleased.

Baxter left the apartment. To say that he was relieved would be an understatement. He did not delude himself into believing that Elizabeth had come over to his way of thinking, but he had managed to buy time. In his estimation, this would enable him to present Bioprimalism in its true light. Moreover, if there were further conversations with Gregory, he could find a way to back the young man into a corner without appearing cruel to Elizabeth. Finally, her infatuation with him would wear off. At the right moment, a new suitor could be introduced.

At headquarters, Baxter disposed of some routine administrative matters. Jorgensen arrived, and they discussed the Harriman case. The junior officer reported on his visit to the *Monthly Gazette*. According to the people he had interviewed, Peter Westlake was on a one-man crusade against the Bioprimalists. It had become an obsession. This, in Jorgensen's opinion, plus Baxter's encounter with the journalist at the scene of the crime, rendered Westlake a prime suspect in the murder of John Harriman. He should be arrested and interrogated forthwith.

Baxter, though agreeing that Westlake should be considered a suspect, rejected his assistant's recommendation for an arrest. He instructed Jorgensen to return to the crime scene accompanied by a forensic expert. At this point in a case, he explained, if nothing of substance had presented itself, an additional pass was advisable. Something heretofore neglected might become manifest. Jorgensen expressed his approval of the idea, and departed with great enthusiasm.

Upon his arrival home, Baxter found Elizabeth engaged in preparations for the festive dinner. She was excited about the delicacies her father had obtained, though she gently chided him for the lavish expense.

The meal passed in exactly the manner Baxter had hoped. Against the background of the sumptuous feast, father and daughter completed their reconciliation. Each of them, however, envisaged the future in a diametrically opposed fashion, and each assumed that the other could be convinced of the error of his ways.

After she finished clearing the table, Elizabeth retook her seat. "Daddy, I've been thinking about what you said."

"What did I say?"

"That we should do something together."

"Oh yes, of course. What will it be, then?"

"A social event is taking place tomorrow afternoon at the medical school. One of my professors, Dr. Benson, is retiring. They're having a surprise party. Other students are bringing family and friends. I'd love it if you could be there."

Baxter smiled. "I'd be delighted," he said, for which response he was rewarded with a hug and a kiss.

Later that evening, Baxter finished reading his scroll on the subject of metaphysics. This was followed by a sweet, peaceful sleep with no interruptions and no dreams of any note.

VII. MOTHER EARTH

The party honoring Dr. Benson took place in one of the larger teaching laboratories at the medical school. In the middle of the room were hefty work tables, upon which normally would be found equipment, tools, beakers, and the like. These items either had been stowed underneath or moved to the shelves and cabinets around the periphery of the laboratory. The work tables now held hors d'oeuvres and beverages.

Elizabeth gave her father a tour of the lab, mentioning that it was her favorite spot on the entire campus. Baxter was shown various implements for cutting, boring, and clamping; a miniature stove; tanks containing creatures and organs submerged in liquids of great viscosity; scrolls depicting procedures for dissection; and assorted human and animal bones. He found the objects to be fascinating, but even more to his liking was the look of enthusiasm and pride on his daughter's glowing face.

Baxter was introduced to students and faculty members, including Dr. Benson. Everyone, without exception, lauded Elizabeth's work. Baxter recognized an orthopedist who, years ago, had provided expert testimony in a homicide case. The two men reminisced about the incident, which in its day was a cause célèbre. As they talked, Baxter spotted Gregory on the other side of the room. The young intern, with Elizabeth at his side, gradually worked his way through the dense crowd until he was standing at close range. When the orthopedist excused himself to go elsewhere, Baxter could not avoid engaging in conversation with Gregory.

It was less objectionable than he had anticipated, as both of them studiously avoided broaching the controversial topics of marriage and Bioprimalism. After chatting for a short while, Baxter admitted to himself that Gregory was an intelligent, educated, and well-mannered fellow, clearly the product of a cultured family. Baxter was still disturbed, however, by the intern's frail and pallid appearance, not to mention his embrace of Bioprimalism.

The discussion was cut short when the formal part of the gathering commenced. After the dean of the nursing program greeted and blessed those present, various students and members of the faculty took turns singing the praises of Dr. Benson. At one point, he interrupted the remarks, thanking everyone but insisting that they stop, as his merit had been grossly exaggerated. The crowd applauded vigorously, and returned to another round of eating and socializing.

Baxter circled the table, picking at the snacks. When he looked up, he saw that Elizabeth and Gregory were talking excitedly with a small group of people. Once or twice, Elizabeth gestured in his direction. He pretended not to notice, and continued his tour of the foodstuffs. Moments later, she appeared at his side.

"Daddy, something really exciting is going on. Two professors and a bunch of students are going to a retreat out in the woods, just a few miles from the city. They have carriages waiting to take them. The professors will be talking about how they use Bioprimalism in their medical practice."

Baxter grunted his disapproval.

"I know you don't like Bioprimalism, but I think it would be really interesting, and it might give me some ideas about alternative approaches to medicine."

"Alternative approaches?"

"Shh, Daddy, you're yelling."

"Alternative approaches?" repeated Baxter, in a forced hush. "You haven't even learned the regular approach yet."

"Yes, but who knows, one little remark by a professor could save someone's life years from now."

"All right, I'm not going to stop you."

"Thanks," she said. "But I want you to come with me."

"What?" he exclaimed.

Elizabeth displayed a sweet, childish smile, and patted her father on the chest, also in a juvenile manner. "It's still part of our day together."

"No, I don't think so."

"That professor you talked to for a long time, the one who worked with you on the murder case, he's participating."

"What good can come of this?"

"Maybe just the two of us being able to share something special, something unusual. You said we should be spending more time together."

Her father was shaking his head in disbelief.

"*Please,* Daddy," she whined.

"Okay, okay."

Elizabeth clapped her hands in celebration. Baxter immediately regretted that he had caved in to her tactics, which had succeeded, as on other occasions, in melting his heart.

"I need to send a parchment to Jorgensen," he declared, "to tell him I'll be away for the rest of the day."

She weaved her way through the crowd to a cabinet along the wall, removed some parchment, a quill, and an inkwell, and returned. Baxter wrote a message and sealed the parchment. Elizabeth gave it to a friend, who promised to take it to a courier station right away.

A short while later, a cavalcade of six carriages holding a group of students, two professors, and one detective set out from the medical school toward the south gate of Nucleus. Being that the university was located near the southern end of town, it was not long before they passed through the gate and onto the main thoroughfare leading away from the city. Compared with the highway that started at the northern gate—the route to Two Scribes—this road was narrower, bumpier, and not as well maintained. The suburbs along the route housed members of social classes that were not among the wealthiest in the Home Cell.

Baxter and Elizabeth shared a carriage with Gregory and three other students. The conversation focused on an incident that had occurred a week before in a lecture hall, during an anatomy class. A teacher was in the process of opening up a cadaver. He apparently made the incision in an odd place, because a jet of noxious fluid streamed into his face. The story produced an uproar of laughter among the students in the vehicle.

The carriage turned from the main road onto a narrow, dusty lane that wound its way into the forest. The conversation stopped, as all present seemed to sense that something of consequence was about to happen. The carriages came to a halt in a small clearing. Someone, from outside, called for the participants to descend. They did so, congregating alongside the vehicles. The coachmen remained in their seats.

The clearing, measuring about a hundred yards in diameter, was tranquil and verdant, covered in soft wild grass. There was a small wooden hut at the far edge; smoke was rising from the chimney. Beyond the perimeter of the open space loomed the forest, dark and foreboding.

The group was first addressed by the orthopedist with whom Baxter had spoken at the party. The man, whose name was Coryell, welcomed everyone to the event. He then turned toward the hut. Its door opened, and a person emerged into the daylight. It was Ross Kinkade, the curator of the art museum. He wore nothing but a loincloth made of dark green linen. This manner of dress was unflattering to his heavy build; the belly drooped over the top portion of the garment. He ambled toward the others, all the while displaying a grim expression.

"Please, sit down," he said.

All present sat on the soft grass. Baxter whispered to Elizabeth that this was the man responsible for the paintings produced by a monkey.

"Thank you, Professor Coryell, for bringing everyone here. For those of you who don't know, my name is Ross Kinkade. Ever since the murder of our dear friend John Harriman, we have been maintaining a low profile. But after some reflection, we concluded that while caution is advisable, total obscurity is not. We will thus amplify our activity over the coming weeks.

"The purpose of the present gathering is two-fold: First, to discuss various Bioprimalist methods of healing; and second, to introduce you to some exercises designed to bring us closer to our blessed benefactor, Mother Earth."

The other professor in attendance expounded upon the contribution of Bioprimalism to the medical arts. This type of healing, he explained, is derived from naturally-occurring material, particularly herbs. Several samples were passed from hand to hand. The speaker decried the overreliance of the medical profession on artificial concoctions. He condemned recent discoveries in pharmacy that he claimed would lead to a "further disregard for the harmony of the human race with Mother Earth." Several students asked questions, which were patiently answered.

"Thank you, professor," said Kinkade, after the discussion had ceased. "Now it is time for our exercise, which we call *earthworming,* after the movement of said creature along the ground."

Baxter stole a glance at his daughter, who had scrunched her face at mention of the animal.

"For who is more intimately familiar with our blessed mother than the humble earthworm? Back and forth, up and down, it slithers its way through the dirt and mud, deriving its nourishment therefrom. Let us draw inspiration from this seemingly base, but in reality noble, life form. Please follow me."

The group rose from the seated position and walked with Kinkade to the other side of the clearing, near the little hut. They stopped at a small depression, about fifteen yards across and one yard deep, the surface of which was entirely bare ground.

"Now, my friends," said Kinkade, glowing with satisfaction, "we commence our earthworming session. We crawl on our bellies, upon the back of our blessed mother. In the process, we issue forth the cry of one of our friends from the animal kingdom. Choose your favorite. For me, it is the rooster. I will demonstrate." The curator of the art museum then fell to his knees, prostrated himself, and began writhing every which way. The frantic movement was accompanied by his rendition of the sound made by a rooster. He carried on for some time in this manner.

The students looked on with inquisitive faces. Elizabeth, however, was viewing the demonstration with an expression of distress. She glanced at her father with imploring eyes, silently seeking his guidance. He leaned over and whispered in her ear: "You can just watch if you'd like, here with me. They'll understand."

Kinkade abruptly stopped his movement and jumped to his feet, seeming to have the sprightliness of a man thirty years younger. His corpulent and mostly-bare body was caked in dirt. "Okay, everyone. Choose your animal, and begin." He again dropped to the ground and continued earthworming, now with even greater passion. Most of the students joined in immediately; the rest, after some hesitation.

Elizabeth, with a grimace, contracted her body and stood alongside her father, so that her shoulder was touching the side of his chest. He put his arm around her and held her fast. Gregory, who had already descended to his knees, noticed his would-be fiancée's demurral. He stood up and approached, staring at Elizabeth with vacant eyes. His mouth opened but he could find no words. He returned to the ground, and set himself to earthworming while emitting the squeaks and whistles of a dolphin. Elizabeth hid her face in her hands, and then turned and ran toward the carriages. Baxter, bursting with glee, maintained a stony expression as he viewed the spectacle.

Eventually, the behavior exhibited by the earthwormers was overly taxing for him as well, and he joined Elizabeth. He found her seated inside the carriage, staring at the opposite bench, muttering something under her breath. He deemed it best to leave her alone, so that she could absorb the scene and process the lesson in her own way. He sat on the footplate and awaited the end of the event.

The others appeared, one by one. They were covered in dirt from head to toe. Everyone dusted off their garments as best they could, and climbed into the carriages. Ross Kinkade bid them farewell, and then approached Baxter to personally thank him for his attendance. Kinkade returned to his cabin. The cavalcade departed.

The trip passed in silence. Baxter pretended to be sleeping. Elizabeth fixed her eyes on the passing scenery. The others, dazed and tired, sat quietly.

When they came to a halt in front of the medical school, Elizabeth raced out of the carriage without saying a word to anyone. Baxter had to hustle in order to reach her. Not once during the rapid march home did she speak.

At that quickened pace, it did not take long to reach their destination. Upon entering the apartment, Elizabeth raced into her room and let loose a bout of sobbing. Baxter sat on the sofa and pondered his next move. He considered going to headquarters, but thought it best to remain with his daughter. It was impossible to foresee the duration of the emotional outpouring, but presumably after some time exhaustion would set in, and she would wish to share her feelings verbally. Baxter recited an abbreviated Declaration of Cognitive Achievement, drank a glass of water, and stretched out, supine, on the sofa. He fell into a deep sleep.

He found himself in front of the tent of the Emperor of Luctor. On either side of the entrance were guards, who thrust their lances forward in acknowledgement of the commander. From inside the tent, a hand grasped the flap covering the entrance, and pulled it aside. It was Baxter's aide, the trumpeter, bidding him to enter. The trumpeter stepped to one side as Baxter moved forward.

In the middle of the spacious tent was an assembly of men, seated around a massive rectangular table made of dark wood. Behind them were lavish tapestries and candelabra of gray metal. The men were dressed in elaborate costumes; the Emperor, seated at the far end of the table, was bedecked with gold and jewels. His chair, or rather throne, was equally resplendent. Baxter approached and saluted by drawing his sword, holding it across his chest, and bowing. He then sheathed the sword and took a seat at the opposite end of the table from the Emperor. In contrast to previous dreams, he knew exactly what to do, and was familiar with the people in his presence.

"Welcome, General Hendrick," said the Emperor from under his thick black beard. "We once again compliment you on a campaign well fought. All of Luctor is in your debt."

"Serving Luctor is all the honor and recompense one could desire," said Baxter. "And I am grateful to Your Highness for allowing my wife special permission to join me here in the camp."

The Emperor smiled. "We know you are anxious to be with her. We will be brief, for surely my brother, your father-in-law, with his ravenous appetite, would scold me for holding you here and delaying the start of his meal."

A chuckle was heard from the assembly.

"Let us go to the heart of the matter. As you know, many of our people have been smitten with the spiritual disease known as Bioprimalism. The leaders have become emboldened, and they now have the backing of several senior officers in your army."

"Yes, Your Highness, I am aware of that."

"I am returning to the capital tomorrow. The last thing I wish to hear is that there has been a revolt in the camp. Many soldiers are on leave, and the agitators are about. It is a vulnerable time. We must prevent disaster from occurring. The Great Sage has a plan." The Emperor looked at the man on his right. "Do enlighten us."

The Great Sage was quite aged, with heavy wrinkles that provided a stark contrast to his flawless and delicately-woven white gown, and to the scarlet velvet that graced his breastplate. "Your Highness, gentlemen," he began. "I believe that we have no choice but to meet at least some of their demands. The least painful course of action would be to allow the construction of a small shrine to Bioprimalism. Let the people become ecstatic over the prospect. When the project is complete, and they are allowed to view it and participate in its cult, they will soon grow bored. One can feel a momentary rapture from Bioprimalism, as with a good wine. But drink too much, and the effect is most unpleasant."

"Thank you," said the Emperor. "Now, General Hendrick, it is our wish that you render your reasoned opinion on the matter. But let us forego further discussion at this time. Go to your wife and enjoy your festive dinner. Meditate on the issue. Tomorrow, just after sunrise, we will reconvene here. You will present your views, and the debate shall commence."

Baxter, with a grim face, stood up, drew his sword, and saluted in the Luctorian manner. He took two steps backward while facing the Emperor, turned, and left the tent with the trumpeter in tow.

"Will you be joining my wife and I for dinner?" he asked his aide, as they weaved their way through the camp.

"I would be honored."

"Good. Did you hear the discussion about the Bioprimalists?"

"Yes, sir, I did."

"What is your opinion on the matter?"

"Kill the leaders," he replied, without hesitation.

They reached the General's tent. The two guards on either side of the entrance thrust their lances forward. Baxter and the trumpeter stepped inside. They came into a small foyer, set off from the rest of the living quarters by a series of hanging tapestries. The trumpeter excused himself to wash up. Baxter was about to withdraw to his private suite, but one of the tapestries was pulled aside, and a person stepped forward. It was Jiliada.

It was clear that she had prepared herself for her husband's arrival. An enticing fragrance transpired from her oiled skin. Her smile was like nothing he had ever seen; desire, love, and devotion all were contained within it. She put her arms around his neck, and pressed her mouth to his. He reciprocated with equal passion, drawing her body close.

"I missed you so much," said Jiliada, after they ended the kiss.

"I missed you too," said Baxter. "Now, I hope, we will be able to relax for a few days and enjoy each other's company."

They kissed again.

"Come, my father waits." She took his hand, pushed aside one of the hanging tapestries, and led the way to the dining area. They stopped at a small basin to wash their hands, and then approached the table. Already gathered there were the trumpeter, Jiliada's father, and two young boys whom Baxter knew to be his sons. He went from one to the other, delivering the greeting appropriate to each, and then took his seat at the head of the table.

He invited his father-in-law to recite a blessing. At its conclusion, servants brought the food to the table. Conversation was lively. The elder son asked his father about the recently concluded military campaign. Baxter, now endowed with memory of events that had taken place in Luctor, engaged his audience with tales from the battlefield. When the conversation switched to domestic matters, and Jiliada was speaking, he combed his memory of life in Luctor for a trace of Elizabeth. He could access only some vague and disconnected images, which he was unable to assemble into a coherent pattern.

Baxter observed his sons with great curiosity. They had inherited some of his features, such as the ruddy complexion and the broad chin, but the overall look was that of Jiliada. There was not much opportunity for them to speak, but when they did, the manner of expression was polite and intelligent.

After the meal, Baxter took a bath. He almost fell asleep in the tub, so exhausted was he from the grueling days and weeks of the campaign. Upon emerging from the water, he donned his robe and headed for the master suite. Jiliada was there, dressed in a transparent nightgown. Baxter was almost breathless from his wife's beauty. As he kissed her, his right hand held her close by the back while his left hand reached for her loins. Suddenly, the scene went dark.

Elizabeth was shaking him. "Daddy, Daddy, wake up!" she implored.

Baxter saw the alarm in her eyes, and sat up on the sofa. "What happened?" he asked.

"You were having a dream, moaning terribly. You must have been in pain. I heard you from my bedroom, so I ran in and woke you."

"Oh, thanks," he muttered, disappointed that events had not run their course. "It was that crazy dream again."

"You really need to go to an interpreter," said Elizabeth, looking concerned.

"Of course. What about you? Are you better now?"

"Yes, Daddy. I felt like such a fool, watching Gregory and the others. Don't worry, I'll never marry a man who crawls on the ground making animal noises."

Baxter smiled. "We all make mistakes, dear. What's important is to catch them, and limit the damage before it gets out of hand."

"By the way, what do you think of Ross Kinkade? He looked so silly in that loincloth."

"I thought he actually turned into a rooster, so convincing was he," said Baxter, who then performed a rendition of the sound.

Elizabeth giggled and giggled, seeming unable to stop. When finally the merriment subsided, her face turned somber. "I'm not going to leave you, Daddy," she announced.

"Now, now, I won't have any of that talk again. We just have to find the right man for you, that's all."

She gave her father a hug. "I need to do some reading, after wasting most of the day."

"That's fine. And I need to get to headquarters."

"But it's late, almost sunset."

"Just the same. I'll try to come back soon, but don't wait up for me."

"Okay."

Baxter left the apartment. Even before he reached the street, his thoughts turned to the dream. It was just as Jiliada had asserted: They were happily married in Luctor. He really was on his way to dinner after meeting with the Emperor, and his father-in-law was the Emperor's brother. All of this occurred in the dream, he concluded, because the ideas were planted in his mind by Jiliada. If their previous conversation in Two Scribes had never happened, the dream surely would have taken a different turn.

When he reached the Plaza, instead of continuing north to police headquarters, he headed west toward the Temple compound. Baxter decided to request an interview with Henry Thompson. He would confront the interpreter of dreams and settle the matter once and for all. It had become intolerable; the madness had to stop.

Baxter reached the security gate and announced his intentions. The guard stepped back several feet and whispered something into the ear of a lieutenant. The latter approached Baxter and informed him that instructions had been left for just this contingency. His arrival had been expected; he was to visit the Great Sage at a residence located a couple of blocks away.

Baxter thanked the security personnel and walked to the address he had been given. A profound dread enveloped him as he approached the elegant apartment building. There were two sentries outside, and another two in the lobby. He presented himself to the doorman, who asked him to turn in his dagger. Baxter obliged, and then continued to the dwelling, which was on the ground floor toward the rear of the building.

A servant answered the door and showed Baxter in. They entered a sitting room, where he was asked to wait. The room contained a few pieces of older, high-quality furniture and some impressive works of art. He heard footsteps behind him, and turned to see the servant helping an old man shuffle across the floor. The elderly individual was thin, fairly short, and hunched over. Stopping in front of Baxter, he looked up, showing his wrinkled face. The Great Sage resembled his counterpart in Luctor as two peas in a pod, all the way down to the fine tunic and the scarlet breastplate. How was it possible, wondered Baxter, to manufacture such a personage in the dream, never having seen the man or his likeness.

The servant helped his master be seated, and then withdrew. "Please, sit down," said the Great Sage, in a throaty voice.

"Thank you, Your Eminence," replied Baxter, who bowed before complying with the request.

"Don't be alarmed. I asked to see you the next time you came to the Temple. It was my intention to converse with you."

"Very well," said Baxter, astonished and honored that he was the recipient of such a rare privilege—a private audience with the spiritual leader of the world.

"I am aware of your situation," said the Great Sage, "and I intend to do whatever is possible to facilitate your transition back to Luctor."

Baxter bristled at mention of the place. He summoned all of his courage. "Your Eminence, with all due respect, I believe there has been a mistake."

"How is that?"

"It is not I that you seek. These elements—a dual reality, other worlds, advising an emperor—are far from my spirit. I am a humble policeman, nothing more."

The Great Sage smiled from under his curtain of wrinkles. "It is good that you are humble; it is appropriate to the task. You did have the dream about the promontory of the rock creatures, did you not?"

"I did."

"Each person receiving a mission sees the promontory in his dream. But the *meaning* of this image varies. May I explain the meaning in your particular case?"

Baxter nodded.

"The strange creatures you saw under the promontory, those speckled lizards with webbed feet, represent our society in its service of the intellect. Little by little, the culture is destroyed from within. First one foot is severed, then another, and finally the creature plummets to its death. The cycle is repeated with additional lizards. At some point, however, when you looked up, all movement ceased. Why is that? Because society can seem deceptively calm; business as usual, as we say. But the subversion continues until most of the creatures drop to their deaths, and it is too late to stop it.

"And so it is with Bioprimalism. Like the rock creatures, blending in with the face of the promontory, it seems peaceful and innocuous, as nature itself often does. Everyone living in harmony—what could be better? Happiness for all, without aspirations or dramatic accomplishments. A recipe for everlasting bliss, one might suppose. Alas, people forget the lessons; they forget about Lensic and the Flood. They march headlong into the abyss. By the time they realize that Bioprimalism leads to bloodshed of the worst kind, it is too late. Do you grasp what I am saying?"

"Absolutely," said Baxter.

"It was one of the primary causes of that horrible war of ancient times that almost destroyed our civilization. One of the reasons we have enjoyed peace for so long is that we have succeeded in holding the scourge in check. But it always dwells among us; what varies is the concrete forms it adopts and the degree of acceptance. Allow me to caution you: as you move forward, do not become ensnared in their traps. There is a little bit of Bioprimalist in all of us—an urge to be part of nature, to dispense entirely with our human consciousness."

"Yes, I can see that," said Baxter. "But what do you mean when you say, *as you move forward?*"

"I am referring to your specific task, as bestowed upon you by the Omnificent Cerebrum. That task is nothing less than saving Luctor from the affliction of Bioprimalism. You must help the Emperor find a way to stop the plague."

"What about here in the Home Cell?" exclaimed Baxter, his nerves getting the better of him. "It's spreading. I've seen it myself."

"We know about it, and it will be stopped. Put your mind at ease on that score. Your own mission involves Luctor, not the Home Cell. The Home Cell, for you, is a theater for demonstrating the dangers of Bioprimalism. And I can see that this part of the plan has functioned flawlessly."

"With all due respect, Your Eminence, I submit that there is no plan, and that my dream is a mistake, a coincidence."

"Is it a coincidence that I have such detailed knowledge of your dream?" responded the Great Sage, now looking at Baxter with inquisitive eyes. "My good friend, you seem to treat me as an adversary. Do you think I have something to gain from your torment? We are on the same team. Here, in my waning years, I have been confronted with the greatest challenge to the Omnificent Cerebrum in many generations. It is my preoccupation, day and night. We have been saddled with grave responsibilities. Entire cells depend on us."

"Your Eminence, I do not for a moment doubt your motives. And, as you know, I fully share your concerns about Bioprimalism. But if Luctor and my life in it are real, then my dream will soon reach the point where I can advise the Emperor to take the necessary measures. And I will do so, within the dream."

"It is not enough. You will have one more dream, maybe two. That's all. The dual reality cannot be held in place without end; it breaks all the rules of interaction between the cells. We may compare it to an archer tensing his bow. He cannot hold the arrow in the shooting position indefinitely. At some point, the tension will be released. The arrow will fly, whether he is aiming or not."

Baxter rose from his seat. "I am sorry, but I wish to leave."

The Great Sage raised his hand in the air, and the servant, in the blink of an eye, was at his side. "Show our friend to the lobby," said the master of the house. He looked up at Baxter. "I urge you to reconsider. Please come see me again."

Baxter bowed, and took leave. The servant escorted him to the lobby, where he recovered his dagger. Shaken in body and spirit, he emerged into the city. Where could he go, with whom could he speak? Not Jiliada, he reckoned; at least not at that moment. He needed all his wits about him to confront her belief in Luctor and the dual reality. Jorgensen? Probably not; the young man's lack of maturity made the proposition a risky one. What about Elizabeth? No, it would be cruel and self-centered to burden her young heart and mind with such bizarre tales. Baxter could think of only one appropriate, sympathetic ear: the journalist, Peter Westlake.

VIII. THE TURNING OF THE TIDE

Baxter headed for the offices of the *Monthly Gazette,* located in the southwest corner of the city. He followed Avenue of the Synapses past the intersection of his own little street, Cortex Lane, and continued for several blocks before turning right onto Ganglia Crescent. The Crescent, as it was known to the residents of Nucleus, was home to noted restaurants, a cluster of nightclubs, and the theater district.

The detective reached the building that housed the *Gazette,* and climbed the stairs to the offices of the news-scroll. He showed his police badge and stated his business. The receptionist informed him that Mr. Westlake had already left for the day. Baxter requested the address of the reporter. The receptionist, and then her supervisor, refused to convey the information, saying that a warrant would be required. Without further discussion, Baxter withdrew, unwilling to antagonize people who wield power over the flow of public information. He returned to the street.

There were a fair number of carriages to be seen, and more than a few pedestrians about. While Baxter was weighing his options, Peter Westlake emerged from the crowd. "I see the troops have arrived," he said, with a wide grin.

Baxter returned the smile. "Don't tell me you were following me again."

"Only with my eyes. I was at the café across the street, enjoying an after-work beverage, of the intoxicating variety of course. I saw you enter the building."

"Why didn't you say something, call out to me?"

"I like to watch the police in action. I thought, well, maybe I'll get lucky and see a body fly out the window, land on the coachman of a passing carriage, and cause an accident. But alas, there was nothing of the sort."

"You have a fertile imagination."

"It comes with the territory. Shall we take a little stroll?"

Baxter nodded. They began to walk.

"So what brings you here today?" asked Westlake, in a friendly voice.

"Off the record?"

"Off the record."

"I had a meeting with the Great Sage."

Westlake stopped in his tracks. "Don't tell me. He said that you're a visitor from another cell, and that you have a mission from the Omnificent Cerebrum."

"Correct," said Baxter.

"And what is your mission, if I may ask?"

"To help save the other cell from Bioprimalism."

"A worthy goal. But the real task that faces you, and all of us, is to save ourselves from Bioprimalism—right here in this spot." The journalist stamped his foot on the pavement to emphasize the point.

"He told me not to worry about that. Bioprimalism will be uprooted from the Home Cell."

"Sure it will," said Westlake, laughing. "He'll lead the charge, right? The guy can't even walk without someone holding him up. You know, Inspector, the scary part is that the Great Sage believes all of this. He really believes it."

"Indeed," said Baxter, with a sigh. "One thing does irk me, though. He appeared in my dream. I had never before seen either him or his likeness, yet the personage in my mind was identical to the real man. How do you explain *that?*"

"Who knows, maybe you did see him once, and forgot. You may have been very young, and were present at one of his rare public appearances. I have some other notions, but let us await the judgment of an interpreter of dreams. It would be improper for me, an amateur, to prejudice your opinion."

The two men came upon a crowd assembled around the entrance to a theater, waiting for the doors to open. It took a few moments to navigate through them and arrive at the other side.

"Are you now ready to work with me, Inspector?" asked Westlake, his eyebrows assuming their disjointed alignment.

"Yes."

"Good. Here's what we need to do. First, find another interpreter of dreams, to finally put yourself at ease. I have someone in mind already. Second, drag Jiliada there. Third, find any others who may be at risk. Fourth, expose the travesty to the light of day, so that no one else will fall prey. Fifth, solve the Harriman case in such a way that the Bioprimalists will not be able to use it in their propaganda. And finally, root out and destroy the cancer of Bioprimalism before it is too late. Are you with me?"

"I am, except for the item about solving the Harriman case in a certain way. I know only one way, and that is to find the murderer and bring him to justice. What the Bioprimalists do is another matter."

"Of course, and I admire your integrity. I assume you are convinced of the havoc the Bioprimalists are capable of causing?"

"Oh, yes. In fact, I had a little taste of it today. Have you ever heard of earthworming?"

Westlake laughed uproariously, causing passers-by to stare. "If I hadn't seen it with my own eyes, I wouldn't have thought such folly possible. And these clowns want to be in charge of our spiritual and cultural development. Now there's a sobering thought."

"Indeed."

"The top priority now, Inspector, is to visit the interpreter of dreams. It holds the key to so much else, for you and for the others. So with your permission, I'll try to schedule something for tomorrow. I'll send you a parchment."

"I look forward to it. Thanks for everything. May your intellect expand."

They shook hands and parted. Baxter decided to go home, figuring it was unlikely that he would find Jorgensen at the office so late in the day. Better to spend more time with his daughter. It might still be possible to join her for dinner, or at least the last segment of it.

Baxter retraced his steps along the Crescent. The conversation with Westlake had buoyed his spirits; he now felt that his reintegration into the life of the Home Cell was well advanced. Seeing people going to the theater, pursuing life's enjoyment, served to amplify the sensation.

Arriving home, he found Elizabeth in the living room, reading. She gave her father a strong hug. He joined her on the sofa.

"How's everything?" she asked.

"I had a meeting, and it went well. Did you eat?"

"No, I wasn't hungry. I had some tea."

"I see."

"Daddy ..."

"Yes, dear?"

"Why do people do things like that? I mean that whole earthworming thing."

Baxter chuckled as he conjured up an image of the curator in a loin cloth. He pondered Elizabeth's question for a long moment before responding. "Maybe it's because they want to lose themselves in something larger. Their responsibility is too great for them. Take Ross Kinkade, for example. When I visited him at the art museum, it dawned on me just how heavy is the burden placed on his shoulders. There he is, surrounded by works produced by the most brilliant and creative minds in the history of the Home Cell. And it falls on him to decide which fruits of the intellect are worthy of joining that illustrious club."

"I think it would be a fun job," said Elizabeth, her eyes open wide and gleaming.

"I'm sure it has its satisfying moments, but it also weighs on the spirit. A release from the tension might be welcome, and Bioprimalism provides it."

They continued the discussion a while longer, and then ate a light meal. Baxter recited the Declaration of Cognitive Achievement, read a passage from the Tomes of Ancient Thought, and turned in.

It was with great surprise that he awoke the next morning—he did not have the dream. In his mind were lingering images of Jiliada, but the scenes had taken place against the backdrop of everyday life in Nucleus. He arose and began the morning routine, taking care not to wake Elizabeth.

Baxter arrived at the office feeling refreshed. He began scrutinizing some documents. Jorgensen walked into the room, sauntered to the other side of the desk, and sat down without saying a word.

"Good morning," said Baxter.

"Good morning."

An uneasy silence passed. "Did you find anything at the crime scene?" asked Baxter, finally.

"Nothing worth mentioning. But when the forensic guy, Jensen, and I came back to headquarters, we paid a visit to the morgue. He suggested that we inspect the victim's clothing one more time. Luckily we keep that stuff around."

"Never a bad idea."

"So we looked it over, and noticed that the collar of John Harriman's tunic was a bit thicker on one side than the other. Jensen slit it open, and found …" Jorgensen shook his head, laughing to himself. "We found a parchment, a letter written from Harriman to our little friend Jiliada, mentioning the Emperor of Luctor. We think that Luctor might be some kind of code name. Here." He handed the ultra-thin parchment to his supervisor.

Baxter, feeling queasy, read the note.

Dear Jiliada,

I am writing you this letter because I cannot see you anytime soon; it is becoming too risky. I must fulfill my cosmic destiny, which is to bring the enlightenment of Bioprimalism to the masses. My personal fate is of little consequence.

Your arguments are unconvincing. It may be true that the Emperor of Luctor will soon order a crackdown on the Bioprimalists, but it doesn't mean that the same thing will happen in the Home Cell.

I realize that you are trying to save me from danger, but I have responsibilities that are greater than myself. I will therefore continue my mission whatever the risk.

With great affection,
Your friend,
John

Baxter returned the parchment.

"Do you know anything about this, boss?"

"Yes," muttered Baxter.

"Does it have anything to do with your visits to Jiliada, or your stroll on the Crescent with Westlake yesterday evening?"

Baxter looked at his partner with indignation, to which Jorgensen responded with a frown. Baxter averted his eyes, and then fixed his gaze on the window, as if a wise bird would fly into the office to advise him. "The answer to your question is yes. It's all connected."

"I didn't mean to be nosy, boss, but obviously there's a lot you haven't been telling me."

"Sorry," said Baxter, dreamily.

Jorgensen leaned forward onto the desk. "Do you trust me?" he asked, in an uncharacteristically soft voice.

"Sure, Phil, I trust you."

"Can I help in any way?"

Baxter looked at the young officer, and felt glad to have him as a partner. "Thanks, but I'm not sure whether you can help. Which, I would emphasize, has nothing to do with what I think of you."

"Are you in some kind of trouble?"

Yes ... well, not really. It's not trouble in the legal sense, or a threat of violence, anything of the sort. Just a complicated personal issue."

"Okay. But don't forget—I'm your *partner*."

"Thanks," said Baxter, with a melancholy smile.

"So getting back to the case. You'll have to explain to me later what all that mumbo-jumbo was in Harriman's letter. In the meantime, I think we need to get a search warrant for Jiliada's house, and turn the place upside down."

"Agreed," said Baxter, with pain in his heart. There was nothing he could do to protect Jiliada. To oppose Jorgensen's will, at this point, would be counterproductive.

"I'll be right back," said Jorgensen. He slipped out the door.

Baxter felt sluggish as he picked himself up and walked over to the window. The outside world seemed peaceful that Sixthday morning, and there was no visible activity at the Institute for Vegetal Symbolism. He pondered the meaning of the letter. Jiliada evidently had warned Harriman about his support for Bioprimalism, and somehow linked it to actions taken by the Emperor of Luctor. What reason could she have to discuss this with him? Would not such exposure of closely-guarded information be forbidden in her eyes? Another possibility was that Harriman also was visited by the dream. If so, was he convinced that the Omnificent Cerebrum had tasked him with *advocacy* of Bioprimalism? That would be impossible, or so it seemed. Whatever Harriman's role in the dual reality, yet another mystery remained: Why was the parchment sewn into the collar of his tunic?

Jorgensen bounded back into the office. "Okay, boss. I've got the paperwork done on this end for a search warrant. Now we just need to go to the Justice building and find a judge."

Baxter, still leaning on the window sill, did not react.

"Ready to go?"

"Why don't you get Jensen to go with you? I can't do it."

"Why not?" asked Jorgensen, joining Baxter at the window.

"Because I'm taking myself off the case."

"No way!"

"I'll tell the Chief later. He'll find someone to replace me, just to watch you from the side. It may be your case now, for all practical purposes."

Jorgensen was silent, looking on in anticipation.

"I have a conflict of interest," said Baxter, solemnly.

"Is it Jiliada?"

"Yes, and Westlake too. They're both involved in my personal issue—which I'll explain to you soon. Maybe I'll take a week off and get everything squared away. But that's not your problem. Execute the search and see the Chief when you get back. I'll catch up with you tonight or tomorrow."

"Okay, boss," said Jorgensen. "I'll have to interrogate Jiliada, you know."

"Of course."

"And Westlake as well."

"Yes."

Jorgensen patted his mentor on the shoulder. "Take care of yourself," he said, before turning to leave the office.

After a short while, Baxter headed for the pavement. Instead of taking his usual route on Avenue of the Synapses, he detoured onto a side street, following it for several blocks until he came to a courier station. He wrote a note to Jiliada, telling her to leave the house immediately and join him at his apartment. He gave the address. Wary of the servants, he signed the letter "Hendrick" and added a postscript saying that he would give her a special bonus if she arrived promptly. He sealed the parchment, and paid the clerk a hefty fee for immediate dispatch as well as non-stop, exclusive delivery.

As he headed back to the office, he came to regret his hasty move. With Jorgensen slated to arrive at Jiliada's house, Baxter's summons of her could be interpreted as an obstruction of justice. Her absence would not prevent the search from taking place, but it would delay the interrogation of her, as well as the clarification of any relevant discoveries. Moreover, thought Baxter, having her come to his own home may not have been wise. Such a thing cannot be hidden. He would have to say that the confluence of events was mere coincidence; she just happened to visit him at that moment. Then again, if the servants got their hands on the parchment and showed it to the police, the veracity of the story could be challenged.

Baxter returned to headquarters to see the Chief. The detective did not explain his situation in great detail, but simply stated that he had personal relationships with individuals who were either suspects or sources of information. He was granted a one-week leave of absence on condition that he be available for consultation with any of the officers involved in the case. Following his own recommendation, Lieutenant Jensen would replace him in a supervisory role.

Arriving home, Baxter informed George of the impending visit of Jiliada. After entering the apartment, he meditated, drank some tea, and awaited his guest. He passed the time reading from a scroll on the history of literature. His ability to concentrate was less than adequate.

When he opened the front door and saw Jiliada standing before him, his heart melted. She smiled in an innocent, girlish way, without a trace of the wiliness that often accompanied her glances. Her warm, loving stare unwound and caressed him. At that moment she seemed to him an exact duplicate of his wife in Luctor. He closed the door with his right hand as his left scooped her into an embrace. He hugged her, and she reciprocated. When at last he placed her in front of him to see her face, she reached up to touch his bearded cheek, but the action was meant to keep him at a distance.

"Simon …"

"Yes?"

"Don't forget where we are, and who I am in this world. When we made love in Luctor, in our tent, it was the most wonderful thing that ever happened to me. It was an earthquake. Even during the meal, I was aroused by your furtive glances, as I believe you were by mine. When you told of your exploits in the war, I could feel your spirit. Indeed, our spirits touched, later to unite as never before. We reached the state of Primordial Oneness." She ceased her discourse, and gazed at him with tender eyes.

"So you had the dream, not merely a waking vision," said Baxter, calmly.

"Yes."

"Come, let us go inside." He led her by the hand to the living room, where he took a seat at one end of the sofa. Jiliada stretched out on her back, and rested her head on his lap. He stroked her soft hair.

"Jiliada …"

"Yes, Simon …"

"I don't want to live in a dream."

"Yes, it's frustrating, I know. But when we're there, it's real."

"No, Jiliada, it's *not* real. Our minds are being manipulated to produce these effects. Someone, somehow, is tapping into our spirit, drawing out our deepest feelings. The feelings are genuine, but the scene is fabricated. It's happening to you and me, and it happened to Michael, and to others, who are now dead."

"Is that what Westlake told you?"

"I don't need Westlake to tell me that something is awry. None of this is consistent with the fundamental qualities of the Omnificent Cerebrum, despite what the Great Sage himself is saying. The cosmic Brain is organized in accordance with intellect and logic, and not with this kind of childish game. If the Omnificent Cerebrum wishes to bestow upon someone a mission, it does so. I've studied the Tomes of Ancient Thought over the course of my life. I'm no expert, but I do know that there is no mention of this dual reality. Not even a hint."

"The Tomes of Ancient Thought speak of dreams, do they not?"

"Yes, but in the way that we commonly conceive of them. They are a prime receptacle of messages, but these are lessons to be applied in one's life—one's normal, everyday, here-and-now life."

Jiliada covered her face with her hands. Baxter gently removed them. "Listen to me, Jiliada. I want you to change your life. Your *real* life, here in the Home Cell. So that we can see each other in the light of day, and walk hand-in-hand in the street. Perhaps we'll find happiness, a type of happiness that we each knew, years ago.

"I am going to see a new interpreter of dreams, someone who will help me figure out the true meaning of the messages. And then I want you to come with me. My goal is for us to understand what is happening, and to emerge stronger for the effort." He placed his hand on her forehead and gazed deep into her eyes. "Are you with me?"

"I'm always with you, Simon."

"Are you with Simon, or just General Hendrick?"

"For me, they are one and the same."

"Will you do as I ask?"

"Yes."

"Can you stop your business?"

"I can try."

"Trying isn't good enough. You have to stop it."

"Okay, I will," she said, as a tear rolled down her cheek.

"I'll assign police guards to watch and protect you at all times."

She smiled. "Thank you, Simon."

"Speaking of the police, your house is being searched, probably at this very moment."

Jiliada's body stiffened.

"I could not prevent it. Jorgensen reexamined Harriman's clothing. Sewn into the fabric was a note to you from the deceased, thanking you for your appraisal of the danger, but insisting that a crackdown on Bioprimalism in Luctor does not imply a similar action in the Home Cell."

Jiliada again covered her face. This time, Baxter let her be.

"I took myself off the case," he continued, "telling my superior that I have a conflict of interest. I probably shouldn't have brought you here; it's risky. The same goes for sending you that message. Tell me, was it you who unfurled the parchment after receiving it from the courier?"

She nodded.

"Do you have it with you?"

She reached into her pocket, removed the parchment, and handed it to Baxter.

"I assume that Harriman had the dream," he said.

"Yes, he did. He claimed that his mission, as received in the dream, was to catapult—that was the word he used—catapult the Bioprimalist movement to prominence."

"Well, that proves that this whole thing is unnatural. How could the Omnificent Cerebrum create a dual reality for the purpose of preaching *on behalf* of Bioprimalism?"

"I don't know," she replied, with an air of bewilderment.

"Of course you don't, because it's inconceivable. Tell me, what was the parchment doing in Harriman's collar?"

"I have no idea."

"Is there anything else you haven't told me? Are you connected in any other way to John Harriman or to the murder?"

"No."

"And you have no additional knowledge of it?"

"No."

"Good."

"Simon …"

"Yes?"

"Thank you for everything. I still can't believe you want me, here in the Home Cell that is, when every day I …"

Baxter placed his fingers over her mouth. "Let's not discuss that. It's over now, relegated to the past."

She nodded.

"We have to get you out of that house and find you an apartment in town, close by. Someone will keep you under surveillance at all times. If any of your patrons—your ex-patrons, I should say—come looking for you, they will be greeted with a very rude surprise." Baxter stood up and faced her. "Right now, I'm taking you with me to headquarters. We need to speak with Jorgensen. Both of us are demonstrating good will by presenting ourselves. Let him question you to his heart's content. Then we'll confide in him, seeking his help with your protection. He's a good kid, well not really a kid, but young and sometimes overzealous. But he cares about me, and, by extension, will care about you."

"All right," she said, sitting up on the sofa.

"By the time that's over, I should have an appointment with an interpreter of dreams. Westlake is setting it up."

Jiliada's face turned sour.

"One thing you need to understand is that Westlake is on our side. Forget the past and whatever he did; at least it was in good faith. I happen to know that he is concerned about your welfare, as he is with the welfare of all the unfortunate people who have been trapped by the dream."

Jiliada walked over to Baxter and hugged him. "Simon, I ..."

"Speak no more. We have much business to conduct, and in a short period of time. A sober state of mind is called for. Let's go."

They left the apartment. On the way to headquarters, they stopped at the office of an old acquaintance of Baxter's, a real-estate agent named Joe Connell. Baxter described the required living quarters for Jiliada. The place would have to be close to his own building, have a doorman, be on the third floor or higher, and have a front door capable of withstanding the assault of a strong man. Naturally, it would need to have a decent level of amenities, with everything in good working order.

Connell could hardly contain his excitement as he described the "perfect flat." It was on Medulla Court, the block parallel to that of Baxter's building. If memory served him well, the two dwellings were separated by no more than a hundred yards, with the possibility of visual contact between them.

The agent and his customers set out to view the fourth-floor apartment, which was vacant and available for immediate occupancy. A few pieces of basic furniture had been left behind: a bed, a sofa, and a kitchen table, among others. There were some dishes and utensils in the cabinets. The dwelling was clean and odor-free. It met with the approval of the future tenant. At the end of the visit they returned to Connell's office. Jiliada signed a short-term lease, and the keys were transferred.

"Well, that's one down," said Baxter, as they headed north on Avenue of the Synapses toward police headquarters.

"I wish I could hold your hand," said Jiliada.

"Me, too," said Baxter, "and there will be plenty of time for that, if we play our cards right. I'm going to be very businesslike at headquarters. Don't be taken aback."

"It's okay, Simon. I understand."

They found Jorgensen sitting at the desk, writing on a small scroll. He rose to his feet as the others entered the room.

"Hi, boss."

"Hi, Phil. You remember Jiliada."

"Yes, of course," said Jorgensen, in a formal but cordial tone. "Please sit down."

Baxter and Jiliada did as requested.

"I'm glad you came in," said Jorgensen, directing his words at the young woman. "We wanted to ask you a couple of questions. I suppose you know we searched your house."

"Yes, I know," she said, softly. "Inspector Baxter told me."

"Do you want me to step out?" asked Baxter. "It's your case now."

"That's okay. Now, let me get straight down to business. We found your diary."

Jiliada turned pale.

"Don't worry," said Jorgensen, glancing at his former supervisor. "I'm only interested in, and only take note of, whatever is relevant to the case. But I know all about the dream, the promontory of the rock creatures, Luctor, the Inspector's role, and your feelings about him. Sorry, boss."

"No problem," said Baxter, trying to sound positive. "I had intended to explain everything to you. You've actually made it easier, not having to reconstruct the entire story."

Jorgensen again looked at Jiliada. "You had discussions with Harriman about his dream, did you not?"

"Yes, I did," she said, the color returning to her face.

"When was that?" asked Jorgensen, recording her responses on the scroll.

"About a month ago."

"What did he tell you?"

"He discovered that he is not from the Home Cell, but not from Luctor either. I can't recall the name of the place. In any case, according to his dream he was sent here to advance the cause of Bioprimalism. Soon it would be time for him to return to his cell of origin; his mission was almost complete."

"Interesting," said Jorgensen, scratching his cheek with the feathered end of the quill.

Baxter noted with satisfaction that throughout the interview, his protégé was sounding much like himself.

"So," continued the junior detective, "if I understand correctly, when it is time for someone to return to his cell of origin, some sort of ceremony is performed by the Great Sage."

"Not necessarily by the Great Sage," said Jiliada. "And not exactly a ceremony. More a facilitation of passage."

"Okay, a facilitation of passage. And is this the same facilitation as the one performed on your husband, years ago?"

"Yes."

"And he died—well, passed to the other cell—but for our purposes, legally speaking, in the Home Cell, he died."

"They're not sure whether he made it to the other cell. But yes, for the purposes of the Home Cell, he died."

"Is it possible that Harriman, at the time of his death, was somehow engaged in this ritual?"

"I don't know. I suppose it's possible."

Jorgensen inhaled deeply, glanced at Baxter, and then fixed his eyes on Jiliada. "In your opinion, could the Great Sage have contributed, even in some small way, to the death of Harriman?"

A look of dread came over Jiliada's face.

"You are on familiar terms with the Great Sage, are you not?"

"Yes," she replied. "I've known him all my life."

"You would not feel comfortable if he were in some way threatened."

"No, I wouldn't. He is a wonderful human being, and a genius."

"Did he advise Harriman about the dream?"

"Yes."

"And what was the interpretation?"

"I don't know. John wouldn't tell me. I know that the two of them met, but what they discussed remains a mystery to me."

"When did they meet?"

"About a week before he died."

"You asked Harriman about it?"

"Yes."

"And he refused to say what they talked about?"

"Correct."

"Would you mind if we left you alone for a moment?"

"Not at all."

Jorgensen rose from his spot, and motioned for Baxter to join him. They left the room, closed the door, and stood together in the hallway.

"Boss, I think we need to talk to the Great Sage."

"I don't see how you can avoid it."

"The best thing would be to involve the Chief, right?"

"Right."

"Do you think he'll approve it?"

"Yes. He may take the case away from you, though. Which is a shame, because you seem to be handling things well."

"Thanks," said Jorgensen. He was displaying a wry smile under his shaggy beard. "I hope that one day, a woman will write about me what Jiliada wrote about you in her diary. She worships you like a god."

Baxter smiled. "May it come to pass, but without the dream component."

"Agreed. The whole idea of passing between cells, dying in one and continuing to live in another, is creepy."

"That is an apt word to describe it. Though it does have its fascinating aspects, I must admit."

"Shall we go back in?"

"Not yet. I need to ask you a favor, Phil."

"Name it."

"I need someone to maintain surveillance on Jiliada, day and night. You could say it's needed to protect a witness. She'll be living on the next block from me, that's twenty-one Medulla Court, fourth floor. I hope to move her in there tonight. She will no longer be receiving patrons, but they might try to track her down. If someone shows up, he needs to be convinced that it's not in his best interests to hang around. Also, she's not to go anywhere near the Temple or the Great Sage. I would take care of it myself, but since I'm not officially on the case …"

"Consider it done, boss. And now I have a question."

"Go ahead."

"You love her, don't you?"

"I guess that's what they call it."

"Her past activity doesn't bother you?"

"No, it doesn't. As I once told you, Phil, I have an admittedly archaic view of her profession, unlike the contemporary notion that confuses the function of courtesan with that of a common street prostitute. Having said that, I cannot deny that the attitude prevalent in our society will constitute a formidable hurdle."

"You really think you can pull it off?"

"It's not insurmountable, of that I am certain. But it's a long shot."

"Good luck."

Baxter shook his partner's hand. They returned to the office and retook their seats.

"That'll be all for now, Jiliada," said Jorgensen. "And by the way, I apologize for my treatment of you when we first started investigating the case."

"That's okay," she replied, after her eyes met those of Baxter.

"We may need to ask you some more questions over the next few days, as the investigation develops."

"No problem."

Baxter and Jiliada said goodbye to Jorgensen, and left the office.

"You handled the interrogation well," said Baxter, once they had reached the street.

"Thanks. Sorry about the diary."

"No need to apologize. One doesn't expect one's personal possessions to fall into the hands of the police. When did you start writing it?"

"When I was eight."

"I'm sure it would make a fascinating book."

"Simon, what about the Great Sage? Is he in trouble?"

"I doubt it, but the answer depends on many things. The police will investigate him, unless the government calls them off. Westlake will have a journalistic feast."

"I must go to the Temple."

"Absolutely not," said Baxter, stopping in his tracks. "It's risky, for a variety of reasons. You don't want to be seen there under any circumstances. The Great Sage can fend for himself, don't worry. The whole matter probably will be settled behind closed doors, at the highest level."

Jiliada was looking despondent.

"Let's not dwell on it. Our next priority is to move you into the new apartment. Come." He led her down a side street, where they soon came upon a livery stable. Baxter secured the rental of a carriage with a large luggage compartment. A coachman was assigned by the dispatcher, and they began the journey to Two Scribes.

At the villa, Jiliada packed two trunks and several sacks with clothing, toiletries, and small valuables, such as jewelry. She said goodbye to the servants, telling them that she was moving and would be back soon to collect the rest of her belongings. They helped her load the items into the carriage.

Baxter and Jiliada returned to Nucleus with all possible speed.

IX. A DISTANT MEMORY

They arrived at the apartment building on Medulla Court. The coachman brought the luggage up to the flat. Baxter was pleased to see that an officer had been posted for guard duty. He introduced the policeman to Jiliada. Then, leaving her to unpack a few things and refresh herself, he sat in the lobby with the officer to review the duties of the assignment.

Jiliada descended to the lobby a while later. She joined Baxter and the officer for a round of tea, prepared by the building superintendent. She seemed fairly relaxed, given the circumstances.

A man appeared at the entrance to the building. He motioned with his head for Baxter to join him outside. Baxter excused himself, and hurried to speak with the man, who was a detective with the police department.

"Well, what is it?"

"Peter Westlake. He's dead; murdered. Poison."

"Where did it happen?"

"At a café on the Crescent."

"Wait here," said Baxter. He entered the lobby and told Jiliada that he needed to attend to some urgent police business. He again exited, and the two detectives ran to the crime scene, located a few hundred yards away.

The café across the street from the *Monthly Gazette* was sealed off by a police cordon. A crowd was on hand; people were craning their necks for a glimpse of the action. The detectives entered the establishment and made their way to a room in the back, where various personnel were buzzing about. Jorgensen was there, along with the Chief. Lieutenant Jensen was carefully scooping a tiny object from the floor. The victim was seated in a chair, hands folded in his lap, head tilted back. The facial muscles were marked by an inquisitive expression, as if the man were analyzing his own demise.

"Well, if it isn't the person I wanted to see," said the Chief. He was an enormous man, half a head taller than Baxter. "You knew this Westlake character, didn't you?"

"Yes, we were acquainted. Are you sure it was poison?"

"Absolutely," said Jorgensen. "This time the perpetrator wasn't so careful. The fatal cocktail was on the table, and some of the liquid had spilled on the victim's leg, and on the floor."

"Jorgensen tells me," said the Chief, "that Westlake was an opponent of the Great Sage."

"Not quite an opponent," noted Baxter. "Westlake was impatient with the slow pace of the Great Sage's reaction against Bioprimalism. But they agreed on the danger it poses."

"What about the dream business?"

"Westlake would have said that because of the Great Sage's misguided beliefs, undue hardship was visited upon certain individuals."

"Like yourself and that Jiliada woman."

"Yes, Chief," said Baxter, the beginnings of a smile on his lips. "You have a precious way of describing things."

The Chief released a deep laugh, something between a grunt and a chuckle. "Okay, Inspector, have a look around. In an advisory capacity, that is. I'll be handling this case myself. Of course I'll need some helpers. But you're supposed to be on leave for a week." The Chief threw his giant arms upward in frustration.

"Are there any witnesses?" asked Baxter. "Someone must have seen whoever was here with Westlake. It wasn't that long ago."

"The answer is yes," said Jorgensen. "Several people saw a man sitting with him shortly before the time of death."

The Chief was called to another section of the café. Jorgensen took Baxter aside. "How's it going with Jiliada?" he asked.

"Not bad. She's in the new apartment. Thanks for the guard. You know, Westlake was supposed to get us an appointment with a certain interpreter of dreams. I should have asked for the name."

"There are plenty of others, boss. You'll find a good one, don't worry."

The Chief returned. Baxter announced his imminent departure from the scene, saying that he could be reached at home. He then left the café, and hurried back to Jiliada's building.

He found the guard in the hallway, just outside the door to the apartment, dozing in his chair. Baxter crept forward, silently, until he stood just behind the chair, and then locked his arm around the man's neck. The guard, awakening with a start, attempted desperately to detach the arm. Baxter threw him to the floor. The young officer, looking dreadfully embarrassed, picked himself up.

"I may have saved your life," said Baxter. "You can sit down again."

The guard did as he was told. Baxter knocked on the door.

"Who is it?" asked Jiliada, from within the apartment.

"It's me, Simon."

The door opened, and Baxter stepped inside. Jiliada greeted him with a smile, but it was tainted with anguish. Her face was damp, and her eyes puffy. Baxter closed the door and led her to the kitchen, where they sat down. He pulled his chair forward so that it was adjacent to hers, and grasped her hand.

"What's the matter?" he asked.

The same pained smile appeared on her face. "I'll be okay."

"I didn't ask whether or not you'll be okay."

"I'm just sad. What about you? How did it go, your police business?"

"Westlake is dead."

Jiliada stared vacantly into the space above the table.

"He was poisoned, just like John Harriman. It happened in public, in a café. There were witnesses, though of course they weren't aware that a murder was taking place. They may, however, be able to identify the man who was seated with Westlake."

Jiliada raised Baxter's hand to her mouth and kissed it. "Thank you for protecting me, Simon."

"I could not imagine any other course of action."

She smiled. This time a hint of joy had returned to her face.

"Come with me, Jiliada," he said. "I want to show you something." They rose from their seats. Baxter brought her to the window, which he opened. It was nearly dark, and lamps could be seen through the windows of the apartments on the adjacent block. Baxter scanned them before pointing to one. "You see that apartment over there, next to the one with the bright light?"

"Yes."

"That's mine. It has three windows facing in this direction. The one furthest to the right is my bedroom."

Jiliada nodded, and then tilted her head back to view the sky. "Look, the stars are coming out. The heavens are so pretty at dusk. I love that dark blue color, appearing with the last rays of light."

"Yes, it is very pretty, and peaceful as well."

"I never understood why the Omnificent Cerebrum gave us stars. They serve no purpose."

"Everything serves a purpose. Imagine if the sky were completely black at night. It would be desolate, and we would be unable to navigate, lacking the points of reference. Fortunately our needs have been met, and we have been blessed with a beautiful and serene addition to our aesthetic field."

"How big are the stars, really?"

"No one knows for sure, but the estimates I've seen range from twenty to about a hundred yards in diameter."

"What about the sun?"

"Probably twice the size of Nucleus."

"I remember my father, that is, my adopted father, saying that our neighboring cell is just behind the stars. That's so close you could almost hear the folks over there talking."

Baxter chuckled. "Well, they may be just behind the stars, but between the cells there's quite a wall. If you were standing right next to it, and a volcano erupted on the other side, you wouldn't be able to hear it."

"Wouldn't it be fun to travel to that cell? I wonder what the people are like, if they're nice or mean, beautiful or ugly."

"Probably a mix, I would imagine."

"You're very practical, Simon."

"I suppose. Why do you say that?"

"Just a thought."

"You're not especially practical, are you?"

"No," replied Jiliada, with a laugh that illuminated her features. "I'm the most impractical woman you'll ever meet. Does that bother you?"

"Not at all," said Baxter, putting his arm around her shoulder and pulling her near. "In fact, it makes for a good balance between us."

She hugged him, and began stroking his back. As passion welled up within, he asked himself whether a practical man would become involved with a courtesan who lives in a world of dreams. Romantic liaisons, he reckoned, are beyond the realm of the rational, as explained in the Tomes of Ancient Thought. Baxter postponed further deliberation of the issue as he placed his hands on either side of Jiliada's face and brought her near. They fell into a kiss so deep that Baxter felt as if he were transported up to the vault of the heavens.

Jiliada abruptly withdrew from his grasp and covered her face. After a few moments, she lowered her arms. "I'm sorry, Simon. That was so wonderful, I have no words to describe it. But we must not go any further. I'm not ready for it; it's too soon. I was with a patron just a few days ago. *A patron!* We have to let some time pass so that I can be normal again. I never want to confuse you with *them.*" She leaned onto the window sill and looked at the sky. "That's why I'm so happy in Luctor. You are my husband, and everything is perfect."

"We'll make it perfect here, too."

They gazed at the sky a while longer.

"You must be hungry," said Baxter, suppressing the ache of desire that had seized his body.

"Yes, I'm a bit hungry," replied Jiliada.

"Let's go over to my place and have a good meal. My daughter will be there, of course. Are you up to it? If not, we could go to a restaurant."

"I'm up to it."

They extinguished the lamps and left the apartment. Baxter instructed the guard to stay put until relieved. They descended the stairs, informed the doorman of their departure, and headed into the street. As they walked to the adjoining cul-de-sac, Jiliada seemed more and more reluctant; upon reaching the lobby of Baxter's building, she looked apprehensive.

"Are you sure about this?" he asked.

"Yes … I'll be all right," she replied, with a hesitant smile.

"Elizabeth is a very sweet and courteous girl; you have nothing to worry about. Just relax and let me tell the story."

When they reached the apartment, Baxter asked Jiliada to remain in the hallway. He opened the door, heard the customary greeting from Elizabeth, and joined her in the kitchen. She was standing over the stove, stirring a pot. He gave her a kiss.

"Perfect timing," she said. "Supper's ready."

"Is there enough for three?"

"Sure."

"I'll be right back." He went to fetch Jiliada, and brought her to the kitchen. The two women were soon facing each other.

"Elizabeth, this is Jiliada. Jiliada, this is my daughter, Elizabeth."

The women said hello and shook hands. Elizabeth received the guest with a warm smile, but her features were marked by a look of perplexity. There was nothing hostile about it; rather, it seemed as if she were trying to recall something.

"It's very kind of you," said Jiliada, "to do this at a moment's notice."

"No problem. We enjoy having guests."

"Can I help with anything?"

"No thanks, just relax. Please sit down," said Elizabeth, pointing to the chairs. Baxter and Jiliada did as instructed.

"What are we having?" asked Baxter.

"Calf-brain stew."

"Excellent," he declared. "It's your specialty, after all."

"Oh, Daddy, you say that about everything I make. Anyway, I'm not a good enough cook to have a specialty." She served the others their bowls of stew, and then one for herself. Baxter recited an abbreviated version of the Declaration of Cognitive Achievement, and the meal commenced.

"It's delicious," said Jiliada, "specialty or not."

"Agreed," said Baxter. A few moments later, he put down his spoon, drank some water, and cleared his throat. "Jiliada and I met when I began investigating the Harriman case. I don't know how it happened, but we started talking about other things. It turns out that we have experienced the same recurring dream."

"Really?" said Elizabeth.

"Yes. It's quite remarkable, actually. Remember I told you that in my dream I saw those bizarre lizards under the promontory, and that I was commanding a detachment of soldiers?"

"Yes, I remember."

"Well, it turns out I'm commanding an entire army. In that capacity, I visited the emperor of this strange place, to report to him. It was there, outside his tent, that I saw Jiliada."

Jiliada smiled. "And I saw your father."

"That's amazing," said Elizabeth, who seemed to find the revelation intriguing. This came as a pleasant surprise to Baxter, who had been expecting a reaction of trepidation.

They continued eating, in silence, until the bowls were empty.

"There's something else we have in common," said Baxter. "Jiliada's husband died at the same time as mother. Both of us had a recurring dream at that time, and we both went to see that same terrible interpreter, Conrad Burton."

At mention of the name, Elizabeth's face acquired a look of distress. Baxter and Jiliada exchanged a glance, but said nothing. Regretting that he had introduced a subject that was painful for his daughter, Baxter steered the conversation to other topics. They discussed family history, Elizabeth's studies, their favorite works of literature, and the annual track and field competition taking place two weeks hence.

At the end of the meal, Baxter thanked Elizabeth, and informed her that he was going to escort Jiliada home. The two women said goodbye, amid a profuse expression of appreciation from the guest.

"That went well, wouldn't you say?" asked Baxter, as they descended the stairs.

"Yes, much better than I expected. You have an exceptional daughter."

"Thank you. She seemed a bit upset when I mentioned Conrad Burton. It doesn't surprise me. She's very sensitive about anything connected with the death of her mother."

They reached Jiliada's building, and climbed the stairs to the fourth floor. The guard was in his chair, looking alert. Jiliada said goodnight, opened the door, and disappeared from view.

"Don't let her out of your sight," said Baxter to the guard. "And remember, she's not to go near the Temple. Furthermore, everything I've told you needs to be conveyed to whoever relieves you."

"Yes, sir," said the young officer.

Baxter returned home, walking slowly. He inhaled the cool and refreshing nocturnal air, and looked up at the stars. It was an unusually clear sky, with visibility that normally would be obtainable only outside the city. For Jiliada, he mused, Luctor was still a reality, somewhere up there, beyond the wall of the Home Cell. It would not be a simple matter to return her to the ground. Was it beyond his capability? Was his statement to Jorgensen a realistic one, that the entire effort was not insurmountable?

He found Elizabeth in the kitchen, washing dishes. "Thanks again for the dinner. And thank you for being so gracious."

"It's okay," she said, sounding melancholy.

"What's the matter?" asked Baxter, joining her at the sink.

She halted her activity and looked at him with a pensive expression. "I don't know exactly. Everything was fine. Jiliada is very nice. But there's something else ... I remember her from somewhere."

"Oh?"

"But I can't recall the place. It's frustrating because the feeling is very strong. I think it was a long time ago. I felt it right away, and then it really hit me when you started talking about mother, and the interpreter Conrad Burton. As if we were all connected."

"Interesting. Well, let me know if you remember."

"All right."

"I'll let you finish up here," said Baxter. "I'm going to do some reading." He started to move toward the living room.

"Daddy ..."

"Yes?"

"Are you just ... well ... just *friends* with her?" Elizabeth blushed and lowered her glance.

"Yes dear, just friends. Jiliada is turning over a new leaf, and I'm helping her get established. I'm not sure what will develop. I do care about her, though."

She looked up at him. "I'll help you, Daddy."

"Thanks. That means a lot to me." He gave his daughter a kiss goodnight, and went to his bedroom. A short while later he was lying in bed, fast asleep.

It was in the most profound darkness of the night that he awoke from a repeated knocking on the bedroom door.

"What is it?" he said, sitting up in the bed.

"Daddy, can I come in?"

"Yes, dear."

Elizabeth opened the door, approached the bed, and sat at its foot. With only the faint light seeping in from outside to illuminate the scene, Baxter could distinguish no more than her silhouette.

"I'm sorry to bother you, but I remember now about Jiliada. I had to tell you right away."

"Go ahead."

"It was after mother died. That's why I got that strong feeling at dinner, when you mentioned those days. You were in the hospital—I mean the sanatorium. I came to see you every day, remember?

"How could I forget."

"I think you *did* forget something."

"What do you mean?"

"Jiliada was there."

"She was there? What, as a patient?"

"I think so, but I'm not certain," said Elizabeth. She paused to collect her thoughts. "Yes, a patient, it had to be. She was wearing that awful brown tunic, the same one that you had, that everyone had. You and I were sitting in the garden, in the courtyard. You were telling me a story. The whole time, Jiliada was strolling about. Every so often, she stopped, and stared at you. I remember her face. She had a beautiful smile. It seemed as though a halo of light were framing her face when she looked at you. I had a feeling it was her, Daddy, as soon as she came into the kitchen, but I had to be sure."

"What did she say to me in the garden?"

"I don't know."

"Did I ever talk about her after that?"

"No. From that time until today, nothing was ever mentioned."

"It's so strange," said Baxter, feeling a coldness in his bones. "You would think that I would recall something. I can picture that garden, but not being there with you. The whole stay at the sanatorium, actually, is a blur in my mind."

"It wasn't a happy time."

"No, it wasn't. I'm glad you came to tell me. That was important information."

"Maybe you're both having the dream because of something that happened at the sanatorium."

"It may very well be," said Baxter. He paused for a moment. "There are many mysteries to unravel, that is for sure."

Elizabeth stood up. "I'm going now. Goodnight, again."

"Goodnight, dear."

She left the room, closing the door behind her. Baxter rose from the bed, and walked to the window. He surveyed the rear of the buildings on the adjoining cul-de-sac. He could see a sliver of Jiliada's kitchen, where they had stood together, gazing at the stars. Now, the spot was dark and lifeless. He tried to recall the scene in the garden of the sanatorium. The most intense concentration was of no avail. With difficulty he remembered the garden itself. As for the visits of Elizabeth, then a ten year-old girl, he could conjure only a vague picture of her running toward him as he stood waiting for her in the lobby.

Might Elizabeth's recollection be a figment of her imagination? Childhood memories, Baxter reminded himself, are notoriously unreliable. In a criminal case, such testimony probably would be rejected by the court. Perhaps another beautiful young woman had been present in the garden, and Elizabeth transformed her into the image of Jiliada. On the other hand, Baxter did have a distinct sensation of familiarity the very first time he met her, at the Obscure Thought Café.

Baxter went back to sleep. He dreamt that he was in the Temple of the Omnificent Cerebrum, watching the Great Sage give Jiliada a poisoned glass of wine. He tried with all his force to warn her, but the words would not leave his throat.

When he awoke, his heart was pounding. He sat at the edge of the bed for some time, trying to calm his nerves and focus his thoughts. After washing and dressing, he took his tea in the kitchen. The day's first rays of light were filtering through the window. Elizabeth was still asleep.

There was a knock at the front door. Baxter moved quickly to the foyer.

"Who is it?"

"It's Phil."

Baxter opened the door.

"Hi, boss," said the young detective. His eyes were bloodshot. "I was checking up on the guard at Jiliada's place, so I thought I'd drop in."

They went to sit in the little bedroom.

"You look as though you were up all night," remarked Baxter.

"I was. We combed every inch of that café on the Crescent, surveyed the entire neighborhood, and sealed off Westlake's office. I'm exhausted."

"That's what happens when the Chief personally supervises a case."

"Too bad about Westlake," said Jorgensen.

"Agreed. He wasn't a bad guy, when you come right down to it." Baxter paused, tugging at his chin. "Do you think that this murder is linked to the Harriman case?"

"I don't know yet what I think."

"Good man," said Baxter, tickled that his protégé was employing one of his own favorite phrases. "You have learned well."

"Thanks, boss. Now, to give you some kind of real answer, it is quite possible that the two crimes are linked. For one thing, the same poison was used. And then we have the connection to the Bioprimalists."

"Yes, but Harriman was a leader of the Bioprimalists whereas Westlake was their sworn enemy."

"That's true," said Jorgensen.

"Did you find any interesting artifacts in Westlake's possession? Perhaps a diary, or some collection of notes? I'm looking for a list of people who had the dream, or related information."

"There's a pile of stuff in his office. I'm going back there very soon to sift through it. You can come with me, if you want."

"No thanks," said Baxter, "there's something else I need to do. I'll join you later, and then you can let me know if you came across any relevant artifacts."

"Sure thing. By the way," said Jorgensen, lowering his voice. "How's it going with Jiliada?"

"The most difficult case I ever solved is child's play compared to this. There are nooks and crannies the existence of which I never suspected. Some of them are in my own mind." Baxter sighed, but the sound emerged as more of a grunt. "I told you once that it was not insurmountable. Now I'm not so sure."

"Maybe you need some help surmounting it."

"Maybe so. As soon as I clarify a few things."

Jorgensen left the apartment. Not long thereafter, Baxter headed out. His destination was the Serenity Sanatorium, located in the far northeast corner of the city. After a brisk early-morning run, he found himself facing the main entrance of the institution where, eight years previously, his fractured spirit was rehabilitated. He had not visited the spot since, and, at that moment, had no desire to do so. He suppressed his reticence and entered the building.

The lobby was smaller than in the mental picture he had preserved. The decor was tasteful, with a number of tapestries and statues around the perimeter. In the center of the room was a reception desk, staffed by a middle-aged woman with a pleasant face.

"Can I help you, sir?" she asked, as Baxter approached.

He showed his police badge. "I'd like to take a look around."

"Certainly. Is there anything in particular you're looking for?"

Yes, thought Baxter, a piece of my memory. "No, nothing in particular," he said. He headed for the corridor that began on the far side of the lobby. Not many guests, as they were called, were out and about so early in the day. The ones he saw looked to be utterly absorbed in their imagination. They were shuffling slowly, dressed in the brown tunic that served as the uniform of the institution. Baxter shuddered to think that once he had also fallen into spiritual disorder. To the credit of the Serenity Sanatorium, he departed in much better condition than when he had arrived.

After walking some distance through the corridor, he stopped at a doorway that looked vaguely familiar. Opening it, he entered the garden of Elizabeth's story. It was peaceful, with lush plant life that included several well-maintained specimens of vegetal symbolism. He took a seat on the bench. Was it the spot where he first beheld Jiliada's lovely features? He still had no recollection of the event.

He returned to the woman at the reception desk. "I need to confirm that a certain person was a resident here, eight years ago."

"I'm sorry, sir, that information is confidential."

Baxter leaned forward so that his face was inches from hers. "Let me explain something," he said in a hush. "I can get a warrant, come back here with three other officers, and turn the place upside down for the rest of the day. Or you can quietly check this for me, and no one will know who I am and what I'm doing here."

Before long, he had the answer to his query: Jiliada had been a resident of the sanatorium for about five months. Two of those months overlapped his own stay.

Returning to the street, he pondered his next move. It was too early in the morning to disturb Jiliada, so he decided to join Jorgensen at Westlake's office. It proved to be a fruitful decision. When he reached the reception desk at the *Monthly Gazette,* he saw Jorgensen waving excitedly from behind a desk in a corner of the large hall. Baxter passed under the police cordon, and joined his junior colleague.

"Good news, boss. As soon as I opened Westlake's top drawer, I saw a parchment with the name Harold Smith. Underneath were the words, *interpreter of dreams for Inspector Baxter."* Jorgensen handed over the parchment.

"Thanks," said Baxter, pocketing the item. "Too bad we never find evidence like that in our homicide cases."

"Nah, that would make it too easy. But speaking of homicide cases, I came across something interesting."

"Pray tell."

"See that?" said Jorgensen, pointing to a basket overflowing with documents. "Everything in there pertains to a single subject: John Harriman's daughter, Margaret."

"Ah, yes, you went to see her once. She works at the art museum, if I'm not mistaken."

"Correct. She's the vice-curator for new acquisitions. Westlake was obsessed with her. And I mean *obsessed.* You wouldn't believe it."

"Try me."

Jorgensen removed a parchment from the basket. "Here's an article written by her, clipped from a recent issue of the *Journal of Art History,* with Westlake's notes scribbled all over it. And this," he said, taking a different fragment in hand, "is an interview with her, as an up-and-coming leader of Bioprimalism. I also found an entire scroll detailing her every movement over the course of about three days. He must have followed her everywhere."

"He was good at that," remarked Baxter. "So what's your next move?"

"Read through some more of these documents, and then go have another chat with Margaret Harriman."

"Sounds good."

"Boss …"

"Yes, Phil?"

"Would you mind coming along?"

"I guess I could. In an advisory capacity, of course."

"Of course," said Jorgensen, smiling.

"I just need to stop off on the way, to see Jiliada. A quick visit, to verify that everything is going well."

"No problem."

"By the way," said Baxter, "are you planning on talking to the Great Sage?"

"The Chief is handling that."

"Good. And what about those witnesses in the café?

"Sergeant Burns got that assignment."

"Well, I see that all of headquarters is keeping busy."

The two detectives spent some time reading the documents found in the desk of Peter Westlake. Other members of the police force periodically visited the area, checking one or another aspect of the murder victim's professional space.

Jorgensen announced that his eyes were saturated. He and Baxter quit the premises. It was a fairly short walk along the Crescent to Avenue of the Synapses, and from there to Jiliada's street, Medulla Court. The doorman informed them that Jiliada, accompanied by the guard, had departed a short while earlier "to get some fresh air and do some shopping." Baxter asked the man to convey greetings, and to let her know that he would stop by again later in the day.

The policemen continued their march along the Avenue. Baxter constantly scanned the street, looking for Jiliada, but she was not to be seen.

X. THE WHIRLPOOL

When Baxter beheld the sparkling steps of white marble and the majestic colonnade, he resolved to increase the frequency of his visits to the art museum. After passing into the lobby, he and Jorgensen approached the reception desk, showed their police badges, and stated their business. An employee led them to the office of Margaret Harriman. The room was a few doors down the hall from the chamber of the curator, Ross Kinkade.

During the introductions and initial round of chatter, Baxter observed this singular woman. She looked to be in her mid thirties, and was quite thin, even skinny. Her height, approaching six feet, accentuated the visual impact, as did the belt around her linen dress, tightened with such severity as to make Baxter wonder how her vital bodily fluids could flow between her upper and lower halves. Her glassy skin glistened from heavy application of cosmetics. Her hair was pulled back into a bun with the same intensity that the belt was tightened, so that she seemed almost bald when viewed directly from the front.

"Well then, officers," said Margaret, with an air of courteous pomp. "How can I be of service to you this fine morning?"

Baxter looked at Jorgensen, who was looking at him, reflexively expecting an initiative. "Did you hear," said Baxter, "that Peter Westlake was murdered?"

Margaret's expression froze momentarily, then her eyes and mouth opened wide. "No ... no, I wasn't aware of that at all."

"It happened yesterday."

"He was sitting in a café," said Jorgensen. "Right across the street from his office."

"Did you catch the killer?" she inquired.

"Not yet," said Baxter. "It seems, Miss Harriman, that Mr. Westlake was somewhat intrigued by you."

Margaret laughed in a restrained little cackling noise. "That's an interesting way of putting it."

"How would *you* put it?"

"He was on a crusade against Bioprimalism," replied the vice-curator, now with a serious mien. "He latched onto me as a representative of the movement."

"Which you are."

"Oh, undoubtedly. And I have no problem with the occasional interview, even if the ensuing article is hostile. That's to be expected in our current climate of ignorance."

"Perhaps the current climate of ignorance is fed by misconceptions of the benefits to be derived when monkeys take over our artistic duties," countered Baxter.

"Or when people writhe on the ground like earthworms," said Jorgensen.

Margaret sighed rather loudly. "I gather you've been talking to Ross Kinkade."

"Your conclusion is well-founded," said Baxter. "Do you not approve of his activities?"

"There are two factions within the world of Bioprimalism. The first is Ross and his merry band, which, by the way—and most unfortunately—included my late father. They want to sing and dance and clap their hands. Who am I to stop them? As you evidently have seen, the results are ridiculous." She smoothed the hair that was nearly pasted against her scalp. "Then there's my own camp, which I call the *macro-thinkers*. We see the big picture; we don't have time for Ross's nonsense."

"And what is the big picture?" asked Baxter.

"That we're headed for disaster. It starts with getting at the truth about Lensic and the Flood. The story in the Tomes of Ancient Thought has been misinterpreted. It wasn't the Omnificent Cerebrum that caused the cataclysmic deluge. No—it was Mother Earth herself, in an outburst of fury, unleashing her waters from the subterranean ocean. And now, we stand on the threshold of a repeat performance. In fact, the waters are already rising."

"Rising?" exclaimed Jorgensen. "How can the waters be rising without anyone knowing about it?"

"Have you been to the Cave of the Abysmal Pool?"

"Of course. Everyone has."

"Recently?"

"No."

"And you, Inspector?"

"No."

"As we all know, the Abysmal Pool is an outlet for the subterranean ocean. And the water level is rising. I'll take you to see it, right now if you wish."

"Yes, that would be interesting," said Baxter. "What do you think, Phil?"

"It sounds good, but I have to get back to the crime scene."

"Very well, then. I will accompany Miss Harriman. Do you have any further questions for her?"

"No, that's it for now."

The three of them walked to the lobby and parted. Jorgensen left the museum, while Margaret and Baxter went to the coach house, located behind the main structure. Margaret ordered her personal carriage to be prepared, and they set off for the Cave of the Abysmal Pool.

Baxter used the interval of travel to gather information about the macro-thinkers within the Bioprimalist world. "What is your conception of Bioprimalist art," he began, "given that you reject the ... how shall I say it ... the simian school?"

"I can provide you with a rough definition," said Margaret, not without a subtle grin of acknowledgement for the pun. "Bioprimalist art would be works produced using the traditional methods, but expressing themes that are essential to Bioprimalism. For example, portrayals of man in nature. Not man divorced from nature—as in so many of the works at the museum—but integrated into Mother Earth's scheme. Are you familiar with the giant canvas by Raleigh?"

"The one in the museum? Absolutely."

"A perfect case of this divorce, of the artist's profound alienation from the earth. The painting is very well done; the technique is excellent. What it portrays, however, is lamentable. The person in the center of the scene is standing atop a mountain. It's a magnificent location, but the natural setting is so gray, so somber. Meanwhile, the man's face is ablaze from his ceaseless cogitation. His eyes burn from the flame of his ego. As if he were saying, Mother Earth produced this spectacular setting, more sublime than anything a human could dream of creating, but I will shamelessly show you my face; hearken to it, as it contains so much wisdom and wondrousness. Bah! Where is the humility? Not in that painting. Raleigh is flaunting his conceit, saying, look at me everyone, how great I am that even a mountain pales by comparison."

Though Baxter had misgivings about Margaret's discourse, he was beginning to find her likable. On the whole she seemed engaging, respectful, and forthright.

"So that was a case of alienation," she continued. "Now consider a different work, one that my brother Theodore has in his gallery."

"Theodore is not a great admirer of Bioprimalism, I would say."

"No, Inspector, he is not. He has had too much exposure to the earthworming wing of the movement. But he'll come around. My dear brother is blessed with great aesthetic sensitivity, and that will provide him with a pathway to enlightenment. In any case, the Bioprimalist work in question is Valeron's *Melding of the Worlds*. There you see the compelling luminosity of our natural environment. Man is present, but he is not the uncontested center of all existence. His presence is balanced and proportional. It is Mother Earth who shines forth her inner light. Man adapts himself, and is happier for the effort."

"Interesting," said Baxter, catching through the window of the carriage a glimpse of The Fisherman's Net, the tavern where he once sat with Peter Westlake. "But is happiness really the goal of our interaction with the natural world?"

A smile appeared on Margaret's face, seeming to crack the smooth, glassy texture of her skin. "That is a profound question, Inspector, and not something we can elucidate in the short time before our arrival at the cave. But suffice it to say that no, happiness is not the primary goal of our interaction with nature. Much more critical is our *survival*, which is not to be taken for granted. When the behavior of the human animal becomes arrogant and self-absorbed, disaster ensues. This is because nature must exist in a state of equilibrium. When that equilibrium is disturbed, the imbalance is going to be rectified, one way or another. If you take a straw and blow air into a glass of water, the air must escape. It cannot become blended with the water. The same applies to humans. We think we can be those air bubbles inside the water, existing in contravention of the laws of nature, but it is impossible. The air is ejected."

They were several miles beyond Two Scribes when the carriage turned from the main highway onto a smaller road, which soon began to descend into a broad valley. The settlement was less dense than along the highway, but still a fair number of houses could be seen among the verdant meadows and patches of forest. Baxter identified most of the young cattle grazing upon the grass as belonging to the breed commonly used for calf's brain. The setting was bucolic; together with Margaret's disquisition, it gave him a taste of the alluring mindset of Bioprimalism. It was calming, as if a burden had been lifted from his shoulders. He recalled the cautionary words of the Great Sage, who had asserted that "there is a little bit of Bioprimalist in all of us."

The carriage came to a halt in front of a massive outcrop of rock that jutted from the surrounding pasture like an arrowhead that had pierced a fragment of green cloth. The two travelers descended from the vehicle. Margaret exchanged a few words with the coachman, and then bid Baxter to follow her toward the outcrop. The two of them slipped through a crevice, which led to a corridor within the stone. It was broad enough for two persons to walk comfortably side-by-side. Lamps, hung at intervals of several yards, provided a dull but sufficient light. At the end of the corridor, Margaret motioned to Baxter to move forward. They advanced a few steps, and beheld the Cave of the Abysmal Pool.

It was a grand spherical space, naturally scooped out of the rock. At its widest point, the cave measured about a hundred feet in diameter. The ceiling towered some thirty feet overhead. In the bottom of the bowl, as it were, water swirled continuously, as if searching madly for an outlet. In the face of the rock were carved images of the cerebrum in cross-section, similar to those on Boulevard of the Mind. Part of the carved surface was submerged.

Margaret allowed her companion an adequate interval to absorb the spectacle. She then faced him, arms folded. "When were you here last, Inspector?"

"Oh, many years ago."

"Am I correct in saying that no part of the carving was underwater at that time?"

"That is correct," said Baxter.

"The same was true as recently as six months ago. I was here myself and can attest to the fact. The level is rising; Mother Earth pours forth her fluid, the fluid of life—but also of death."

"I don't think anyone would die from this water, even if it overflowed into the surrounding valley."

"The cave and its environs are not the problem. What we see here is merely a window onto the inner workings of Mother Earth. This is nothing less than the imminent fulfillment of a prophecy in our great scroll, *Humanity and the Harmonious Earth*." Margaret took a deep breath and gazed at the water. "It is written: In those days, if the arrogance be not corrected, the waters will gush forth from the ocean of the depths, and Mother Earth will reabsorb her children into her womb." Margaret returned her penetrating glance to Baxter. "We have another two months, no more. The water will overflow; the jet will tear the rock formation asunder. Nucleus will be underwater in a matter of days. Now you understand why I spoke of survival. You see it with your own eyes. And, I might add, how fitting that the unctuous sages chose this very spot to rape Mother Earth with their chisels."

After viewing the scene for another short while, they returned to the carriage. The coachman cracked his whip, and they began the slow ascent to the main road. Fortunately, the carriage was hitched to a team of four sturdy horses.

"Are you going to ask me any questions about my father?" inquired Margaret.

"Not at this time," replied Baxter. "Officer Jorgensen interviewed you after the crime, and we discussed the subject at the museum earlier today. It seems to me that this is sufficient. That being said, if there is something you wish to state for the record, I would be more than willing to listen."

"No, nothing to add," she said, with a glum expression. "I just wish it could be solved already, and the killer brought to justice."

"I think we're getting closer. And it may be linked to the Westlake case. Just a little longer to wait."

Some silence passed before Margaret again looked at the detective. "What kind of art do you like, Inspector?"

"Well, let's see … I suppose that my personal favorite would be the statuary of the Old Crescent school, particularly Davis and Liander. In painting, the Formulists have always caught and held my interest."

"Ah, yes, the Formulists. Masters of the highest rank. My only criticism would be their overuse of the palette knife. It tires the eye."

"Would you not agree, Miss Harriman, that the production of these masterpieces, and others like them, is dependent upon a society being firmly grounded in intellect, with nature relegated to a subordinate status?"

Margaret's face turned somber, almost to a scowl. "My answer is no. The grounding of which you speak has produced impressive works, it is true. But this is only a stepping-stone on the way to still greater achievements. When Bioprimalism permeates the culture, art will burst its chains; it will become the proving-ground of humanity in its ultimate and highest phase of development. We shall one day look back upon the

Formulist paintings and the Old Crescent sculpture as quaint relics. They will have archival value, good for reminiscing and teaching art history, but nothing more."

When they arrived at the museum, Baxter thanked Margaret for the trip and the stimulating conversation. They parted with a handshake and an exchange of blessings.

Baxter headed for Jiliada's apartment. Along the way, he reflected on the discussion with Margaret. She spoke of a "misinterpretation" of the story of the Flood, as recounted in the Tomes of Ancient Thought. This sounded implausible. The famous passage was explicit, leaving no doubt that the cause of the Flood was the Lensic rebellion, designed to usurp the authority of the Omnificent Cerebrum. His followers refused to perform—or even acknowledge—their duties in the realm of intellect, be it art, music, poetry, or theater, not to mention the proper maintenance of the Temple. It seemed to Baxter that Margaret had inverted the meaning of the passage to make it fit the Bioprimalist narrative.

As he passed the busy shops along Avenue of the Synapses, his thoughts turned to Jiliada. He needed to uncover the truth regarding their purported encounter in the garden of the sanatorium. He also needed to secure Jiliada's cooperation in the interpretation of the dream. It was his hope that within a day, they could visit the interpreter recommended by Westlake.

Baxter arrived at her building. The doorman smiled and pointed upward with his thumb. Baxter climbed the stairs and emerged into the hallway. The guard was perched on his chair next to the door of the apartment. He stood up as his superior approached.

"How's she doing?" asked Baxter.

"Safe and sound," replied the young officer, his voice shaky. "But … well … she got away from me as we were crossing the Plaza, and ran toward the Temple gate. I couldn't catch her, I'm sorry. She's faster than lightning, that one."

Baxter pounded on the door with great force. It opened almost immediately, and he stepped inside. With his fury barely held in check, he beheld Jiliada. Her face radiated melancholy; her eyes implored him for mercy. She moved forward, and hugged him.

"Don't be angry, Simon."

"Why did you go to the Temple?"

"I needed answers."

"That is the last place you will find them."

Jiliada ended their embrace, took Baxter's hand, and led him to the window in the kitchen. "Remember, Simon, when we stood here and contemplated the stars?"

"Yes, I remember," he replied, but the enchantment of the previous occasion was lacking.

"The situation in Luctor has become a crisis," she said, in a somber tone.

"Oh, I see, we're back to Luctor again. A perfect encore for my last conversation. I was just speaking to Harriman's daughter, who tried to convince me that Nucleus will be underwater in a matter of weeks unless we all embrace Bioprimalism."

"Simon," she said in a hush, "that's exactly the problem—Bioprimalism. What happened in your dream last night?"

"I didn't have the dream last night. I haven't had it since the last one I described to you."

"That's not good."

"Why not?"

"Events there are taking a turn for the worse, and you must act."

"Let General Hendrick handle it."

"That's not funny," she said, looking insulted. "You wouldn't joke like that if you had seen Elizabeth."

"Elizabeth?"

"Yes. She came from the capital to see us in the camp. You were away at the time, with your troops. I learned that in Luctor, she's your daughter from a previous marriage."

"Why didn't Elizabeth have the dream, if this is so real? And why didn't I have any memory of her while I was in Luctor? I concentrated on it with all my mental strength."

"I don't know," replied Jiliada. She paused, her face turning grim. "Simon, you must allow the dream to visit you again. You must not resist it."

"And why is that?" he asked, in a sarcastic voice.

"Because the fate of Luctor hangs in the balance."

Baxter felt a weakness in his knees. He sat on one of the chairs next to the little table. Jiliada did likewise.

"I am weary of this Luctor business," he said. "I thought we were beyond that."

"I'm sorry, but …"

"Now I have a question," he interrupted. "Do you remember me from the Serenity Sanatorium?"

Jiliada's expression reflected her incomprehension.

"I was a guest at the sanatorium," continued Baxter, "at the same time as you. Our residency there overlapped for two months. Elizabeth said that she saw you strolling in the garden, when she and myself were sitting there. But I confess that I have no recollection of it."

"Neither do I. But if we were both there, we probably met."

"It seems likely."

"Our lives have so many intersecting lines, don't they?"

"I don't know," he replied. "It seems that the lines are more parallel than intersecting."

"No," moaned Jiliada, throwing herself onto his lap and embracing him. "Don't say things like that. I love you, Simon."

Baxter could not muster a verbal response. He closed his eyes, tilted his head back, and began stroking Jiliada's soft hair.

"Do you love me?" she asked.

"You know I do. The first time I saw you, in that café, it was sealed. It was as if I were reconnecting with something that I had once cherished, and lost."

"Maybe it started at the sanatorium."

"Maybe it did. That's why I want to visit the interpreter of dreams recommended by Westlake. Something's missing from the equation, and I'm going to find it. I'm not giving up on you, Jiliada. Since you love me, I know that you'll trust me. You don't have to take any initiative, just do as I say."

She remained silent.

"I'm going to see the interpreter alone, for the first visit. Which I intend to do right away, if possible." He leaned forward, and looked into her eyes. "Can I trust you to wait for me here?"

"Yes, Simon. I will wait for you."

"Good. It won't be long now. I have a feeling that answers are close at hand." Baxter kissed her on the cheek, and then pressed the side of his face against hers, savoring the sensation of her warm, soft flesh. He kissed her one last time, and then rose from his spot. A few moments later, he was closing the door of the apartment behind him.

After reaching the pavement, he began walking rapidly, and then broke into a jog. He turned onto the Crescent, soon arriving at the building that housed Westlake's news-scroll, the *Monthly Gazette*. He found Jorgensen at the deceased journalist's desk, looking over some papers.

"How's it going?" asked Baxter.

"Not bad, boss; I'm almost finished. I'll be going back to headquarters in a little while. We just received a message from Sergeant Burns. He's there, interviewing witnesses. Says he may have identification on the man seen with Westlake at his table in the café, around the time of the murder."

"Sounds good. Listen, Phil, I need some simple information, and I think they might have it here, in the archives of the news-scroll."

"Just let me know what it is, and I'll ask someone for it. They've been very cooperative."

"Okay, two things. First, the address of Harold Smith, the interpreter of dreams recommended by Westlake."

"Sorry, boss, I should have gotten it for you when we found the parchment with Smith's name. It slipped my mind."

"Mine, too. I would also like to obtain the name of an expert on the subterranean ocean."

"Does this have anything to do with your visit to the Cave of the Abysmal Pool with Margaret Harriman?"

"Yes, it does. I'll explain it in detail later, but the condensed version is that the water level is rising, and she says it's the fulfillment of a Bioprimalist prophecy. We'll all be underwater very soon."

"So now might be a good time to invest in the shipbuilding industry."

"Yes, and in high-altitude real estate. Can you get me that information?"

Jorgensen nodded, and went to speak with an employee of the news-scroll. Baxter passed the time chatting with two officers who had been assigned to the case. The conversation did not have time to ripen, however, for Jorgensen soon returned, parchment in hand.

"Here's the address of Smith, along with the name of a professor at the university, said to be the leading expert on the subterranean ocean."

"Thank you, my friend," said Baxter, pocketing the parchment. "May your intellect expand."

He left the offices of the *Monthly Gazette*, descended to the street, and began the walk to the interpreter of dreams, Harold Smith. The address given to him by Jorgensen was at the northern end of town, not far from the city gate. Baxter's step was brisk, eager as he was to attain closure. If only the thorn of the recurring dream were removed from their side, he figured, he and Jiliada would have a reasonable chance of success in their life together. As long as the fantasy of the dual reality loomed overhead, any attempt at normalization would be futile.

He arrived at Harold Smith's office. The secretary, a young woman dressed in a light gray tunic, informed Baxter that the interpreter was with a client, but would be free very soon. Baxter took a seat on the sofa in the waiting area. Moments later, he heard raised voices coming from the inner chamber. They became louder. The door flew open, and a man emerged, clutching the top of his head. "I can't take it anymore," he yelled, before storming out of the office.

Another man emerged from the chamber. This one was a short, middle-aged fellow dressed in the traditional blue and white tunic of the learned classes. His face and balding scalp were reddish and moist from sweat. He gazed at the door leading into the hallway, as if waiting for his distraught client to return.

"Mr. Smith," said the secretary.

"Yes," he replied, turning his head after a momentary delay.

"This is Mr. Baxter. He's here to see you."

Baxter rose from the sofa and approached Smith. They shook hands and went into the chamber. The interpreter took a seat behind the desk as he motioned to Baxter to sit in one of the armchairs. Smith removed a handkerchief from his desk drawer, wiped his face and scalp, and returned the fabric to its place. "You're probably wondering what happened out there," he said.

"It did cross my mind."

"Sometimes a person has difficulty coming to terms with an interpretation."

"That's understandable. I would like you to know, Mr. Smith, that you were recommended to me, and quite highly, by Peter Westlake."

"Ah ... You're the detective?"

"Yes. He told you about me, then."

"Just briefly."

"You are aware of the fate that befell him, I presume."

"Yes," said Smith, shaking his head. "Poor guy. I suppose it was bound to happen. He was drawn to controversy as a woman to jewelry. Anyway, Mr. Baxter, tell me about your dream."

Baxter recounted the saga: his earlier, disastrous dream after the death of his wife Eleanor; the bizarre and cryptic promontory of the rock-creatures; his emerging identity as General Hendrick of Luctor; the parallel dream of Jiliada; the explanation offered by the interpreter of dreams at the

Temple, subsequently backed by the Great Sage; and his current efforts to convince Jiliada that the dual reality was an illusion.

Smith listened carefully to every word. At the conclusion of his new client's recitation, he leaned back, pressed his fingertips together, and pondered the story for some time. "Mr. Baxter," he said, finally. "This is a complex case. There are multiple elements that need to be analyzed. But right now, at the outset, I can put your mind at ease by assuring you that this notion of passing between worlds, between cells, is sheer nonsense."

"I'm glad you think so."

"Why the Great Sage is involving himself in this affair remains a mystery. It is very uncharacteristic."

"Why is that?"

"It does not correspond to his philosophy and to the overall tenor of his administration. Tell me, how long have you known Jiliada?"

"Not long at all; about a week. But we may have been acquainted eight years ago, when we were both patients at the Serenity Sanatorium. We don't remember each other from that place, but my daughter, who was ten at the time, recalls seeing the two of us together."

"Interesting," said Smith. "And you never had the dream about Luctor before these past few days?"

"No, definitely not."

"It started after you met Jiliada?"

"Not quite. I had the very first dream, with the lizards, just before I met her. But it was only after we were acquainted that I took on the identity of General Hendrick, and saw Jiliada in Luctor."

"When did she first have the dream?"

"A couple of days ago. That was when she imagined Luctor for the first time in a dream. But she has been experiencing it for years already in what she calls a waking vision."

"I will need to speak with her."

"Of course," said Baxter. "I can fetch her right away."

"That would be fine."

"Do you have a preliminary evaluation?"

"It's very hard to say at this time. I will meditate while you are gone, and then speak with you again, and with Jiliada, upon your return."

"Very well."

Smith again leaned back and pressed his fingertips together. "Tell me something. Have you ever held a position of command in the police force?"

"Yes. On several occasions I led small groups of men on special missions."

"They were dangerous, these missions?"

"Some of them were dangerous, yes. Once, we were tasked with storming a house in which criminals were holed up, refusing to surrender. There were hostages as well. Two of our men were killed. I myself was stabbed in the leg."

"Was your good work recognized by the higher-ups?"

"Absolutely," said Baxter. "After that mission, the Chief of Police asked me to take charge of special operations, to replace someone who was about to retire."

"And your answer?"

"My answer was no."

"Why?"

"It's not for me. I don't like the fanfare and the politics that surround every person in a position of authority. I prefer to be a simple detective."

"Would part of you, though, prefer to be in command?"

"I suppose. You know, it would be appropriate if I were a different type of person. But alas, I am not." Baxter reflected for a moment before continuing. "You evidently believe that this is connected with the dream."

"Quite possibly," said Smith. "But it is too early to reach a conclusion. First I must digest the information. Anyway, I will let you go now."

Baxter stood up. The two men shook hands and exchanged blessings. Baxter opened the door, passed into the waiting area, and thanked the secretary. He exited the office suite feeling relieved and optimistic. Buzzing with energy, he headed for Jiliada's building, not intending to stop along the way. His plan, however, was scuttled as he was crossing the Plaza.

"You over there," shouted a speechmaker from his pedestal.

Baxter turned to look, and saw that it was the same speechmaker who had addressed him on Fifthday, as he was returning home from Theodore Harriman's art and antique gallery. This time, a sizable crowd had gathered.

"What say you now, my good man, about dreams?"

"Which aspect?" replied Baxter, enervated by the faces turned in his direction.

"I am referring to our previous exchange, when I asserted that dreams are a manifestation of an additional personality."

The detective could not muster a response.

"I see that you are no longer prepared to deny my theory outright. Allow me then, good sir, to expound upon the notion. I submit to you that we all have numerous personalities—no, let us call them *tendencies*—that alternately come to the fore. Some are stronger, and thus tend to dominate our lives, and to give us the appearance of a certain personality type. Yet the secondary tendencies are always present, bubbling beneath the surface." The speechmaker scanned the crowd, making eye contact with as many of his auditors as possible. "Did you ever wonder, my friends, what would have happened, in a given situation, if you had acted in a different way? Did you ever consider an alternative outcome, and perhaps wish that it had occurred, or sighed with relief that it did not?"

Many heads were nodding in agreement.

"Well," continued the speechmaker, "there is a reason, beyond mere curiosity, why we long to know these other outcomes. It is because they actually exist. Yes, my friends, somewhere in the vast cosmic Brain, every one of those alternative outcomes are taking place. In other words, our diverse personalities are living their lives." He paused and looked Baxter in the eye. "In our dreams, we catch glimpses of these parallel realities."

Baxter, now feeling emotionally drained, bowed in the direction of the speechmaker, and then turned and continued on his way. He regretted having stopped, and wondered, in line with the idea of alternate scenarios, how pleasant it would be if he were now caressing Jiliada's lovely face instead of crossing the Plaza.

Like a horse with blinders, Baxter did not veer from his path. He walked briskly at first, and then began to run. By the time he reached Jiliada's building, his body was covered in a light sweat.

"Get ready to move," said Baxter to the guard, who was seated at his perch in the hallway. "The three of us are taking a little stroll. If she tries to run away, catch her."

"Don't worry, sir, I'll be ready. I'll walk behind you, so that I see everything."

"Good," said Baxter. He knocked on the door, entered the apartment, and notified Jiliada that they were leaving to visit the interpreter of dreams. She consented, but her eyes betrayed deep misgivings. Baxter repressed all sentimentality. The mission was clear; it was essential that Jiliada be disabused of her notions about Luctor. The anguish involved was well worth the expected benefit.

They began the walk, with the guard trailing closely behind. Jiliada made no attempt to run away. Periodically, Baxter made eye contact and smiled, trying to put her at ease. Despite these efforts, her expression grew more pained with each city block that they traversed.

Smith took them immediately into his chamber. He did his best to be friendly and nonchalant, given the young woman's evident distress. "Jiliada," he said softly, "Mr. Baxter told me that you also had the dream about Luctor. Would you mind describing it to me?"

"Okay," she replied, her eyes cast downward. "Where do I start?"

"Anywhere you'd like. It's important that I hear the story from you, in your own words."

Jiliada embarked upon a long and detailed recitation. The tenor of her remarks annoyed Baxter, as the emphasis was on the dual reality, and on the impending return to their true home, Luctor. Baxter did not interrupt, preferring to let the calm professional handle the situation.

When she finished, Smith removed the handkerchief from his desk, and wiped his sweaty face and scalp. "I know it isn't easy for you, and I appreciate your candor. This case is by no means unique. Others have dreams in which they, like you, adopt new identities. Each person fashions the scene according to his personality and background. One man I counseled a couple of years ago was convinced that he had broken through the wall between the cells, and subsequently dropped down to us from the vault of the heavens.

"It is important to understand that in a recurring dream, the Omnificent Cerebrum gives us messages that are shrouded in metaphor. This is not to be taken literally. We are instructed in the matter by the Tomes of Ancient Thought as well as by experience. The use of metaphor is an effective device for embedding profound lessons. It compels us to dig down, deep within our spirit, for answers to the riddles of life.

"Let us now address your specific riddle. Clearly, a major theme in the dream is Bioprimalism. It is revealed as a threat to society. Both of you have been given the task of combating it. It is now incumbent on you to contemplate your lives and your future, in order to determine where you can make the most significant contribution to the demise of Bioprimalism.

"But a question presents itself: Why the double identity? What is the Omnificent Cerebrum trying to teach you? It is my conviction that it wants you to imagine a life that is unlike the one you have now. If the dream would have taken place in the Home Cell, you might not have stretched your imagination enough to conceive of the alternative career, lifestyle, or attitude that is required in order to fulfill your destiny. For example, you,

Mr. Baxter, are portrayed as a general. This is a position of command, of great influence. I need to know more about you in order to speculate as to what that could represent, but it seems clear that you are destined to take a leadership role. And you, Jiliada, have an equal share in that responsibility, to construct a supportive household, the equivalent of General Hendrick's tent, right here in Nucleus."

Smith leaned back in his chair. He pressed his fingertips together as his eyes flitted back and forth between the two clients.

Baxter looked at Jiliada. The color had drained from her face. "You don't understand," she mumbled.

"Pardon me?" said Smith, leaning forward.

"You don't understand," she declared, quite a bit louder. "It is real. The Great Sage said it's real. Not everything is written in the Tomes of Ancient Thought."

"I agree that not everything is written there, but if something *does* appear, I see no reason to contradict it."

"Do you see a reason to contradict the Great Sage?" countered Jiliada, her tone becoming shrill.

"That aspect of your story does concern me," replied Smith. "I would need to speak with him to find out exactly what is transpiring. Perhaps there has been some sort of misunderstanding."

"Misunderstanding?" exclaimed Jiliada, rising abruptly from her chair. "The only misunderstanding is yours. How can you listen to us for one single day, and then decide that you know everything?"

"Jiliada, please ..." implored Baxter, reaching out to grasp her forearm.

She yanked away the arm. "And why have I had this vision for eight years, and knew exactly what my husband would look like, so that I could recognize Simon immediately?"

"To answer that question," said Smith, calmly, "perhaps the three of us ought to visit the Serenity Sanatorium."

Jiliada let loose a wail of anguish. Baxter extended his arm to touch her, but she raced out the door, through the waiting area, and into the hallway. The guard sprang to his feet and bolted after her.

"Stop!" shouted Baxter.

The officer halted in his tracks.

"Let her go. And you can go, too. Return to headquarters. Ask your supervisor for a new assignment."

The guard saluted and left the premises.

"I'm sorry," said Smith.

"There's nothing anyone can do. She's too far gone. I give up."

"Well, if you would like to discuss it further, just let me know."

Baxter thanked the interpreter, settled his account, and headed for the street.

XI. THE SCIENTIST

Strange as it seemed to Baxter, his most vibrant emotion at that moment was a sense of relief. Though he felt frustrated and saddened by the scene with Jiliada, a heavy burden had been lifted from his spirit. The battle against her belief in Luctor and the dual reality was over, and with it the exasperation of trying to rescue someone from a campaign of self-destruction.

After returning home, however, the emotions switched places: The feeling of relief faded into the background, to be replaced by a resurgent melancholy. Baxter stood at the window in the living room, reticent to do so in his bedroom, which faced Jiliada's apartment. He gazed at the street as his consciousness became filled with images of their embrace in the tent, in Luctor. How perfect it had been at that moment, he mused—how absolutely perfect. Jiliada was right about one thing: inside the dream, events are as real as everyday life in the Home Cell. How could he blame her for refusing to let go?

Baxter reclined on the sofa and began to doze. He was treated to a sweet and peaceful nap. When he awoke, the outside light was dim, and a cool breeze was blowing in from the window. A lamp had been lit in the kitchen. He savored the moment of domestic comfort.

Elizabeth peeked out from the kitchen and smiled. She walked over to her father and gave him a kiss. "You look exhausted, Daddy."

"An accurate description of my condition," he grumbled, not budging from his position.

She sat in the adjacent armchair. "Dinner's almost ready."

"Thanks, but I'm not hungry."

"Did something happen to you?"

"I took Jiliada to an interpreter of dreams. Remember when she had dinner with us, and we told you that we had been experiencing the same dream?"

"Yes …"

"Because of an incident years ago in the Temple involving the death of her husband, she believes that this dream is taking place in another cell, which she calls Luctor. She claims that our real life is there. The Great Sage, unfortunately, agrees with her."

"Do you believe all that?"

"No, I don't. And neither does the interpreter we just consulted. He said that Luctor is purely symbolic. Jiliada screamed at him and fled the building. I let her go. I can't pursue it any further."

"Oh, Daddy," said Elizabeth, with a sigh. "I'm sorry to hear that."

"Maybe she'll come back, but I doubt it."

"One never knows. But I think you made the right decision. You can't force people to change their minds."

"True."

"Are you sure you don't want something to eat?"

"I'm sure. But I'll sit with you."

They moved to the kitchen. Elizabeth served herself and began to eat. Baxter recounted the events of the day: his visit to the sanatorium and the subsequent confirmation of Jiliada's residence there; the trip with Margaret Harriman to the Cave of the Abysmal Pool, and her prediction of the impending flood; and the two consultations with Harold Smith, ending in the flight of Jiliada.

"That's quite a day," remarked Elizabeth.

"Yes, it is. I also found the name of an expert on the subject of the subterranean ocean, a Professor Lucien Hart. He's at the university, in the Faculty of Physical Sciences. Perhaps he can help me learn more about the ideology of Bioprimalism—specifically, their belief in an impending flood—so that I can more effectively fulfill my mission from the Omnificent Cerebrum."

"Your mission?"

"Yes, as explained by the new interpreter. The Omnificent Cerebrum has instructed me, via the dream, to assist in the effort to halt Bioprimalism. So perhaps you could take me to Professor Hart's office tomorrow morning, on your way to class."

"Sure. Can I go with you? To see the professor, I mean."

"Absolutely, dear. I'd be delighted."

"You know," said Elizabeth, her eyes glimmering, "I've been thinking about the sanatorium, and about Jiliada when she was there."

"What do you remember?"

"On her tunic, those horrible brown tunics, she painted something. Some kind of symbol, with gold and black in it."

"Gold and black ... What shape was the symbol?"

"I don't know. I only recall the colors. Yes—the gold was quite vivid. You stared at it for a long time, as if you were trying to decipher it."

Baxter moaned as he covered his face with his hands.

"Oh, Daddy, I'm sorry."

"There's no reason to apologize," he said, lowering his hands. "Now I know the origin of the colors on the standard of my troops. Yes ... it started at the sanatorium. Everything is from the sanatorium."

"I think you're right."

"If you remember any further details, tell me immediately."

"I will."

Baxter walked over to the family's Cerebral Shrine, to recite the Declaration of Cognitive Achievement. After washing up, he read from the scroll on the history of literature. He avoided passing next to the bedroom window.

The night brought no coherent dreams; only a few disjointed images danced within his unconscious mind. But lying in bed early in the morning, Baxter experienced a powerful longing for Jiliada. He arose and prepared himself as quickly as possible, hastening the arrival of the distractions to be expected in the day ahead.

He ate breakfast with Elizabeth, and they set out for the university. The sky was overcast, and a light drizzle was falling. They walked quickly through the back streets of the city's south side and soon reached the main gate of the campus. After passing through the gate, Elizabeth pointed to their destination: the Faculty of Physical Sciences, which contained the office and laboratory of Professor Lucien Hart. The building was a classic structure with a broad colonnade, similar to the art museum, only smaller.

A crowd had assembled around the main entrance. It was a group of students sitting on the ground, wearing sackcloth, wailing and shrieking and waving their arms every which way. In the middle of the ruckus was Gregory, Elizabeth's ex-suitor. Baxter and his daughter stood in the rain and watched the spectacle.

"Have you come to join the vigil?" asked a young woman who had approached from the side.

"No," said Baxter. "We're on our way into the building. What's all this about?"

"It's a vigil to save our society."

"Save it? From what?"

"From the flood. It's only weeks away, or even days. The subterranean ocean is rising, and we're all going to be underwater."

"Speaking of which, could you direct us to the office of Professor Lucien Hart?"

"Lucien Hart!" hollered the young woman, as if Baxter had threatened her with bodily harm. "Hart is a *negator*. You must stop him, or we'll all be dead."

"Why?" asked Baxter, now amused. "Does Professor Hart control the flow of water?"

"No, but he controls the minds of government officials. He told them that nothing is happening."

"Okay, I'll see what I can do. Now, how do I get there?"

The young woman pointed to a side entrance. Baxter thanked her, and made his way into the building with Elizabeth in tow. A few moments later, he was knocking on Lucien Hart's door.

"Who is it?" said a voice from within.

"Inspector Simon Baxter, Nucleus Police Department."

The door opened just a crack, revealing a pair of suspicious eyes. Baxter showed his badge. "Come in, come in," said Hart. "I hope you're not arresting me for flood negation."

"No, no arrests today," replied Baxter, smiling as he shook the professor's hand. "This is my daughter, Elizabeth. She's a student in your nursing program."

"Nice to meet you," said Hart. He showed them into the large room. Around the periphery were a number of work tables, on which were strewn maps, scrolls, rocks, and a variety of instruments. Hart guided his guests to a seating area at one end of the room.

The professor was tall and lanky, with a tunic that was too short for his frame. His curly brown hair was unkempt, and his beard seemingly out of control, growing every which way. He reminded Baxter of Jorgensen, but a quarter of a century older.

"What can I do for you?" asked Hart, after the three of them were seated.

"I am investigating two related homicide cases," said Baxter. "Both of them are connected to Bioprimalism. The victims are John Harriman and Peter Westlake."

"I am familiar with both of those mind carriers. Harriman actually came to see me several times, in an effort to convert me to Bioprimalism."

"Without success, I presume. It seems that Westlake had been monitoring, rather intensively, the activity of John Harriman's daughter, Margaret."

Hart rolled his eyes at mention of the name.

"So I paid Margaret a visit," continued Baxter. "She took me to the Cave of the Abysmal Pool. I need not recite to you the thesis presented to me at that time."

"I'm quite aware of it. These people are implacable, Inspector. I assume that you got an eyeful and earful of their antics in front of this building. It's been going on, nonstop, for weeks. They have several teams that rotate their shifts. So far there has been no violence. A student by the name of Gregory appears to be the ringleader."

Elizabeth lowered her eyes and blushed.

"You know him?" asked Hart.

"Yes," she replied. "We used to be … uh … friends. He's an intern at the medical school."

"Lovely girls like you shouldn't be anywhere near those fanatics."

"My sentiments precisely," said Baxter. "Tell us, professor, what is it that drives them to this madness?"

"An adequate discussion of that subject would require days. But I can summarize much of it in one image. You seem to be a cultivated man, Inspector. Are you familiar with the Tree of the Spirit, as set forth in the Tomes of Ancient Thought?"

"Yes. Man is an inverted tree. His branches cover the earth while his roots reach into the heavens."

"Exactly. The branches represent our everyday activity: farming, manufacturing, construction, and so on. These spread across the earth. But our roots, our spiritual being and our intellect, stretch into the heavens, where they are at one with the Omnificent Cerebrum. Now let us switch to the Bioprimalists. In their infamous scroll, they have taken our inverted tree, and inverted it once again. In other words, it has become a tree like any other from the natural world. They call it the Tree of Harmony. Its branches, representing practical activity, are in the heavens. And of course its roots are in the earth. For the Bioprimalists, the human spirit serves the earth, not the other way around."

"Interesting," remarked Baxter. "What about the Abysmal Pool?"

Hart chuckled. "Could anyone have imagined that the fluctuation of the water level in a subterranean spring would be presented as evidence of an imminent, cataclysmic deluge? It's as though one were saying that the phases of the moon are proof that a piece of it is about to fall off and land on our heads."

"Have you tried to convince them to change their minds?" asked Elizabeth.

"Numerous times. But they refuse to listen to reason. And Margaret Harriman, she's the worst. At least her father had some grip on reality. I saw him a few days before he was murdered, and at the time he expressed doubts about certain aspects of Bioprimalist doctrine."

No wonder, thought Baxter, that John Harriman never sent to Jiliada the parchment that was sewn into his collar. "Do you know, professor, whether Harriman had any conflicts with his own people over these doubts?"

"I have no idea. One thing is certain, though: there wasn't much time for the strife to develop. His doubts appeared only at the very end."

"What about Ross Kinkade? I heard that he had a very contentious relationship with John Harriman."

"Yes, but Kinkade is a harmless idiot. He just wants to feel good, so he snorts around in the mud like a pig."

Elizabeth giggled, covering her mouth.

"You know about it?" asked Hart.

"We saw it for ourselves," said Baxter. "A full session of earthworming."

"One might question the appropriateness of such behavior for the curator of an art museum, but it's not going to destabilize the social and political fabric of the Home Cell. The situation is altogether different when we speak of Margaret Harriman. She's smarter, and much more dangerous."

"I can see that," said Baxter. "But I wouldn't underestimate Kinkade, either. He's on a crusade to disrupt the very art that has been placed in his care."

"That is true. Now, please accept my apologies, but I have a class to teach. Come back any time you wish."

"Thank you, we appreciate that," said Baxter. "Allow me to propose that you join us at our home tomorrow, for Brainday. We can relax and discuss these issues in depth, over lunch. I know this is very late to ask— but could you? You can bring someone, if you'd like."

"Much obliged, Inspector. I will take you up on your kind offer. A single plate at your table is all that I require. Until tomorrow, then. May your intellect expand."

Baxter conveyed his address, and returned the blessing. He and Elizabeth left the office, descended the stairs, and exited the building. Although the precipitation had abated, the sky was still overcast and the air a bit cool. The Bioprimalist vigil was going strong, now reinforced by a supplement of wailers.

"Is everything ready for Brainday?" asked Baxter. "Did you have a chance to shop?"

"Oh, Daddy," replied Elizabeth, with an expression of pity. "You ask me every week, and every week I give you the same answer: it's all set."

Baxter smiled, kissed his daughter, and said goodbye. He left the campus, though he was unsure of what his next move ought to be. He considered reporting to the Chief for a new assignment. This would have the advantage of distracting him from his heartache over Jiliada. On the other hand, he could not rule out the possibility that she would return to him. In that case, some extra free time might prove to be useful.

His rumination was for naught. As he entered the lobby of his building, George waved him over. "A parchment just arrived for you, sir," he said, handing it to Baxter. The detective broke the seal and unfurled the document. It was from Jorgensen: *Come to headquarters immediately. Major break in the Westlake case.* Moments later, Baxter was heading northbound on Avenue of the Synapses.

The sergeant on duty at the front desk instructed him to go directly to the Chief's office. Baxter hurried up the stairs, and soon reached the inner chamber. The Chief was there, with Jorgensen at his side.

"Well, well," said the Chief, "if it isn't our crack investigator."

"It isn't," said Baxter.

The Chief laughed, his deep voice sending reverberations into the atmosphere around him. "Jorgensen, tell this wise guy what's going on."

"Yes, sir. We have witnesses who identified the man who was seated with Westlake in the café around the time of his death."

"Anyone I know?" asked Baxter.

"Yes. Ross Kinkade."

"Interesting."

"I'll say it's interesting," said the Chief. "He's in his office at the art museum. We haven't approached him yet, but we have personnel in the area to make sure he doesn't disappear. There's more. Tell him, Jorgensen."

"At Westlake's apartment, we found the draft of an article he was writing about Kinkade. Westlake alleged that he was spending the museum's money on all sorts of Bioprimalist projects, most of which had nothing to do with the museum, or even with art for that matter. Now get this—alongside the article was a message from Kinkade, pleading with Westlake to delay publication until they had a chance to meet. The proposed meeting time and place were those of Westlake's murder."

"Bingo," said the Chief, snapping his fingers. "He's our man."

"Nice work," remarked Baxter, looking at Jorgensen.

"Thanks, boss," said the junior detective, his face aglow. "The article also had a few paragraphs on the raging conflict between Kinkade and John Harriman. This corroborates what Jiliada said."

"What did she say?" asked the Chief.

"That Kinkade and Harriman hated each other's guts. They were the fiercest rivals."

"Make sure that's all documented."

"It already is, sir. Westlake also wrote that Kinkade doesn't get along with Harriman's daughter, Margaret. The two are in competition for leadership of the movement. She works at the art museum, as well; her office is right down the hall."

"What does she do again?"

"Vice-curator for new acquisitions," replied Jorgensen. "The two of them have been at each other's throats for weeks about some painting, called *Melding of the Worlds,* that she wants to acquire for the museum. Kinkade hates it. We know that the painting is now hanging in the art gallery of Margaret's brother, Theodore."

"Margaret told me about it," said Baxter. "She considers it to be a masterpiece of Bioprimalist art."

"While we haul in Kinkade," said the Chief, directing his speech at Baxter, "why don't you pay a visit to Theodore? Maybe you can get something concrete out of him. This Kinkade-Harriman feud gets bigger every time we turn around. See what you can do. We'll all meet back here to work over Kinkade. Who knows, we may have a confession to both murders tonight."

"Perhaps," said Baxter.

"Okay, let's get going," bellowed the Chief. "Any questions? No? Get out of here, then."

Baxter and Jorgensen left the office, walked down the stairs, and exited the building. A light drizzle was falling once again.

"Are you doing all right, boss?" inquired the junior detective.

"Jiliada ran away, and I let her go. There was nothing more I could do."

"Sorry to hear that. Maybe she'll regret it, and come back."

"We'll see. I doubt it, but we'll see."

XII. THE PAINTING

They parted in front of the art museum. Jorgensen entered the premises to arrest Kinkade. Baxter continued on Avenue of the Synapses, crossed the Plaza, and turned left onto Boulevard of the Mind, at the far end of which was his destination, Theodore Harriman's art and antique gallery. Baxter walked the entire length of the Boulevard within the arcade to shield himself from the rain. Many others were doing the same, making the route crowded and noisy.

Upon reaching the gallery, he noticed that the previously missing unit of vegetal symbolism had been replaced. The new shrub, planted in a shiny earthenware pot, was cut into the shape of a reading stand. He observed it for a moment, and then entered the shop.

Theodore was busy with a customer, so Baxter took the opportunity to view the captivating objects on display. One in particular caught his fancy: a small, hinged box, made of black onyx with gold trim. The lid was emblazoned with a coat of arms. He was scrutinizing the interior of the box when Theodore approached.

"That's a charming little item. It's about four hundred years old, originally owned by one of the families who built Nucleus."

"Yes, it is quite intriguing," said Baxter. He replaced the box and advanced to a table that held a collection of bronze statues, each about a foot tall. "I like this piece," he said, taking one of them in hand.

"Your taste is impeccable, Inspector. That is a unique exemplar, and one of only three known pieces from that sculptor."

Baxter carefully rested the priceless statue on the table. "I heard that your father was having doubts about Bioprimalism shortly before his death."

Theodore's slender face turned pensive. "Yes, that is true. But it was only during the last few days of his life, and he was never totally disabused of his faith."

"Is it possible that someone within the movement felt threatened by his ambivalence?"

"I suppose it's possible, yes."

"Whatever happened to that Bioprimalist scroll you had, what was the name …"

"*Humanity and the Harmonious Earth* by Conrad Burton. Margaret is now in possession of it, much to my relief."

Baxter moved deeper into the gallery, stopping in front of an enormous painting. "What can you tell me about this one?" he asked.

"Another of my sister's obsessions," replied Theodore, as he straightened his gangly frame to its full height. "She loves it because the flora and fauna are so prominent. I've got to sell it; I can't afford to keep giving her these expensive toys. This one is called *Melding of the Worlds.*"

"Ah, yes. She told me about it."

"Is that so? In what context?"

"She cited it as an example of sophisticated Bioprimalist art, as opposed to the low-brow taste of Ross Kinkade."

Theodore chuckled. "It's amusing to hear that Margaret is deriding the taste of another Bioprimalist as low-brow. The whole movement is low-brow, as far as I'm concerned."

"It seems that Kinkade and Margaret are not particularly fond of each other."

"No, not at all. They represent two completely different approaches to everything. It's hard to believe that they belong to the same organization."

Baxter resumed his examination of the canvas.

"It's not a bad painting, actually," said Theodore. "It was produced by a legitimate master, and it is inconceivable that he was purposefully creating a Bioprimalist work. That designation was stamped onto it by Margaret and her fellow disciples."

"What is this?" asked Baxter, pointing to a tiny pair of human figures in the background of the scene. One was standing, holding a knife, while the other was sprawled on the ground, bleeding.

"It does not surprise me that you noticed this detail, Inspector. It's a portrayal of a homicide that took place long ago. I've been told that the story, recounted in the Tomes of Ancient Thought, is about a son murdering his father."

"The passage is known as the Filial Destruction. I've never seen it depicted in art," said Baxter. He turned toward Theodore. "Tell me something. What was Margaret like growing up?"

"She had the most settled spirit of all the children. She was self-sufficient, calm, wise, and always helpful. A brilliant student. I would have to strain my memory to remember her being subjected to parental discipline. On the contrary, I think my parents, especially my father, relied on her for emotional support. And she adored him, idolized him. She was daddy's little princess from day one. Whenever my father made a mistake, and it wasn't often, she covered up for him, and directed her anger at whoever had the temerity to point out the fault. If one of our relations made fun of the slaughterhouse, she reminded him, like an old schoolmarm, that many of the advantages the critic enjoyed in life were derived from that business and the hard work that went into it."

"She's a pretty hard worker herself, wouldn't you say?"

"Oh, absolutely. In fact, she does little else but work."

"How did she get mixed up with people who think that the water level at the Cave of the Abysmal Pool is a sign that we're all going to die in a flood?"

A wry smile appeared on Theodore's lips. "Science was never Margaret's strong suit. She let herself get swept away by the new faith, to the point where logic no longer carries any weight."

"Did she ever mention Peter Westlake to you?"

"Yes, on one occasion, about a month ago. Westlake was hounding her for an interview. She said that he was as annoying as a mosquito. Those are the exact words she used."

Baxter continued his stroll among the objects, returning to the little box of onyx and gold. "I have nothing further to ask you, sir. Is there anything you wish to add?"

Theodore picked up the box and surveyed it. "If only life were as simple as appreciating and cataloging the beautiful objects produced by the great masters."

"Indeed," said Baxter, in a solemn tone. "Thank you for your time. May your intellect expand."

After exiting the gallery, Baxter passed through the arcade and the colonnade, emerging into the broad, open thoroughfare that is Boulevard of the Mind. The rain had abated, and the sun was peeking through the dissipating clouds. The air had a fresh, pleasant aroma. Baxter began to walk the route to headquarters, but slowly, enjoying the sensations of the moment. The wet tiles under his feet, depicting the cerebrum in cross-section, glistened in the newly-arriving light. In the distance, the Temple of the Omnificent Cerebrum, like a giant pearl, radiated its splendor across the urban space.

Without being fully conscious of his action, Baxter scanned the crowd, looking for Jiliada. He became aware of what he was doing, and recognized that it was futile, but continued the search nonetheless. The heartache that propelled him was more powerful than any calculation of utility.

At headquarters, there were no messages waiting for him at the front desk. He climbed the stairs, and soon reached his office. Jorgensen was there, leaning over the desk, reading a scroll. "Hi, boss," he said, in an energetic voice.

"Hi, Phil."

"How did it go?"

"Not bad," said Baxter, taking a seat. "I learned about the internal rivalries within the leadership of the Bioprimalist movement. And I saw the painting that Margaret is anxious to acquire. So I assume that you arrested Kinkade?"

"Yes. He's down in the lockup."

"How did he react?"

"He laughed, thinking at first that it was a joke. Then he went on about the low intellectual level of the police force. He even asked me what my intelligence grade was."

"Did you tell him?"

"Sure, why not? He was impressed, and said that when I lose my job as a result of this false arrest, I should come see him about employment at the art museum."

"Tell me something, Phil. Do the last couple of days qualify as *real police work?*"

"You bet. This is great."

"Good, I'm glad to hear it. Shall we visit our prisoner?"

"Let's go," said Jorgensen, hurrying out of his chair.

"Just one thing," said Baxter.

"Yes …"

"I am not fully convinced of his guilt."

"Why is that?"

"There's no hard evidence. It is quite possible that he's guilty, but not certain. We must be careful not to alienate him. So we have to walk a fine line, okay?"

"You got it, boss."

They stopped by the office of the Chief, but found that he was absent, having been summoned to an urgent meeting outside of headquarters. The two detectives descended to the lockup, located in the basement. The jailer had moved the prisoner from his cell to the interrogation chamber, which was little more than a small room with a few simple chairs. The space was humid, and a smell of mildew permeated the air.

Ross Kinkade was seated in the middle of the room. His eyes darted from one to the other of his accusers. "So, Inspector," he said, "I guess you didn't care for our little earthworming session out in the forest."

Baxter placed a chair next to Kinkade, while Jorgensen did so on the other side of the prisoner, so that the two policemen faced each other. A scribe sat in a corner of the room, under a lamp, quill at the ready.

"Actually," said Baxter, "it was my daughter who reacted rather strongly to the earthworming. I myself found it fascinating; a fine addition to the catalog of oddities that one encounters over the course of one's life."

"Speaking of oddities," countered Kinkade, "I would say that the present occasion qualifies for the designation."

"Let us begin. You were seen with Peter Westlake, at a café on the Crescent, around the time he was poisoned."

"I was there, yes."

"Please describe to us the nature of the business you conducted with him."

"Certainly," replied Kinkade, sounding convivial. "I had asked Westlake for the meeting in order to dissuade him from publishing an article in which he was going to expose all sorts of alleged wrongdoing at the art museum. I pleaded with him to give me a chance to explain my side of the story."

"I see. And after you presented your explanation, how did Westlake react?"

"Favorably. He said that he would delay publication. We scheduled another meeting, set to take place the next day, in his office."

Baxter was tugging at his chin. "So he really wasn't such a bad guy."

"Not at all. I think he has—*had* a few screws loose. But he also had integrity, I'll grant him that."

"Where did you go after you left the café?" asked Jorgensen.

"Do you always interrogate this way, from either side of the prisoner?" retorted Kinkade.

"Please answer the question," said Baxter, softly.

"I took a walk around the Crescent, and then I went home."

"And when you left Westlake, everything seemed normal," said Jorgensen.

"Absolutely. We parted on a positive note. He was still nursing his drink, and he looked perfectly healthy and alert."

"Nothing suspicious going on around you?"

"Not that I can remember. By the way, gentlemen, is this going to last much longer? I need to get back to my office, or at least send a parchment, so that my assistant knows what to do in the morning."

"What about John Harriman?" asked Baxter.

"What—that too?" exclaimed Kinkade, throwing his hands into the air.

"Yes, that too. This time, though, level with me. I heard some stories about the two of you."

"All right, I couldn't stand him. I admit it. John was well-intentioned, but a complete idiot. You know what I mean—the sort of person who files a document or makes you a cup of tea, but does it for the cause, so that his action takes on cosmic significance. Quite pathetic, but he was valuable to me. I have a real problem replacing him."

"Wasn't Harriman having some doubts about Bioprimalism, toward the end?"

"Yes, but nothing irreversible. If I had been able to spend an entire Brainday with him, I could have returned him to the fold."

"What about Margaret?"

"Why?" said Kinkade, with a chuckle. "Was she also murdered?"

"I hope not," said Baxter, suppressing a grin. "Do you get along with her?"

"What does this have to do with anything?"

"Just answer the question," said Jorgensen.

"We don't get along very well. But I'm sure you know that already."

"But why not?" insisted Baxter. "You're aligned ideologically, aren't you?"

"That's not enough. You know as well as I do, Inspector, that compatriots often find themselves at loggerheads."

"Indeed. Well, Mr. Kinkade, I think that's enough for today. We'll escort you back to the art museum."

"You mean I'm free?"

"Long enough to take care of your duties at the museum. Then we'll come back here and see about a permanent release. It depends on my superiors, but I think the chances are favorable. You've been cooperative, and we appreciate that."

"Well, thank you."

Baxter dismissed the scribe. The two policemen and their suspect exited the interrogation room. Baxter informed the jailer that he needed to "borrow" the prisoner for a while. The jailer pulled a long face, but acquiesced. Jorgensen, though maintaining silence, was looking perturbed by the prospective liberation of the prime suspect.

The three men left the building. The sun had set, but there was still a substantial volume of pedestrian traffic. They headed south on Avenue of the Synapses, and, in short order, were crossing the great yard of the art museum. Kinkade led them to the rear of the building, where he opened a simple door with his key. They walked through a long hallway, passing at its midpoint the door leading to the basement, where the curator had revealed the paintings produced by a monkey. Finally, they came to a halt in front of Kinkade's office.

"I wonder if Margaret has already left for the day," said Baxter.

"Probably not," said Kinkade. "Why do you ask?"

"Would you mind if we paid her a visit?"

"No, not at all."

They continued walking down the corridor. Kinkade stopped at a door and knocked.

"Yes," said a woman from inside.

The curator and the two detectives entered the office. Margaret, who was seated at her desk, rose to greet them. "Well, well," she said. "To what do I owe the pleasure of receiving this esteemed delegation?"

"Just a little question for you, Margaret," said Baxter, his demeanor as cold as ice. "Where were you when Peter Westlake was drinking his poison?"

"When he was drinking … oh, you mean when he … when he died?"

"That's exactly what I mean."

"I was at home."

"But you always work late, don't you?"

"Usually, but yesterday I had to run an errand."

"To where?"

"Down the avenue, to buy some food," said Margaret, smiling. "I'm having some friends over for Brainday."

"Can a merchant over there vouch for you?"

"Absolutely. I conducted business with Marvin at Bailey's Delicatessen, and then with Mrs. Johnston at the fishmonger across the street."

Baxter paused, then looked intently at Margaret. "We have witnesses who were in that café on the Crescent when Westlake was murdered."

Her face froze.

"That's right. And they saw you. Now, do you wish to change your story?"

"No, not at all. After I went shopping, I went to the Crescent to buy theater tickets."

"For which show?"

"*The Mathematician's Wife.*"

"Which performance?"

"Next Seconday evening."

"So you still have the tickets, then."

"No, it was sold out."

"None of the theaters were sold out for the performances on Seconday."

Margaret's lips were quivering. "How do you know that?"

"We know every single thing that happened along the Crescent on the fateful day that someone squeezed the last drop of life out of a mind carrier named Peter Westlake."

Margaret's rate of breathing had increased noticeably.

"Okay," continued Baxter, "so you went to see about tickets. Then you entered the café."

"The café," mumbled Margaret, as if talking to herself.

"Yes, that's what I said. Why did you go in there?"

"I ... I sometimes go there, just to get a tea or something."

"What were you doing in the kitchen?"

Her countenance fell.

"In the kitchen, Margaret," said Baxter, raising his voice. "Only men work in that kitchen, but we found a strand of hair, of a woman's hair. And it matches yours perfectly."

Margaret descended slowly into her chair. She was nearly panting, and her pupils were dilated. Baxter moved to her side, and then inclined his upper body so that his face was alongside hers. "Westlake deserved to die, didn't he?"

"Yes ... yes ... he's an evil man."

"He's a flood negator, isn't he?"

"The worst."

"He had to be taken out."

"It was critical."

"You did it to save the world."

"Yes!" shouted Margaret. She jumped to her feet. "I was doing it for you, for everyone. You should thank me. Someone had to get him. At least he died peacefully, though he deserved to have his head smashed to pieces."

"Margaret ..." muttered Kinkade. "What have you *done?*"

"Shut up, you wretch! All you know how to do is crawl along the ground like a beast and bring monkeys to the museum. You're a fool, a simpleton! But I'm different, I took real action. I'm the one who had the guts to take out Westlake."

Kinkade leaned his bulky frame against a scrollcase as a look of anguish spread across his face.

"Who else did you take out?" asked Baxter, in a hush. "There was someone else, wasn't there? Someone who was overcome with doubt, who wasn't so sure about Bioprimalism anymore."

Margaret's look of anger turned to one of despondency. She started to wobble. Baxter grabbed her arm and guided her into the chair. Her face was contorted from grief; the emotion burst forth in a torrent of tears.

"Oh, Margaret ..." moaned Kinkade. "Your own father?"

The three men remained still as Margaret cried herself to exhaustion. Kinkade, with an air of sickness about him, excused himself and left the room. Baxter instructed Jorgensen to run the few blocks back to headquarters and return with a carriage. In his absence, Baxter sat silently with the woman who had confessed to the crime of homicide.

Upon Jorgensen's return, he and Baxter escorted Margaret, now incoherent, to the vehicle, and ferried her to headquarters. They brought her down to the jail, where she was formally charged with two counts of first-degree murder. The jailer handled the formalities of the incarceration.

The two policemen climbed the stairs to their office. The junior detective lit the lamps while his fatigued mentor plummeted into one of the chairs.

"Nice work, boss," said Jorgensen, also taking a seat.

"Thanks."

"You really took a chance, saying we had witnesses who identified her."

"Yes, I took a chance."

"And that was a great story you made up, about the woman's hair."

"I made up the part about the kitchen," said Baxter, "but not the hair." He opened a drawer and pulled out two envelopes. From each he removed a strand of hair, and held them up. "In my left hand is a hair I found at the café, near Westlake's table. In my right, one I took from Margaret's carriage, when we went to see the Cave of the Abysmal Pool. It's not hard evidence, but it made me think."

"There must have been something else that made you think."

"Indeed there was," said Baxter, as he returned the hair to the envelopes, and the envelopes to the drawer. "When I visited Theodore Harriman's art gallery earlier today, we had a little discussion about Margaret. He showed me the painting, *Melding of the Worlds,* with which she is enthralled. In a corner of the scene is a portrayal of the Filial Destruction, a murder of a father by his son. Again, not proof of anything, but further grounds for suspicion.

"But the clincher was entirely analytic. Of all the people connected with the case, only one possessed a personality capable of the crime. It had to be someone cold and calculating, highly intelligent, and driven by an unrelenting force. Margaret alone fit the profile."

"So you decided to lunge at your prey, with no hesitation and no trimmings."

"Exactly."

Jorgensen had a pensive expression. "One thing bothers me, though."

"What's that?"

"Why didn't the folks in the café see her? We interviewed everyone there. Do you think she was wearing a disguise?"

"Possibly. Then, at some opportune moment—such as Westlake going to the restroom—she slipped the poison into his drink."

"Maybe she was disguised as a waiter or a busboy. That place can get pretty crowded, and an extra staff member might not be noticed."

"Quite plausible. I am sure you will hear the entire story soon, from the killer herself. Anyway, Phil, always use your intuition, and consider the improbable."

"I'll be sure to do that," said Jorgensen. "Are you going to call a press conference?"

"No, the Chief can do that. I don't mind keeping the reporters at bay during the investigation, but the final announcement of success must be issued by a higher echelon. When the case is solved, the real police work, as you would say, is over, and politics abound." Baxter released a prolonged yawn.

"I can take the hint, boss."

"Sorry, I'm exhausted. It seems as though an extraordinarily long time has passed since sunrise. It's hard to believe that today, only this morning, I visited the sanatorium, and then met up with you at Westlake's office."

"Yes, and we saw those documents, showing his obsession with Margaret. Naturally, they also made you think of Margaret as a suspect. I should have figured that out myself."

"Next time. There will be many more cases coming your way."

"You know, it's creepy and sick that she killed her father."

"That is an apt description of the deed. In our line of work, we encounter the darkest recesses of the human spirit. And it isn't always pretty." Baxter stood up and stretched his stiff back. "Time to go home."

"You deserve it, boss. Any plans for Brainday?"

"Nothing extraordinary. As usual, I'll try to finish as much reading as possible. We invited Professor Hart from the university to join us for lunch. If you recall, he's the expert I went to see about the subterranean ocean. He seems to be very knowledgeable about Bioprimalism, as well."

"Sounds interesting."

"Would you like to attend?"

"No thanks, I already have plans. I'm going with a friend of mine to a recitation of poetry."

"Who is the poet?"

"Robert Haines."

"Ah, yes. I've read some of his work. A rising talent, without question. Well, Phil, thanks for all your help. Have a great Brainday, and I'll see you on Firstday morning. May your intellect expand."

Baxter left headquarters and walked home, enjoying the sparsely populated streets and cool nighttime air. The Plaza was almost empty of mind carriers. A tenacious speechmaker was attempting to generate interest in his theories. Baxter did not stop, despite the invitation that came his way.

Reaching home, he found that Elizabeth was asleep. Because of his fatigue, it required an effort to prepare some light food, wash up, and recite the Declaration of Cognitive Achievement, before collapsing into bed.

There were no interruptions during the night, and no dreams of any significance.

Baxter awoke to bright rays of light streaming into the bedroom. He sat up in bed and stretched his arms and upper back. It was an unusually late time to be rising, even on Brainday. He felt well rested.

After dressing himself, Baxter meandered into the kitchen, where Elizabeth was busy preparing lunch.

"You really slept!" she exclaimed, before giving him a kiss.

"Yes, I was exhausted. How are things going?"

"Very well. Everything is in the oven. Would you like some tea?"

"Yes, please. By the way, I have some good news."

"What's that?"

"We solved the murders. They were both committed by Margaret Harriman, the vice-curator of the art museum. She confessed."

"That's great … wait … Did you say Margaret *Harriman?*"

"Yes. She's the daughter of one of the victims."

A look of dread crept over Elizabeth's face. "Daddy, that's terrible."

"I know."

Baxter took a seat at the table while Elizabeth prepared the tea. He savored the moment, realizing how fortunate he was. Pushing fifty, he was in good health. He was at the pinnacle of his career, and had just demonstrated that his professional competence was of the highest grade. His daughter was developing into a cheerful and beautiful young woman. He lived in a city at peace, endowed with a rich and thriving culture. Last but not least, one of the great scares of his life—the recurring dream about Luctor—finally had been removed from view.

Of course, Baxter regretted the rupture of his relationship with Jiliada. Though hurtful, it was for the best, he concluded. Clearly, she was mentally unbalanced, never having recovered from the spiritual disorder that, eight years previously, had caused her to be committed to the Serenity Sanatorium. She believed with all her heart in the dual reality. Nothing, apparently, was going to alter her view.

After finishing his tea, Baxter adjourned to the little bedroom, where he remained until the arrival of the guest, Professor Lucien Hart. The time was spent in study. His relatively relaxed and lucid mind was able to race through the remaining text in the scroll on the history of literature. He completed it a few moments before Professor Hart knocked on the door.

Baxter showed the distinguished scholar into the living room. Elizabeth came in to say hello, and served some light refreshments. Baxter noted that the professor's tunic was clean and well-pressed, unlike his garments at the time of their previous meeting. In addition, he had trimmed his hair and beard. The two men explored their biographical profiles, finding several points of convergence, such as having grown up in the same area of Nucleus, the northwest quadrant. They also had attended the same gymnasium, though at different times.

It was later, over lunch, that Baxter broached the topic of Bioprimalism. "Tell me, professor, how did Margaret Harriman and her people latch on to the Cave of the Abysmal Pool, making it a key element of their doctrine?

"I have two answers to your question," replied Hart, as he took a sip of the excellent wine that his host had uncorked for the occasion. "One is that the Abysmal Pool contains a strident reminder of our society's customary relationship to nature. I speak of the famous carvings on the face of the rock. They extol cerebral activity in a spot where nature offers a demonstration of her savage ways. This provokes a strong reaction among the Bioprimalists, who then feel compelled to formulate a contrarian theory to explain the flow of water."

"Yes," said Baxter, "I can understand how a Bioprimalist might feel dismayed when viewing the imprimatur of our cerebral culture in such a setting. It is one thing to display such art forms on Boulevard of the Mind, in a thoroughly urban and human environment; quite another in a place where nature reigns supreme."

"Precisely," acknowledged Hart.

"What is your second answer?" asked Elizabeth.

"The second answer is that there is something mysterious, even other-worldly, about the Cave of the Abysmal Pool. For someone not imbued with the spirit of science, the whirlpool begs the imagination to invent a source of power and to endow it with consciousness. In other words, to make it human. Only then can one arrive at the absurd conclusion that if mind carriers do not change their behavior, Mother Earth will become angry."

"But is it really that different," said Elizabeth, in a hesitant voice, "from saying that the Omnificent Cerebrum brought about the Flood because of the Lensic heresy?"

Professor Hart smiled. "I see that your father's faculty of discernment has been transmitted to his progeny. Yes, on a certain level, the cases are similar. The similarity evaporates, however, when we consider that there are only two entities in the cosmos that have consciousness: the Omnificent Cerebrum, and man. Everything else exists to serve man, and man in turn serves the Omnificent Cerebrum. Other living things and objects, including the earth, cannot possibly exist for their own sake because they have no mind. Therefore they cannot be subjects. No form of reason can originate with them. To say that the earth seeks revenge has the same connection with reality as saying that a rock can practice law, or that a spider can compose a poem."

"Interesting," remarked Baxter. "That kind of thinking, so typical of the Bioprimalists, may have driven Ross Kinkade to devise so-called art that is produced by a monkey. Are you familiar with his efforts in that domain, professor?"

"I am, much to my chagrin. Kinkade is attempting to abrogate one of the immutable laws of existence, that art is the purposeful product of a mind. Though Margaret Harriman would be loathe to admit the fact, Kinkade's primate campaign is no different, at its core, than her attributing a form of consciousness to changes in the behavior of the whirlpool. Margaret's, I admit, is a more elegant formulation, but both represent the same attempt to attribute a form of will, along with the capacity to generate ideas, to entities that lack these capabilities.

"This has an analogy, Inspector, to something in your line of work. Forcing a paint brush into the hand of a monkey is no different from wrapping the fingers of a murder victim around the handle of a dagger thrust into his chest by someone else, to create *post facto* the impression of suicide. In the case of the monkey, an idea—that a beast could produce art—already was formulated by a human mind before the animal ever saw the brush."

"Well put, professor."

"Thank you. By the way, the food is delicious."

"I'm glad you're enjoying it," said Elizabeth, smiling.

"Let me ask you something else," said Baxter. "You are at the university, in the thick of the intellectual warfare that takes place day in and day out. How far advanced, would you say, are the inroads made thus far by the Bioprimalists in the academic and cultural realms?"

"Do you want the optimistic or the pessimistic view?" asked Hart.

"I want the accurate view."

"It is dire, in my opinion. The Bioprimalists have recruited new disciples in numerous fields, and at an alarming rate. Mind carriers whom I would have described, no more than a year ago, as pillars of rational thought, have hurled themselves into the cauldron with abandon. It is unlike anything I have ever witnessed."

"Fascinating," said Baxter, tugging at his chin. "We are all acquainted with the stories in the Tomes of Ancient Thought describing similar periods of crisis, some of which precipitated horrendous wars. It is quite different to bear witness to the same phenomenon in one's own society. In some ways it has the quality of a nightmare; that is, of an appalling, uncontrollable force that overtakes us, leaving us powerless, or at least with the sense of being powerless."

These words were followed by a period of silence. The participants turned their attention to finishing the meal. Lighter conversation ensued, and then, after dessert and tea, all present adjourned to the living room.

Later in the afternoon, Elizabeth excused herself to take a nap, while Baxter and Hart departed for a stroll to the Plaza. They deepened their acquaintance, touching upon a wide variety of personal and societal topics. The day ended with a pledge to keep in touch, and to work together, along with other concerned citizens, to stem the tide of Bioprimalism.

XIII. THE CHASE

Brainday was followed by a peaceful sleep with no memorable dreams. But then Baxter awoke, for no apparent reason, during the latter part of the night. His mind was focused on one thing: Jiliada. First, he imagined her eyes, and then recalled the texture of her hair, the sound of her voice, that adorable little frown, and her expressions of wonderment when they were observing the vault of the heavens. He relived the scene from one of the dreams—taking place in the tent, after dinner—which ended in their loving embrace.

Baxter tried to banish the images, but to no avail. They became ever more vivid. He sat up, and then moved to the window, where his eyes focused on Jiliada's apartment. All was still. Had she returned since running away? Unlikely, he concluded.

A cup of tea did nothing to calm his nerves. His spirit was saturated with Jiliada. Something had to be done. He placed himself in the living room, at a window overlooking the street, and gazed at the little sliver of the city that was available to his eyes. Where could she be, he asked himself. He was a detective, and had just managed to crack a complex case. Surely he could mobilize these same talents. But where to find her? Where to start?

An idea struck him that very instant: appeal to the Great Sage. If anyone in the Home Cell could lead him to Jiliada, it was that esteemed personage.

He left the apartment in a hurry. The street was dark and deserted. He broke into a trot on Avenue of the Synapses, and in short order arrived at the building that housed the living quarters of the Great Sage.

"My name is Simon Baxter," he said to the doorman. "I must see him."

"Yes, sir, he's been expecting you."

Baxter reached under the breastflap of his tunic and extracted his dagger and its sheath, and placed them on the counter. One of the two guards present in the lobby escorted the visitor through the hallway to the front door of the residence. He rang the bell. A servant opened the door, dismissed the guard, and led Baxter to the study.

The Great Sage was hunched over a scroll that was unfurled upon his desk. A large but simple lamp, on a shelf above, bathed the text in light. The rest of the room, packed with scrolls of every description, remained relatively dark.

"Please, sit down," said the Great Sage, looking up at his guest with a little smile that peeked out from within the flowing gray beard.

"Thank you, Your Eminence," said Baxter, bowing to the man who in all likelihood was the most intelligent mind carrier in the Home Cell. The detective parked himself in the vacant chair. "Do you always work at this time of night?" he asked.

"Yes. The most lucid thoughts arrive in the nocturnal air."

"When do you sleep?"

The Great Sage pushed a laugh out of his throat, but not without some effort. "I am like a horse, who can sleep standing up. In my younger days, I would do just that—sleep while standing at my lectern. Now, in my old age, I doze right here in this chair."

Baxter tugged at his chin. "I need your help," he declared.

"I will do what I can."

"Your Eminence, I implore you to return Jiliada to me."

"I already have."

Baxter attempted to process the words he had just heard.

"Jiliada is with my wife," continued the Great Sage, "at our country home. She is resting from her ordeal. Yesterday, she was here with me, and I said all that was necessary to return her to you. Allow me to explain."

"Yes, please do."

"Eight years ago, a beautiful young woman was starting her adult life in decidedly favorable circumstances. Granted, she had been an orphan, but was raised from earliest infancy by an elderly childless couple who were the most generous, loving, and cultivated mind carriers one could possibly imagine. They married her off to a young man, an apprentice sage, who matched her in intelligence, beauty, charm, and upbringing.

"But misfortune arrived. The parents, having reached a ripe old age, died within weeks of each other. Needless to say, Jiliada was devastated. Unfortunately, her young husband was in no position to furnish the requisite emotional support. This is because he had fallen in with an element at the Temple who were experimenting with some dangerous ideas. I mean dangerous in the sense of being harmful, first and foremost, to one's self. A member of the group lost his mind, and is still institutionalized today. One died at the Cave of the Abysmal Pool, in mysterious circumstances. Michael, Jiliada's young husband, committed suicide, in the Temple no less.

"My wife and I took Jiliada into our home, in an effort to salvage her battered spirit. The main obstacle to her recovery was not the grief over the loss of her husband and her parents, staggering as it was. Nor was it the tragedy of the stillborn child. Rather, it was an idea planted in her head by some of the rogue sages, in their carelessness. They convinced her that both she and Michael had come to the Home Cell from other worlds. Michael had returned to his, and soon she would be sent back to hers. Her spirit, weak and desperate, clamped itself onto the notion like a lion locking its jaws into the flesh of its prey. I tried to dislodge the idea, but to no avail. Jiliada became agitated, shrieking and wailing and pulling her hair out.

"We had no choice but to bring her to the sanatorium, where she could receive professional help. It was only with difficulty that they managed to subdue her, and then lead her down the path to recovery, or at least to a modicum of stability. But even as the worst of the storm subsided she remained delusional, clinging to her dream world.

"A fateful turn of events ensued. A man, a widower approaching middle age, arrived at the sanatorium. His spirit was also shattered, though a strong thread held him to reality, probably because of his young daughter, and because of his experience as a clear-thinking police detective. There was, shall we say, some strong chemistry between the two forlorn individuals. I saw it with my own eyes. One day, in the garden of the sanatorium, they were seated next to each other on a bench. The smiles they exchanged expressed their feelings for each other more convincingly than the greatest love-poem ever composed. And all the while, a little girl stood alongside her father, unsure how to interpret the behavior exhibited in her presence.

"Later that day, my wife and I sat with Jiliada in her room. She talked about the wonderful man with the red beard. She conveyed her sensation of love without calling it by name. Then she broke down, sobbing like a child, agonizing that she would soon have to leave him, when it was time to return to her world of origin.

"Her condition deteriorated. The doctors feared a relapse. I decided that action must be taken immediately to save our beloved Jiliada. I told her that the man with the red beard was her husband from the other world. She would not lose him in the end, I explained, because he would be making the same journey. To ensure that all goes well, however, it was necessary to approach the matter with great prudence. This meant, first and foremost, not divulging the details to anyone.

"Thus I launched her on a project that would absorb her excess emotional energy. It worked, but with a singular flaw: She—how shall I say it—*infected* the man with the story of Luctor. He let himself participate in the fantasy, but only for a while. I learned from the physicians that at the time of his release from the institution, he already had purged the notion from his mind. His conscious mind, that is.

"Jiliada forgot, or seemed to forget, the man she had met in the garden of the Serenity Sanatorium. He was never mentioned until these recent days. Apparently, she had mentally repackaged the entire episode so that the existence of her husband belonged exclusively to her life in Luctor." The Great Sage paused, breathing deeply as he mustered his strength.

"And so," said Baxter, "we arrive at the murder of John Harriman, the circumstance that reunited the man and the woman."

"Correct. But there is one more intervening detail to recount. Despite his leadership role in the Bioprimalist movement, John Harriman was a very decent fellow. Decent, and gullible. Jiliada infected him with the dream. Not long ago, Harriman came to see me, at her behest, for the purpose of interpretation.

"I recognized the golden opportunity that had fallen into my lap. I respun the story so that Harriman believed that the Omnificent Cerebrum had tasked him with *infiltrating* the Bioprimalist movement. In other words, I convinced him that the movement is evil, and that he is uniquely positioned to subvert it. Naturally, I did not suspect that he would pay with his life for the subsequent about-face.

"You know, Inspector, there is something very powerful about the Bioprimalist doctrine. It is not to be underestimated. And the proof: it drove a woman to murder her own father. Margaret believed that she was accomplishing nothing less than the salvation of humanity."

"Yes, it is quite shocking."

"By the way, I persuaded Harriman not to divulge to Jiliada his role as *agent provocateur*, lest she be put in danger. But he did, unfortunately, confide in Margaret."

And in Professor Lucien Hart, thought Baxter. "One cannot foresee everything," he said.

"I suppose not," said the Great Sage. "I have now brought you up to date. Yesterday, I told Jiliada the same story you have just heard. She was upset, but the reaction was less severe than expected. I asked her to stay with us at our country home, and she agreed."

"There is one thing I fail to understand, Your Eminence," said Baxter.

"Yes …"

"With all due respect for the soundness of your motives, why did you not previously inform me of this background, when the two of us met? And why make the story of Luctor even more entrenched by involving the Temple's interpreter of dreams?"

The wrinkles in the Great Sage's face deepened, expressing the profundity of his sorrow more keenly than any words. "I apologize for the irritation I have caused you. First, allow me to set the record straight regarding Henry Thompson, our interpreter of dreams. Henry has always been an advocate of the dual reality. He honestly believes everything he told you. As for my withholding of information, it was for Jiliada's sake. I needed to be certain of your commitment to her before overturning the comforting tale I had been reciting for eight years."

"I see."

"Now, looking ahead, I will not rest until you and my dearest Jiliada are reunited, with no dreams or alien worlds lurking about. We will do whatever it takes to put the past behind us, and transcend the unfortunate events and circumstances of her tortuous life."

Baxter nodded.

"Will you accompany me to my country home?"

"Yes, Your Eminence, gladly. But first I must go home and inform my daughter of what is happening. I shall return forthwith."

"Very well," said the Great Sage, shaking Baxter's hand with all the strength that remained in his aged body. "I await you."

Moments later, Baxter's feet hit the pavement. He moved quickly through the awakening city, now coated in the soft light of dawn. Pondering the conversation, his first impulse was to feel jubilation. But the detective's pragmatic side soon dominated. What guarantee did he have that Jiliada had come around to his way of thinking? None whatsoever, he concluded. She may yet reject or misconstrue the Great Sage's revelation.

After entering his apartment, Baxter washed up and changed his tunic. As he completed the task, Elizabeth emerged from her bedroom.

"Are you all right?" she asked.

"Oh yes, everything's fine. In fact, something good has happened."

"Tell me, please," she said.

"I have just returned from a private meeting with the Great Sage."

Elizabeth's face adopted an aspect of perplexity.

"He has a lifelong connection with Jiliada, about whom he cares deeply. In an effort to help her, he was instrumental in perpetuating the story of the dual reality. Now he decided to break the news that it was all a fantastic tale. She's resting at his country home. I've been invited to accompany the Great Sage, right now, to go there and see Jiliada, and settle the whole matter once and for all."

"I'm coming with you."

"You are? I mean, why?"

"You may need help. I feel that I understand her. Don't worry, I'll stay in the background."

"What about your classes?"

"I have only one lecture and a lab today. The lecture notes I'll copy from a friend, and the lab I can make up later in the week."

Baxter smiled. "You're a sweetheart."

Elizabeth returned to her room to prepare herself for the day ahead. She then joined her father, and they set off toward the residence of the Great Sage.

As they approached the building, a guard requested that they wait on the sidewalk. A large carriage, hitched to a team of four horses, pulled to a halt. Baxter and Elizabeth ascended. Soon, the Great Sage emerged from the apartment house, accompanied by his servant. Baxter helped lift the elderly man into the cab. The servant joined the coachman at his perch, and the carriage departed.

The Great Sage seemed delighted to find himself in the company of a gracious and perceptive young woman. He inquired of her studies, and listened patiently to the response. The conversation turned to her and her father's experience with the Bioprimalists at the university. The Great Sage related some anecdotes of his own, painting a grim picture that corroborated the prognosis offered by Professor Hart.

The country home was located north of Nucleus, beyond Two Scribes, and farther even than the Cave of the Abysmal Pool. The property was circumscribed by a high stone wall, in the midst of which was a gate adorned with the coat of arms of the Temple. Once inside, the visitor traversed several hundred yards of verdant meadow before reaching the central compound. The home itself was a stately, though mostly unadorned, three-story brick structure.

No sooner did the travelers descend from the carriage than a man hurried over to them from the house.

"Jiliada ran away," he declared. "She's fast, and got a good jump on us. The gardener spotted her just as she was passing through the gate. We sent out a search party."

The Great Sage, already hunched over, sagged onto his cane. His servant helped to steady him.

"Okay, listen," said Baxter, directing his speech at the man from the house. "Send someone to the police station in Two Scribes. Tell them what happened, and ask them to summon Officer Jorgensen from headquarters. Bring some men. Orders from Inspector Baxter."

"Will do," said the man.

"In the meantime," said Baxter, "I'll join the search."

"We have a small carriage you can use, or a chariot if you prefer."

"I'll take the chariot. Where are the stables?"

"Over there," said the man, pointing to an outbuilding at the edge of the compound.

"Good. Get going. Elizabeth, come with me." Baxter and his daughter moved rapidly to the stables. The stable hand prepared a chariot with a pair of horses. The vehicle was in excellent condition, barely used, and the animals looked healthy.

"You need to hold on tight," cautioned Baxter, as Elizabeth mounted the footplate. "The ride can be very rough."

"Don't worry, Daddy, I'll be okay."

Baxter cracked the whip, and they flew across the compound, heading for the gate. He felt a surge of exhilaration. The woman he loved was in flight, goading him to rein her in. He figured that Jiliada was merely venting her rage and frustration. If he might only talk to her and hold her close, the fury would be assuaged. Her emotion spent, she would have no choice but to surrender. The Great Sage had divulged the truth. There could be no further refuge in the grand illusion.

Acquiring the opportunity to speak with Jiliada, however, proved to be no simple matter. Baxter spent a considerable portion of the day combing the countryside searching for her. He was assisted by members of the Great

Sage's household, and then by a detachment of police officers brought to the area by Jorgensen.

At mid afternoon, all forces reassembled at the country estate, at the very spot where Baxter and Elizabeth had arrived that morning in the carriage of the Great Sage. It was soon clear that Jiliada had successfully eluded everyone. A new strategy was called for. One and then another of the participants offered their conjecture as to the possible escape route of the young woman, and her most likely current location.

It was in the midst of this discussion that a carriage entered the scene. All present ceased their banter as the vehicle came to a halt. The door opened, and out stepped Ross Kinkade. The silence continued as the curator made his way over to Baxter, who was flanked by Elizabeth and Jorgensen.

"Good afternoon, Inspector," said the new arrival.

"Good afternoon."

"Judging by the little phalanx I see before me, you must be engaged in a manhunt."

"That is correct."

"Might you be searching for a young lady named Jiliada?"

"Yes," replied Baxter, his heart racing.

"I will bring you to her," said Kinkade, surveying the group around him. "But we must not be obstreperous. I suggest that only you and Mr. Jorgensen accompany me."

"Understood. Can my daughter Elizabeth come with us, as well?"

"Certainly. Let us make haste."

Baxter thanked all present and released the police officers. The reconstituted search party climbed into Kinkade's carriage. Elizabeth sat next to her father, while Jorgensen and Kinkade occupied the opposite bench.

"She's at the Cave of the Abysmal Pool," began Kinkade, after the carriage had lurched forward from its parking spot. "This morning I decided to visit the site, driven by curiosity about Margaret Harriman. On the way, I saw servants of the Great Sage running about, frantically conducting their search. When I arrived at the cave, Jiliada was there, standing at the edge of the whirlpool. I inquired as to the reason for her presence. She said that she had escaped from the country home of the Great Sage. Then she told me that Simon—that's the name she used—had convinced the Great Sage that Luctor is not real. The two of you, Inspector, are allegedly conspiring to prevent her from accomplishing her mission. I assume that all of this makes sense to you."

"Yes," said Baxter, softly. "But what does it have to do with the Cave of the Abysmal Pool?"

"Some sages believe—this is what she said—some sages believe that the cave represents a link, a tunnel if you will, to the other world."

Baxter, overcome with distress, leaned forward and buried his face in his hands. Elizabeth placed her arm over his back and held him tight.

"Thank you for helping us, after what we put you through," said Jorgensen.

"Don't mention it," said Kinkade. "You were just doing your job."

Soon, the carriage pulled into a clearing near the entrance to the Cave of the Abysmal Pool. The passengers hurriedly descended from the vehicle, and then entered the stone corridor that led to the whirlpool.

Baxter, first to arrive at the cavernous bowl, experienced a severe letdown when he saw that the space was uninhabited. The roar of the violently swirling water accentuated the despair in his spirit. Elizabeth appeared at his side, and, after a brief interlude, pointed to a spot along the face of the rock. "Daddy, look!" she exclaimed.

Jiliada was crouching on a stone shelf recessed into the rock face. Only a sliver of her profile was visible. Baxter surmised that she had traversed the twenty feet or so of wall that separated them by grasping and stepping on the small pieces of rock that jutted from its surface.

"Jiliada!" he shouted.

She turned toward him.

"What are you doing?"

"It will be good for us in Luctor," she hollered. "That is where I am going. You must make the journey as well."

"No," responded Baxter, forcefully. "Our life is here, right here. You are to come back at once. Elizabeth and I are taking you home."

She was shaking her head, as the tears began to fall.

"I love you, Jiliada. You will be my wife." Baxter waited several moments for a response that did not arrive. He moved to the spot where the edge of the cave floor met the wall of the pool, and then tested the closest protruding rocks for their fastness.

"No, boss," said Jorgensen, grabbing Baxter's tunic. "If you fall, it's certain death. No one can survive that whirlpool."

Jiliada was now standing on the edge of the little shelf. "I love you too, Simon," she cried. "I'm going to Luctor. We will be together there." She leaned over the edge.

"No, Jiliada!" screamed Baxter. "The Great Sage has forbidden it. Stop!"

She leapt into the air and plummeted feet first into the thunderous vortex. Baxter released a scream that reverberated between the walls of the cave, filling the space with the sound of sheer horror. He dropped to his knees and leaned over the precipice, looking everywhere for a sign of his beloved. Upon discerning a patch of color in the swirling water, he jumped to his feet, shouted her name, and dived toward the spot.

Now it was Elizabeth who shrieked in agony. Kinkade, fearing a repeat of Baxter's futile rescue attempt, retracted her from the edge. She looked at him, her face contorted, before staggering and losing her bearings. He grabbed her, and carefully lowered her onto the ground. Jorgensen, meanwhile, was scurrying to and fro along the brink, as if somehow his action would cause the impossible to happen. He continued his frantic pacing until it was evident that even the most miraculous feat of survival was no longer possible. The young police officer then stood motionless, staring into the furious waters of the Abysmal Pool.

Kinkade approached. "Let's get her out of here," he declared, pointing to the young woman lying insensible on the ground.

It took Jorgensen a moment to react. "I'll get her," he said; with Kinkade's assistance, he raised Elizabeth, and carried her in his arms. They walked through the stone corridor and emerged into the daylight. The two men lifted the unconscious woman into the carriage, took their seats, and instructed the coachman to return to the country estate.

* * *

Upon hearing the news of the death of Jiliada and Baxter, the Great Sage fainted into the arms of his servant. The household staff removed him to his bed. They also carried Elizabeth to one of the guest rooms. A physician was summoned. When the Great Sage regained his senses, he vowed in the presence of witnesses that he would provide Elizabeth with a lifelong pension.

Ross Kinkade, on his return trip to Nucleus, dropped Jorgensen off at the police station in Two Scribes. The station commander, with a detachment of officers, hastened to the Cave of the Abysmal Pool. They brought equipment necessary for extracting a corpse from water. The gesture was futile, however. All they could recover were fragments of clothing.

Elizabeth was given the finest medical care available. Despite the best efforts of all concerned, her condition deteriorated rapidly. She lapsed into fits of hysteria, and would not eat or drink. Days passed with no improvement. On the fifth day after the drowning of her father, the young woman succumbed.

Phil Jorgensen pursued his career in the police force with great vigor, considering himself to be the heir to Inspector Simon Baxter. He was also an heir in the financial sense. Unbeknownst to Jorgensen, he had been named in Baxter's will; the portion he received was enough to provide the young man with a respectable nest egg.

Theodore Harriman, the art and antique dealer, was driven to the brink of nervous collapse by the revelation that his sister had murdered his father, and by the subsequent trial and execution of Margaret. Somehow, he managed to keep the art gallery functioning, but did it without gusto or ambition.

Ross Kinkade redoubled his efforts within the Bioprimalist movement. With the demise of his two chief rivals, Margaret and John Harriman, he became the undisputed leader of the cause. Years would have to pass before Gregory, Elizabeth's erstwhile suitor, could amass enough power to challenge the veteran's position. The failure of the dreaded deluge to arrive was interpreted by Kinkade and his cohorts as a reprieve granted by Mother Earth, in her infinite mercy, to allow the Bioprimalists sufficient time to reform humanity.

Professor Lucien Hart, fearing for his safety, resigned his post at the university and accepted a job offer at a less renowned institution of higher learning located far from Nucleus. Taking into account the deaths of Westlake and Baxter as well as the burgeoning and increasingly strident Bioprimalist presence on campus, Hart decided that fading into obscurity would be a wise policy of self-preservation.

The other residents of Nucleus, for the most part, went about their lives as if our saga had never taken place.

XIV. A FULLY-DEPLOYED INTELLECT

Baxter perceived that he was suspended in a realm of darkness. It was an absolute darkness, without a trace of sound or light, as if he had been returned to the womb, but with his adult consciousness intact. He felt neither pain nor discomfort. In fact, there was nothing to feel; no space in which to expand. Movement lacked purpose in a medium that had no beginning or end, no up or down, and in which measurement of any kind was impossible.

At times he felt minuscule, as narrow as a strand of hair, so slender he could fit through the eye of a needle. Alternately, he had the sensation of being a giant; nay, a Leviathan, larger than all of the Home Cell, even including the vault of the heavens and the subterranean ocean.

He found it impossible to gauge the lapse in time between the incident at the Cave of the Abysmal Pool and the present moment. Time might be standing still, or it might be rushing by. Either way, it didn't matter. There was nothing to accomplish. What could be the difference, for all practical purposes, between one moment and another?

This existence, reasoned Baxter, must be the passage between death and reassignment of his spirit. If so, he was now covered by the Cloak of the Omnificent Cerebrum, as it was called in the Tomes of Ancient Thought. Where would he be sent? It could be anywhere; for all he knew, his next life was destined to be lived as a shepherd in a primitive society lodged in a distant nook of the cosmic Brain. But alas, all such speculation was pointless. The intelligence required for such calculations was unfathomable to a mind carrier.

A question presented itself to Baxter's spirit: How much longer would he be generating thoughts from within his existing consciousness—that is, as Simon Baxter of the Home Cell? When would his memory be erased; when would the slate be wiped clean? In effect, when would he cease to be himself?

As he pondered these enigmas, a subtle change occurred in his sensory field. The darkness now exhibited a lighter tint. It was a greenish black, but still dark and uniform. And then he heard a sound. Like the color, it was undifferentiated; a deep buzzing, very faint, off in the distance. Baxter adopted an attitude of anticipation, yet there was no corresponding physical form in which the anticipation could manifest itself.

Next came a sense of orientation. He felt an above and a below; in other words, a type of gravity. But it acted exclusively on his consciousness, which was all that seemed to exist. This consciousness, much to his surprise, was still that of Simon Baxter.

Expecting the imminent termination of his old self, he concentrated with all his might on Elizabeth. He sent forth a muted cry into the cosmos. It was a confession and an apology: Through the impulsive and ill-advised act of diving into the whirlpool, he had caused what must have been unendurable agony to his beloved daughter. He begged her to believe that he loved her with all his heart, despite the appearance of reckless indifference.

The buzzing sound ceased to be uniform; it became intermittent, and variable in its tone. Also variable was the location of the points of sound. This reinforced an emerging sense of depth. In his visual perception as well, greater movement and variation were discernible. The dark green became lighter, and it acquired a grainy texture. Despite the perception of sound and light, he possessed neither eyes nor ears; in fact, all corporeal existence was denied him.

But this, too, arrived. As the focal point of his attention shifted between the various stimuli, Baxter noticed that he was breathing. He concentrated on his lungs, and then detected a heartbeat. He followed the pulse outward from the heart to his ill-defined extremities. A body was taking shape, though its precise contours could not be determined.

That is, until pressure was applied by an outside force onto a spot close to his consciousness. There was no pain; on the contrary, it was a source of great comfort. His spirit rushed, like moths to a flame, to meet the foreign object, seizing upon this foothold in the exterior world. The sensation became steadily more clarified until there remained no doubt that a hand was touching his forehead.

Suddenly, like a fetus at the end of its term, Baxter was hurled into the new reality. The Cloak of the Omnificent Cerebrum had been lifted. He was lying in bed, on his back, dressed in a light tunic, with a blanket pulled up to his chin. Some distance above him was a smooth, taut fabric;

it was the ceiling of a tent. He glanced to the right, and saw Elizabeth, displaying her clever, ironical smile.

"Hi, Daddy," she said.

He turned his head to the left and saw Jiliada, looking more beautiful than ever.

"General Hendrick, welcome to Luctor," she declared, before tilting her head back and releasing a laugh that enveloped the surrounding space in its carefree zest.

In one swift motion, Baxter sat up on the bed, removed his arms from under the blanket, and pulled the two women down onto him. He held them fast as the tears streamed from his eyes with a force as mighty as the waters at the Cave of the Abysmal Pool.

After some time, he began to feel dizzy. He relaxed his grip on Jiliada and Elizabeth, prompting them to ease him back to the supine position. The women knelt at either side of the bed, each holding one of his hands.

Baxter looked at Jiliada and at his daughter, and laughed. "Is this really Luctor?" he asked.

Jiliada squeezed his hand. "You know it is, my husband. There is no other possible explanation. You surely did not survive the whirlpool, and if you were dead, you would have been reassigned by the Omnificent Cerebrum."

"This is true," admitted Baxter. "But how do you know that I jumped into the whirlpool?"

"It was imperative that you come to Luctor. It had to happen. Anyway, Elizabeth told me."

"Did you also pass through the whirlpool?" asked Baxter of his daughter.

"No, I fainted. They brought me to the home of the Great Sage. I couldn't eat or drink. The end came five days later."

"I am sorry for the terrible grief I caused you."

"It doesn't matter now, Daddy."

"How did you get here before me?"

"The process isn't uniform," explained Jiliada. "Not everyone spends the same amount of time in the transition phase."

"How could Elizabeth be sent to Luctor without having had the dream?"

"The Great Sage spoke of a mirrored existence that is often provided for family members of those who have the dream. But I never quite understood how it works."

"Who can fathom the ways of the Omnificent Cerebrum?" said Baxter, with a sigh. "Come to think of it, Jiliada, I never renounced my life in the Home Cell, and neither did Elizabeth. Wasn't that a prerequisite for returning to one's cell of origin?"

"Yes, but your actions reflected your intentions more powerfully than any vows. When you leapt into the whirlpool, Simon, it was clear that you were ready to follow me into another existence. As for Elizabeth, I believe that her refusal or inability to eat was a way of renouncing her former life."

"I suppose so. Tell me, what day is it here, in Luctor?"

Jiliada smiled. "It is still the same evening as in your last dream. Remember our lovely family dinner, with the boys and my father? Well, much later, Elizabeth entered the tent. I woke up, but you were exhausted, and continued sleeping. She and I chatted for a short while, and then we came in here so that I could give her a hair brush. You were still deep in slumber."

The short blast of a trumpet was heard.

Baxter sprang into the seated position. "That's my aide, the trumpeter."

Elizabeth stood up. "I'll go see what he wants."

"Tell him to wait at the table. I'll be there shortly."

She exited the room. Baxter returned his attention to Jiliada. She was still kneeling alongside the bed; her face was not a foot away from his. "How could you possibly stay the course?" he asked.

"Because you are my husband."

He kissed her on the lips, and then pulled her toward him. "Jiliada, I ..." His words were interrupted by another, stronger blast of the trumpet, this one from within the tent. Baxter threw off the blanket and sat on the edge of the bed. "I must go."

"I know," said Jiliada. "I will fetch your clothes." She removed the pieces of her husband's uniform from his wardrobe, and brought them to him. He hurriedly dressed himself, fastened his sword, and went to meet the aide. Jiliada followed close behind.

The trumpeter rose at the sight of his superior officer. "I am sorry to disturb the General at his tent so late at night. Unfortunately, circumstances demand it."

"Tell me what happened."

"The Bioprimalist revolt has begun. The Emperor was taken prisoner. An entire brigade has defected. Rebel forces are mustering a few miles from here, preparing to take the camp."

"We must defeat them at once. Assemble the troops at the western field."

"Already in progress, sir."

"Good. Let us go quickly. But first, allow me a moment of privacy. I will join you momentarily outside the tent."

The aide saluted, took one step backward, turned, and exited.

Baxter motioned for Jiliada and Elizabeth to approach. He grasped their hands in his. "Will we ever know tranquility?" he asked.

"Perhaps not," said Jiliada. "It is time to go, my husband. You must lead the people of Luctor against the Bioprimalist insurrection."

Baxter gave Jiliada and Elizabeth each a hug, and hurriedly left the tent. He and his aide headed for the western field, moving at a brisk pace. It was still nighttime, and quite cool. The camp was almost deserted.

They came upon the Great Sage, who was standing outside the entrance to his tent. Baxter stopped in front of him and bowed, and again requested a moment of privacy. The aide retreated several yards.

"I see that you have completed your voyage," said the Great Sage, his sharp eyes glistening under the heavy wrinkles.

"Indeed I have, Your Eminence."

"And now I must complete mine. After this day, we shall never meet again."

"Are you saying that you will live out the rest of your days in the Home Cell?"

"Yes. My existence in Luctor will be terminated."

"I will regret that circumstance," said Baxter. "Did you always know that this day would come?"

The Great Sage took a deep breath. "You have posed a difficult question. The Home Cell is my cell of origin. Luctor is my secondary existence. The split lasted so long—most of my life, in fact—that I hardly knew which was which. When Jiliada and I first discussed Luctor, I was already having doubts about the dual reality. Not long thereafter, I became convinced that it is an illusion, existing solely within our dreams. I continued to vacillate, finally settling about a year ago into a comfortable state of denial.

"That all changed today, however, when I was apprised of your death in the Home Cell and subsequent presence in Luctor. This evidence in favor of the dual reality cannot be denied."

"No, certainly not," said Baxter. "I gather that you are now prepared to renounce your existence in Luctor."

"Absolutely, and I will do so with great relief. The tribulations that you have experienced these recent days have accompanied me throughout my adult life. The long years of doubt and anxiety are, I hope, coming to an end."

"Why was it necessary for your dual reality to last so long?"

"The Omnificent Cerebrum was obliged to introduce me to a broad range of concepts, the command of which can be a life's work. For example, one intuitively thinks of the various cells in the cosmic Brain as being entirely separate, each with a distinct character and function. To some extent, this is true, but not in its essence. The cells are more accurately described as different shades of human potential."

"Fascinating," said Baxter, as he recalled a similar assertion made by one of the speechmakers on the Plaza. "So we're talking about the alternative paths that seem to lie dormant within us."

"Yes. Within us individually, as well as collectively."

"Tell me something, Your Eminence. Why Luctor? What did you need to learn in this cell, specifically?"

"Something similar to your mission in the Home Cell. We both were required to learn about Bioprimalism, but in different ways. You, being a more practical person, a man of action, needed to be steeped in the underlying ideology. Myself, being ensconced in the world of scholarship and disputation, needed to become acquainted, somewhat brutally, with a Bioprimalist bid for power."

"There is still one thing I don't understand, Your Eminence," said Baxter.

"What is that?"

"Why does the Omnificent Cerebrum allow a destructive concept like Bioprimalism to spread so widely? Does it not hinder mind carriers from fully realizing their intellectual potential?"

The Great Sage looked into the distance and sighed. "It seems to hinder that realization, but only for undisciplined minds that are not capable of expansion and creative force. For the keener minds, it acts as a stimulus. This is because intellect can be fully deployed only when it is forced to struggle."

"That seems logical," said Baxter. "The Tomes of Ancient Thought were written by men who had experienced great upheaval."

"Precisely. And now, my son, go forth to meet your own struggle—and deploy your intellect."